FEARLESS JONES

ALSO BY WALTER MOSLEY
AND PUBLISHED BY SERPENT'S TAIL

FEARLESS JONES

Walter Mosley

A complete catalogue record for this book can be
obtained from the British Library on request

The right of Walter Mosley to be identified as the
author of this work has been asserted by him in
accordance with the Copyright, Designs and Patents
Act 1988

First published by Little, Brown and Company,
Boston and New York in 2001

Published in 2001 by Serpent's Tail,
4 Blackstock Mews, London N4 2BT
www: www.serpentstail.com

Printed in Great Britain by Mackays of Chatham, plc

10 9 8 7 6 5 4 3 2 1

Dedicated to Clyde Taylor
and Manthia Diawara

FEARLESS JONES

1 MY USED-BOOK STORE had been open for just about a month when the police showed up. I hadn't called them, of course; a black man has to think twice before calling the cops in Watts. They came to see me late that afternoon. Two well-built young men. One had dark hair and the other sported freckles.

The dark one wandered around the room, flipping through random books, looking, it seemed, for some kind of contraband.

"Where'd you get all these books, son?" the other cop asked, looking down on me.

I was sitting in my favorite swivel chair behind the makeshift table-desk that I used for book sales and purchases.

"Libraries," I replied.

"Stole 'em?" the dark-haired cop asked from across the room. There was an eager grin on his face.

"Front'a each page marked DISCARDED," I said, editing out all unnecessary words as I spoke. "Library throws away thousands of books every year."

I reached for a paper folder at the far end of the table, and the cop standing over me let his right hand drift toward his holster. I removed a sheet of paper and handed it over slowly.

"This letter," I said, "is from the office of the head librarian downtown."

The freckled and frowning cop used his left hand to take the letter from me.

I was put out by the roust but not surprised. The police weren't used to a Negro in Watts going into business for himself. Most black migrants from the South usually got jobs for the city or did domestic work or day labor. There were very few entrepreneurs active among us at that time. That's why I had asked Miss Ryan, assistant to the president of the county library system, for a letter of explanation. She had written the letter on official letterhead, addressed "To whom it may concern," stating that any library book marked DISCARDED was no longer the property of the library and could be disposed of in any way that the current owner saw fit.

Upon reading this the officer's hand moved away from his gun.

"The law says that you're supposed to post business hours clearly on the front door," he said, letting the letter fall back on the table.

There was no such ordinance, and I knew it, but I said, "Yes, officer. I'll take care of it tomorrow."

I felt no rancor toward them. Being challenged by the law was a rite of passage for any Negro who wanted to better himself or his situation.

• • •

I HAD OPENED my nameless bookstore on Central just down from 101st Street. It was the only one of its kind for miles. I carried everything from Tolstoy to *Batman,* from Richard Wright to *Popular Mechanics.* No new books, but a used book is just as good as a new one as far as the reading goes.

At first I was scandalized by the thought that a library would discard a book, but once I realized the possibilities for business, I made the rounds of every library in L.A., carting off almost two thousand volumes in just over three months. Then I paid first and last month's rent on a storefront that was down the street from a Holy Roller church called Messenger of the Divine.

My friend Fearless Jones helped me throw together some pine shelving and I was in business. I bought magazines two for a nickel and sold them at twice the price. I traded one book or magazine for two of equal worth.

Business wasn't brisk, but it paid the rent and utilities. And all day long I could do the thing I loved best — reading. I read *Up from Slavery, Tom Sawyer Abroad, Journey to the Center of the Earth, Mein Kampf,* and dozens of other titles in the first few months. Whole days I spent in my reclining swivel chair, turning pages and drinking Royal Crown colas. Every once in a while I'd have to stop in order to sell an encyclopedia to proud parents or a romance to a woman who needed more than her husband had left at the end of a hard day's work. I had a whole army of little children helpers who'd sort and alphabetize for comic book privileges and maybe a free taco now and then.

For a solid three months I was the happiest man in L.A., in

spite of the cops. I had a checking account, and for the first time in my life I was caught up on my bills.

But then Love walked in the door.

It was a cloudless day in October, the year was 1954. It wasn't hot or cold outside, but her dress was definitely a summer frock, white with a floral pattern. The thin straps lay loose on her brown shoulders. She didn't seem to be wearing anything under that dress — not that she needed to. The sunglasses had been pushed up to the top of her head, nestled in the big, floppy curls she'd had done at some beauty shop.

Her face is what scared me. It was too wide to be pretty and too flat to be handsome, but she was beautiful anyway. I wanted to feel my cheek rubbing up against hers.

The last time I'd felt like that about a woman I almost got killed. So the fast beating of my heart was a coin toss between love and fear.

"Is Reverend Grove here?'" she asked me in a breathy voice.

"Who?"

"Reverend William Grove. He preached with Father Vincent and Sister Thalia."

The skirt came down to the middle of her knees. Her legs were bare and her ankles were bound with thin straps of white leather snaking up from delicate sandals.

"I don't know any Grove," I said, forcing my eyes back to her face.

The name had some meaning to me, but it felt so distant that I thought it must be someone from long ago, maybe from down in Louisiana. Certainly not anyone this beautiful girl and I would both know.

She looked around the room, twisting at the waist to see for herself. She had a figure made for that kind of movement. Her eyes lit on a burlap curtain that hung over a doorway.

"Where's that go?" she asked.

"My back room," I said. Then it came to me. "You must be talking about the Messenger of the Divine."

"Oh yes. Yes."

The hope in her voice brought me up out of my chair. She moved toward me. Her hands reached out for me.

"They had a place look like mine down the street," I said. "But they moved out. Must be two months ago now."

"What?" Her face went blank.

"Moved," I said. "Went away."

"Where?"

"I don't know. They moved out in the middle of the night. Took everything. All that was left was an empty space and a few paper fans."

I was sad to make my little report because now there was no reason for her to stay and twist around. I realized that I had spent a little too much time lately wrapped up in books. I had the notion that I should go out to the Parisian Room that night.

Just then the young woman leaned backward and then crumpled forward, into my arms. As I stood there holding her steady, the fear fled my heart. At close quarters her scent was floral, but it was also sharp, like the smell after lightning strikes.

"You got some water in the back?" she whispered.

I nodded and led her through the heavy burlap curtain to the back room and put her on my cot. She was mumbling and crying.

"Are you okay?" I asked, perching next to her.

"Where did they go?"

I couldn't find the words to hurt her again.

"What am I gonna do?" she cried, turning her head, looking around in the dark as if the room might somehow transform itself into the church she sought. "Reverend Grove is the only one who can help me now."

"What's wrong?" I asked, thinking, even then, that I didn't really want to know.

"I have to find William. If I don't —" She broke off in tears. I tried to console her but she was bereft.

After a moment or two I heard the front door to the store come open. She heard it too and took in a quick breath. Her fear made me wary again. I rose up and went through the curtain to the store.

The man standing there was a study in blunt. His hairless head was big and meaty. The dark features might not have been naturally ugly, but they had been battered by a lifetime of hard knocks: broken nose, a rash that had raged and then scarred over the lower left side of his face. His eyebrows seemed to be different sizes, but that might just have been the product of a permanent scowl.

"Wherethegurl?" he said in a tone so guttural that for a moment I couldn't make out the words. "Wherethegurl?"

He was about six feet tall (I'm only five eight), but he had the chest and shoulders of someone who should have been much taller. He was a volcano crushed down into just about man size. His clothes were festive, a red Hawaiian shirt and light blue pants. The outfit was ridiculous, like a calico bow on an English bulldog.

"I don't —" I said.

"Wherethegurl, muthahfuckah!" He had the build of a fire-plug but moved like a cat. He had me by the arm and in the air before I could invent a lie.

"Where is she?" He looked around the room and saw that the burlap curtain was the only exit besides the front door. He threw me at the curtain, and I tore it down falling into the back room. He came in right behind me, looking at all the corners and then at the bed.

My eyes were on him.

"This your last chance," he said, threat heavy in each word.

I dared a glance at the bed and saw that it was empty.

"I don't know, man," I said as bravely as I could. "She come an' asked about a church used to be around here. I told her that they were gone. So then she said she had to go to the bathroom."

I gestured with my hand. He saw the door and flung it open with so much force that one of the hinges ripped loose from the wall. All that was revealed was a lidless commode and tin sink.

"Where is she?" He dragged me to my feet with one hand.

"She must'a gone out the back, man. I don't know."

I think he slapped me, but I've been hit by blackjacks that had more give than his fingers. The taste of salt came into my mouth and the lightbulb on the desk multiplied into a thousand stars.

"Wherethegurl?" a parrot somewhere said.

"She must'a gone out the back," I repeated.

"I'll kill you, niggah, no lie."

He slapped me again and I tried to think of what I could say to save my life. But I didn't know anything, not even the frightened woman's name. I decided that, since he was going to kill me anyway, I would go out bravely. For once I would be as brave as my friend Fearless. I had never stood up to a bully in my life. So at least this one last time, in a back room in Watts, Paris Minton would show some backbone. *Fuck you, asshole,* was on the tip of my tongue.

"Please don't, brother." My trembling words betrayed me. "I don't know nuthin'."

He slapped me again. My head turned around so far that I was sure my neck had broken.

"You a dead man," my attacker said.

A child's voice squeaked, "Mr. Minton, you okay?"

"Who's that man?" another child screamed.

I fell to the floor, noticing as I hit that my killer wore leather sandals on bare feet. As I lost consciousness I thought that if a man was going to kill me, he should at least wear grown-up men's shoes.

2 | "MR. MINTON? Mr. Minton, are you okay?"

It was a man's voice. A familiar voice. There was concern, not mayhem, in the words. I opened my eyes and saw Theodore Wally, the clerk from Antonio and Sons Superette next door. He was a young man, but his face was ready for old age. It was medium brown and soft with fleshy weight around the eyes.

"Mr. Minton?" he asked again. "Are you okay?"

I didn't answer because I was preoccupied with the miracle of my survival. The killer, I figured, was still human enough not to want to murder children. When he saw them he decided to spare me. I lifted my head, and a pain as sharp as Fearless Jones's bayonet traveled the length of my spine.

"Help me up," I said, fearing that I was paralyzed.

The little shopkeeper pulled as hard as he could and I sat up. When I got to my feet the pain was even worse, but I could take steps without falling.

"Damn! Ow!"

"You okay, Mr. Minton?"

"Why don't you call me Paris, Theodore?" I said, angry at the world.

"I don't know. It's the way I was raised, I guess."

"You call Freddy at the hot dog stand Freddy." A wave of pain crashed in my head. I almost lost my footing, but Theodore held me up.

"You okay? You want a doctor?"

"No. But thank you. Thank you. How come you came in here?"

"Those kids, Elbert and them. They come in the store an' said you was dead, that a big, ugly man killed you."

"Where the kids?"

"Outside."

I tripped over the downed burlap curtain going through the doorway from my back room. When I got outside the sunlight made my eyes feel as if they were going to explode.

"You okay, Mr. Minton?" a too-tall-for-his-age eight-year-old cried.

"Okay, Elbert. Okay. You see him?"

"That man that hit you?"

"Uh-huh." The pain from the sun was so great that everything was tinged in red. I wondered if that meant I was bleeding inside my skull.

"He drove a blue car like my daddy's, only it was a light blue and it had horns."

"Horns?"

"Yeah."

"What kinda horns?"

"Like the cows in the movies."

"Longhorns?"

"Uh-huh."

I fell to my knees and threw up, hard. The boys skittered away, but Theodore knelt down and held me by the shoulders, then helped me back to my back room.

"You should go to a doctor, Mr. Minton."

"I just wanna sleep, Theodore." They were the truest words ever spoken. "Do me a favor and pull the shades and lock the door. And put up my closed sign. Please, Theodore." I added the last two words because I was a transplanted southern boy who learned manners before he knew how to talk.

Theodore moved quietly around the bookstore pulling down the dark yellow shades. I turned out the lamp on the desk and then lay down on my cot. The back room had no windows and so became very dark. When I heard the front door close I made a powerful effort to stand. At first I thought I might throw up again, but the urge passed. I staggered to my desk and let myself down on one knee. It was an old maple desk, heavy and cramped. I only used it to store and stack papers. Store and stack and secret away a .38-caliber pistol on a ledge behind the center drawer. It was Fearless's gun. I held it for him when he was between apartments. It was in my possession in that capacity when he was sent to jail.

For the first time I lamented Fearless's incarceration.

They had arrested him for felony assault on three crooked mechanics, convicted him on a lesser charge, and given him the choice of paying five hundred dollars or spending nine months as a guest of the county. He opted for the fine but had no money to pay and so asked me for a loan.

"I'm sorry, Fearless," I said through the visitor's grille at the county jailhouse. "But, man, I just can't do it."

Fearless's lean, dark face didn't show the disappointment I know he must have felt. He had put his life on the line saving mine eight years earlier, but over the years since then, I had risked my own skin many times for him — and I was no war hero the way he was.

Fearless was the kind of person who attracted trouble. He didn't know how to look away or back down. He couldn't even spell the word *compromise*. Whenever he called me, I didn't know if we were going to get drunk at a party or get jumped down some dark alley.

To protect my interests as a businessman, I decided to cut my ties with probably the best friend that I ever had.

"Okay," he said. "I understand. But you know them men did me wrong, Paris."

I CHECKED to make sure the pistol was loaded and took off the safety. Then I climbed into the bed with the gun under the covers next to me. I didn't fall into a deep sleep but instead drifted on the edge of a nervous doze.

WHEN I FELT a feathery touch against my forehead I feared that it was a rat, that I was dead and he came in from the alley to eat my flesh. The thought of food caused me to writhe from nausea, and when I moved I felt her flowery dress.

I knew it was her. That was my kind of luck. The kind of woman I wanted most, the kind of woman I should stay away from at all costs, that's the woman who I will awaken to from a slumber that might have been death.

"Are you okay?" she asked.

I could barely see her in the darkness.

"No."

"Does it hurt much?"

"Like a toothache set in a broken jaw."

"I'm so sorry," she said, reaching out to touch my brow again. "What's your name?"

"Elana Love. What's yours?"

"Paris Minton. Paris Minton." The repetition was my attempt to extricate myself from the trouble in that room. But I wasn't going anywhere, and neither was she.

"That's a nice name."

"How did you get back in here?" I asked.

"I never left," she said. "When Leon came in I looked for a back door, but I didn't see one, so I squeezed in behind the file cabinet and waited until he left. I was going to run out, but then that other man came in."

"Why didn't you say something?"

"I thought you might be mad that I didn't help you against Leon."

"Who is this Leon?"

"Leon Douglas. We used to see each other before they sent him to jail. He was in for armed robbery and attempted murder, but a lawyer got him out."

"What did you do, cheat on him or something?"

"No," she said in a flash of anger. "I broke it off with him before he robbed that store. I told him that no love was gonna make me live with a criminal."

"Maybe he didn't like that."

"He thinks I have somethin', but I don't have it. I don't, but he won't believe me."

"But Reverend Grove knows where it is?"

"How did you know about him?" She was suddenly wary. "Oh, yeah. I told you."

"Does he?" I asked. For some reason talking made me feel better. I sat up.

"Does who?"

"Reverend Grove. Does he have what Leon wants?"

"Uh-uh," she said, but I wasn't sure that I believed her. "I told Leon that he did though. I was seein' William for a while back there, and I thought he could help me against Leon. But when the church was gone I didn't know what to do."

Silence brought back the awareness of pain. I didn't care about Grove or Leon either. I didn't care what they were hiding or looking for.

"Why are you still here?" I asked.

"When you went outside I looked for a back door, but there wasn't one, and where could I go anyway?" she asked. "Maybe Leon's waiting around outside somewhere."

The thought of that killer lurking outside my door made me queasy again.

"How did he know you were here?"

"He made me come," she said in a pained tone. "He told me to come in and get his property from William or else he was gonna break somebody's neck."

"Yeah," I said. "I got that."

"You have to help me, Mr. Minton."

"I can go to the market next door and use their phone to call the police," I offered.

"No. No, not the police."

"Why not? He's threatenin' you and he almost killed me."

"Leon has a lot of friends," she said. "Even if he gets arrested, he'll send somebody after me, and maybe you too."

"Me? Honey, I don't know either one'a you. All I was doin' was sittin' here mindin' my own business." I thought of Fearless then, of how he was always saying how he was minding his own business when all hell broke loose.

"But now that he's seen you, he might think that you're in this with me."

"In what? I don't even know you."

Elana reached out and touched my chest then. It might sound like a silly gesture, but when a woman like that lays hands on you, it's hard to ignore.

"Listen, honey," I said, despite my thrumming heart. "You're gorgeous. I only meet a woman like you about once every five years or so. But when I do, somebody always ends up wantin' to kill me. And you know I could find me an ugly girl, be half as happy, but live ten times as long. I don't want anything to do with you or your boyfriend or your ex-boyfriend. So please, go back out the way you came and shut the door behind you."

My eyes had adjusted to the darkness enough to see the struggle in her face. She wanted to convince me, to make me her protector but couldn't quite figure out how.

"I don't even have bus money. If I go out there alone he could kill me," she said.

That was my downfall right there. I took pity on her the way I did time and again with Fearless. I came to a compromise in my head even though I knew that what I should do was throw her outdoors.

I made it to my feet and said, "Okay, I'll give you a ride wherever you need to go to get away, but that's it."

3 | ELANA DIDN'T COMPLAIN when she saw me pocket the .38.

"Might as well go out the back," I said. "I mean, he'd probably be covering the front. Does he have any friends?"

"He was with two friends." Elana sounded defeated. I clearly wasn't the protector she needed.

"What're their names?"

"What difference do that make?"

"Well, let's go out the back door," I said. My head was still light and my stomach was churning. I swallowed once and gazed at a piece of wall with a cabinet handle screwed on at just about waist height. The reason that Elana hadn't found her way out was that my back door was almost invisible. It was just a rectangular slat that swung on three rusty old hinges.

My red Nash Rambler was parked against a salmon-pink stucco wall that ran the length of the alley separating the houses on the residential street behind. There was no sign of Leon, his horned car, or his nameless friends. Elana slid into the passenger's seat and laid her head against the window. She was a picture-perfect damsel in distress.

If I were Fearless Jones I would have run headlong into the fray, taking any blows and doing anything to protect her. But I didn't believe that even Fearless would have stood long against Leon Douglas.

I started the motor and we slid off into the afternoon.

"Where to?" I asked.

She rattled off an address on a street named Hazzard.

"Where's that?"

"It's off Brooklyn Avenue in East L.A."

"What's there?"

"Prob'ly nuthin'."

I WAS CUTTING left and right on side streets, making my way east, looking up into my rearview mirror from time to time. We'd driven for more than five minutes in silence.

"What does this Leon guy want from you?" I asked.

"You don't want to get involved, remember?" she said.

"Have it your way, honey. All I thought was that maybe I could give you some advice."

"The only thing anybody could give me is manpower or money. Either that or Leon Douglas is gonna kill me."

I looked over into the side mirror and saw the flash of a powder blue Chrysler with horns on its grate as it swerved, aiming to cut me off.

"Shit!" I hit the brakes, narrowly avoiding the collision. He banged into a parked car at a wide angle, blocking the street. I hit the gas and drove up onto the sidewalk. The lawns on that block were small hills leading up to the little homes. I put deep ruts across three of these lawns, fishtailing as I went. As soon as we cleared Leon, I cut a hard left back down to the street. Once on the asphalt, I gunned the engine and we took off. I would have felt good about the maneuver except by then Leon had straightened out also. He was barreling down on us.

I careened left, scraping an oncoming Ford. Leon did the same thing. Then I heard something that sounded like a chicken bone breaking.

"They're shooting at us!" Elana cried.

I made three more wild turns. Shots popped off at irregular intervals. There were no cops anywhere.

"Take the gun outta my pocket!" I yelled.

Elana wasn't slow. She didn't resist or think or pretend that it was too much for her. She just jammed her hand into my pocket and rolled down her window.

A bullet ricocheted off the side of my door.

I made a right turn and Elana leaned out, taking four fast shots at the rampaging bull of a car. I had turned onto Edison, a warehouse street with very few pedestrians. I remembered, too late, that most of the side streets off it were dead ends, so I couldn't afford a turn. We were on a straightaway with only two bullets left.

"Did you hit anything?" I shouted.

"I don't think so."

The Chrysler was coming on strong for three blocks, four, five. I swerved and banked to pull around cars ahead of me. Leon matched me move for move. After Leonard Street the bull slowed. By the next block there was smoke from the car's hood. They pulled to the curb soon after that.

I almost fainted when I realized we'd survived.

I turned onto Hooper and headed downtown.

"Where are you going?" she asked me, the steely calm of her voice in deep contrast with my racing heart.

"You'll see when we get there."

After half an hour or so we came to an underground parking lot on Flower. It was expensive, thirty-five cents an hour, but I wanted to be careful now that I had a killer on my trail. A killer with whom I had just been in a running gun battle in the streets of L.A.

I reached out to Elana Love and said, "Gun, please."

She looked down at the pistol in her hand and considered a moment before handing it over.

We went to a small diner called Guardino's on Hope. It was a nice place with an Italian flair. Larry, the owner, liked me and Fearless because we'd come there on double dates and buy big dinners with fancy wines for our girls. Fearless could eat antipasto all day if you'd let him.

"Paris," Selena Karsky said in greeting. She was Larry's girl-friend, bottled blond and fifty. She still looked good though. "Where's Fearless?"

"He went away," I said.

"Oh, that's too bad. Is he coming back soon?"

"No," I said. "I don't think so. He got a job outta town."

"You must miss him."

"More every day."

Selena took us to a booth in the dark corridor of the restaurant. Of the eight booths, six already had customers. All of them were white, and a few gave us surprised looks.

"We're not too hungry, Selena," I told her. "Just beers, minestrone, and an antipasto plate for two."

"Okay," she said, smiling.

"Friend of yours?" Elana asked when Selena was gone.

"She smiles and serves me spaghetti and seats me even though some people complain. I like her okay."

"Why did you bring me here?" Elana asked.

"Because I'm a fool."

"Excuse me?"

"If I had sent you away instead of offering you a ride, none of this would be happening. I'd be sleepin' off my lumps, and you'd be all snugly with Mr. Douglas."

My words made her uncomfortable, which was just fine by me.

"So," I continued. "Tell me about Leon and why it's his business to kill me."

"Are you going to help me?"

"No. I'm gonna help myself. You got Frankenstein and his brothers stakin' out my store. If I don't do something, I'll either lose my business or lose my life. You know I don't like either one'a them choices." I spoke in a whisper that had all the weight of a shout.

"What could you do?" Her sneer reminded me that she had witnessed my humiliation under Leon's threats and violence.

"Go to the cops for one thing."

That wiped the smug off her face.

"No, don't," she said.

"Why not?"

Elana Love struggled with the truth. It was all caught up with lies and fears. She couldn't tell me everything, but she had to let up on something or I'd blow the game.

"Leon had a cellmate in prison. A man named Sol Tannenbaum. Sol was in for embezzlement, but, you know, he wasn't a criminal type, never even been in jail. Leon's tough. He promised Sol that he'd protect him. But Sol had to give him something." Elana stopped a moment.

"What?"

"It was a bond. What they called a bond of deposit. It was issued by some bank in Switzerland."

"How much?" I asked.

"It was ten thousand francs, about two thousand five hundred American dollars."

"So? What does all this have to do with Leon?"

"Sol didn't have the bond in jail. He set it up so that I got it from his wife."

"I thought you broke up with Leon before he got sent up?"

"He asked me for a favor. An' maybe I didn't exactly tell 'im that we were through."

"And so you took the bond and . . ."

"I gave it to William to hold it for me."

"I thought you said he didn't have it."

"He didn't think he did, that's what I meant," she said. "I didn't tell him what it was or anything. It was just in a whole bunch of papers I left with him for safekeeping."

Selena came with the beers and a basket of white bread.

When she was gone I asked Elana, "Why didn't you keep the money with you?"

"Not money," she corrected, "a bond. After Leon got sent to jail I was having trouble making my rent, and I didn't wanna take a chance and lose it if the landlord changed the locks and took my stuff."

"But couldn't Grove go through your papers, find the bond, and cash it in?" I asked reasonably.

"No," she said as if talking to a fool. "It was made out to Mr. Tannenbaum. Only he could cash it. That way everybody was covered. I couldn't get the money and neither could Leon if he got out before Sol. He didn't though. Leon told me that Sol got out on good behavior last week."

"So you think Reverend Grove went to this Sol guy an' got him to sign over the bond?" I asked her.

"No," she replied, looking down into her beer.

"Why not?"

"'Cause William don't know he got the bond."

I knew she was lying. Why would she tell me the truth?

"Why didn't you go to find Grove yourself?" I asked. "And take the bond to Sol for him to sign it?"

"I didn't even know that he was out of jail," she said. "And even if I did, he would'a been a fool to sign it without Leon's say-so."

"There's something else I don't understand. You said that Leon was in for armed robbery and attempted murder. How's he gonna get out anytime before twenty years?"

"Leon had a bad lawyer. He was sure that if he got a new trial he could beat the charges."

"So now you sayin' he didn't do the robbery?"

"He did it all right, it's just that they didn't have no evidence."

"Uh-huh. And the bond was gonna pay for the new lawyer?" I was trying to make some kind of sense out of her story, but it wasn't easy.

"Yeah. Leon told me that he told his lawyer that he could pay him a thousand dollars when he got out. He was gonna use the bond for that."

"And now he needs the money to pay his lawyer?" I asked.

Elana nodded. "Otherwise the lawyer'll drop the case an' he's back in jail."

"I'm sorry, honey, but your story still don't add up," I said. "Here you tell me that you're close enough to Reverend Grove for him to store your things, but you don't even know his church's address."

"I knew where Messenger was" — there was acid on her tongue now — "I knew that William had cleared out too. But I needed to get away from Leon. The church store was padlocked, so I told him that your place was the church office. That way I could leave him outside and get away through the back."

"Why wouldn't he just come in with you?"

"Because he's out on bail waitin' for his new trial and he don't wanna get that revoked."

"Out on bail?" I said. "How much was that?"

"I don't know. I didn't go to the hearin'. All I know is that the judge turned over his conviction and set bail. I told him that the people in the church would call the police if he caused trouble. He said he'd wait ten minutes, but I guess he didn't trust me."

"No kiddin'? So all that shit you said about lookin' for Grove, that was just actin'?" As I said the words I realized that I was no more a match for Elana Love than I had been for her boyfriend.

"Maybe I already knew the church was gone, but I really was scared. You saw Leon. You can't blame me for tryin' to get away."

"Here you are, hun." Selena appeared with our soup and antipasto on a wide, cork-lined tray. She set the plates out in front of us and stared admiringly at Elana. "You're a beauty."

"Thank you," the siren said.

"Are you an actress or model?"

"No," she answered. But there was something else. The way her eyes moved and her body twisted, a whole volume of mystery passed from her to the waitress.

When Selena was gone I said, "So tell me something."

"What?"

"Did Leon have money from that robbery? Is that what he's after?"

She shook her head again. "They let him out of jail today and he was at my door an hour after. All he said was that he wanted his bond."

I wrapped a slice of salami around a semi-sour gherkin and popped it in my mouth. I chewed for a while, enjoying the loud crunching in my ears.

"I didn't mean to get you into trouble, Mr. Minton. I was just looking for a way out."

I took Elana to that restaurant instead of putting her out on the street because I wanted to know about the trouble I had fallen into. I had found out a few things, but they didn't help much.

"So what do you intend to do now?"

"I don't know." She made a gesture of hopelessness with her hands, but I had learned by now not to trust when she was acting weak.

"What about that place on Hazzard you wanted to go before? You wanna go there?"

"No."

"Why not?"

"Are you going to help me?" she asked.

"I don't know. I can't go back to the store because of Leon. That's where he'd go for sure."

"We could go to your place," she suggested.

"I live at my store," I said.

"Oh."

"But there's a motel down at Venice Beach take us. It's cheap and there's the ocean outside. The waves help me think."

"Let's go there." She reached across the table and laid her hand over mine. And damn if my fingers didn't curl around hers.

4　THE MUSSEL BEACH INN was half a block up from the water, perched on a small hill. You couldn't see the ocean in the darkness, but you heard and smelled it just fine. I left the sliding doors open because of a false sense of security I had. I mean, Leon wouldn't find us at the beach if he searched for seven years.

The lights were down and the linen curtains were waving in and out from our little cement patio. Every now and then the moon appeared in a curve of the flowing fabric.

Elana told me that she was from Georgia, that her mother had brought her to live in L.A. when she was only twelve. But then, just three years later, her mother moved to Jackson, Mississippi, with a merchant marine who later abandoned her.

"She left you on your own when you was just fifteen?" I said, sounding more concerned than I actually felt.

"We didn't see eye to eye, my mama and me," Elana said rather callously. "And anyway, I had a boyfriend I was livin' wit' when she left."

I said that that was sad and tried for a kiss, but she turned away before I got there.

Leon, she said, was a strong arm and a robber. She worried that Sol Tannenbaum had to give up part of his life savings for his thuggish protection. That's why she left him. She wasn't going to be a moll or an accomplice. She needed a man who was going to be sweet and gentle.

I didn't believe a word she said, but that didn't matter. I told her that my mother raised me as a gentleman. "A gentle man," I said before launching another kiss. That one missed too.

It was late, and there was no immediate danger. She was a young woman, and I was the young man who had just saved her life. I couldn't see where a kiss was out of line.

"I'm too upset to do that, baby," she said after my third awkward attempt. "Why don't we try an' get some sleep. I'll feel better tomorrow."

The only vacancy the motel had was furnished with two single beds. I could see that I was destined to sleep alone and so crawled under the covers of the one nearest the window.

"Aren't you gonna take off your clothes?" she asked.

"No."

"I won't look."

"I wish you would. You might see somethin' you like. But I'm not taking off my pants until I know that I won't have to run any minute with some killer on my ass." I wasn't really afraid, but I had my car key, money, and Fearless Jones's pistol in my pockets. I wanted all of that close at hand.

She made a little humming sound and then got under her bedclothes. She did take off her dress, but I couldn't see anything because of the blankets.

"G'night," she said softly.

I switched off the lamp on the night table next to my bed, closed my eyes, and concentrated on the sound of the waves. After a while my mind began to drift.

In the reverie my thoughts kept returning to Fearless Jones.

Fearless Jones. Tall and slender, darker than most Negroes in the American melting pot, he was stronger than tempered steel and an army-trained killing machine.

I learned just how deadly he was one night after a big rainstorm in San Francisco. I was coming down a dark street dancing to the jazz I knew I'd be hearing soon. When the cops stopped me, I guess I must have been a little too cocky. They didn't like my attitude and were correcting it with their nightsticks when Fearless showed up to meet me. He jumped in the middle of the fracas as if he were still under Bradley fighting the Germans hand to hand. He disarmed both men and beat them to their knees.

He would have let it go at that if one of the cops hadn't put a knife in his thigh. After that there was no hope. One cop fell unconscious, facedown in a pool of water. The other, the one who stabbed Fearless, well, his windpipe busted.

Fearless still had a small limp from that knife wound. There's never a day that goes by I don't wish that I'd taken the beating and Fearless had missed the whole thing.

But for all that he was a killer, Fearless was a good man too. Too good. He was generous beyond his means. This generosity often led to trouble that I got pulled into. Loan sharks and wife-beating husbands, con men and shady landlords. Fearless brought me into conflict with every kind of lowlife and thug. And I am not a courageous man.

Maybe that's why I had Fearless on my mind instead of the sensuous curves of Elana Love. I was scared, and Fearless was the only person I really trusted. I considered going to the police about Leon, but the cops were an iffy bet at best. Maybe somebody had reported the shoot-out. Maybe, if they couldn't find Leon, the cops would decide that I shot at myself. There was no way that I could rely on Elana telling them the same story she told me. And if they got me into an interrogation room, I'd confess to anything they said.

No, I couldn't go to the police. And I wouldn't go to Fearless either. In the morning I'd take Elana anywhere she wanted to go and then I'd go on vacation for a few weeks, maybe down in San Diego. I had enough money for a holiday. And by the time I returned, Leon would either be back in jail or on easy street. Either way he wouldn't be worried about me.

With that decision made I dozed off, but I didn't relax. In my dreams someone was chasing me through the main library downtown. I ran from room to room with my unknown pursuer close behind. I knew that in one of the books there was written the secret of my success and salvation, but I couldn't stop to search for it for fear I'd get caught and drown in the waters outside the Mussel Beach Inn.

"Paris." Her lips were touching my ear.

I tried to jump, but her arms were around me. Her breasts were heavy against my back.

"I thought you said —" I started to say.

"Shhhh," she whispered. "What you got down here?"

I heard the zipper from under the blanket and then I felt the silken warmth of her hand.

"Dang," she said in what I knew was real surprise. "I could use three hands on you."

There are no two lovers alike. Every man and woman has different needs and pleasures in bed. I've always known this. It's part of the reason that I have so much anticipation the first time with a new woman. But that night I realized that everybody is different with every new love they meet. Coming together with Elana made me into a new man. I was jumping through hoops I hadn't known were there. Elana gave me pleasure in places I never associated with sex.

Together we were like an overripe peach, just dripping with sweetness and sticky with love. My orgasms were so strong that I didn't even feel the ejaculations. But they were in no way superior to the feel of her teeth at the back of my neck.

From a worried sleep to passionate love to a deep slumber she took me. The ocean was crashing, and the cool air drove me deeper into the blankets. At the first moment of consciousness I was smiling and placated. But then I began to sense that I was alone.

Morning light was coming through the wavy curtains. Elana was not in my bed and neither was she in hers. The bathroom was empty. My pants were strewn in the middle of the floor. My wallet was laid open, emptied of cash. The .38 was gone too.

She hadn't taken the five-dollar bill that I keep in my shoe. I always thought it would come in handy if I was mugged late one night and had to pay for a taxi ride home. I never imagined that a mugging would come in the form of sex. And, as much as I wanted to be mad, as much as I was mad, I still appreciated the way she had robbed me. At least I did until I realized that she had also stolen my car.

The blacktop lot to the motel was completely empty. It was ten A.M. and I was marooned in Venice for no reason other than I was a fool.

I took a bus directly to the Bank of America branch on Normandie. I made a withdrawal, which took a while because I was closing out my account, and carried my money back home.

THERE WAS no crowd, and so I figured the fire must have happened either the night before or early in the morning. Whenever it happened it must have raged, because there weren't ten books out of over three thousand that survived the blaze. My storefront rental was razed to the ground. Only the metal fixtures and the extra thick wood of my desk and filing cabinet left any vestige of the life I had been trying to build.

I wept like a child. The tears ran down my cheeks, and my hands hung down. I stood there in the middle of the blackened lot that had been my future, quivering from the diaphragm.

"Mr. Minton." It was Theodore Wally from the Superette. He was standing at my side ready to catch me in case I were to fall again.

"What happened?" I asked.

"It was a fire last night," the old-faced youth told me. He seemed almost as upset as I was. He might have even shared a tear or two with me. "The fire inspector came and asked me questions about you. I told him what happent yesterday. I hope that wasn't bad."

"What am I gonna do now?" I moaned. "That was everything I ever owned."

"Your insurance'll pay for it, won't it?" Theodore asked hope-fully.

"Insurance? Man, I didn't have no insurance." I laughed a little too loudly.

"Can I do something for you?" Wally asked. "Anything you want."

"Did the inspector say anything about the fire?"

"He said suspicious. Suspicious."

I didn't need to ask him any more questions. Wally went back to the store and brought me a Royal Crown cola and a ham sandwich. I sucked on the bottle and inhaled the odor of my life gone up in smoke.

5 MILO SWEET'S BAIL BONDS, Tax Filing, and Financial Advising office was on the fourth floor of a warehouse building on Avalon. At that time an illegal poultry distributor occupied the ground floor, so there was the general odor of chicken shit and grain feed throughout the upper rooms.

Milo's office had a frosted glass door with black letters stenciled at the top:

OTTO RICKMAN

LIFE INSURANCE AGT.

&

NOTARY PUBLIC

I was never sure if that was the old sign or if Milo purposely had it printed to mislead creditors and others who might have held a grudge or a marker.

The room was maybe twenty feet wide and ten deep. There were three windows across the back wall and a desk on either side of the room. Wooden filing cabinets filled in the spaces between the windows.

"Hello, Mr. Minton," Milo's secretary, Loretta Kuroko, said from the desk on the right. She'd been Milo's secretary since his lawyer days. She stayed with him after he'd been disbarred, imprisoned for three years, and then when he went through a series of professions. She was a hostess when he had been a restaurant owner, a bookkeeper when he'd tried car insurance sales. Even in Milo's brief stint as a fence Loretta answered his phone and ran interference with the fiercest of clients.

They had never been lovers as far as I knew, and that was odd because Loretta loved Milo and she had a kind of perpetual beauty, thin and elegant with no wrinkles or lines. She was Japanese-American, a victim of America's little-publicized Japanese internment camps during World War Two.

"Loretta," I replied.

"Hey hey, Paris," Milo growled from his desk to the left. He sat in a haze of mentholated cigarette smoke, smiling like a king bug in a child's nightmare.

Milo was always the darkest man in the room, except when he was in the room with Fearless. He was taller than I but not six feet. He had big hands and long arms, bright white eyes and teeth and the complexion of polished charcoal. His short hair was always loaded with pomade and combed to the right. He knew the definition of every word in the dictionary and every once in a while managed to beat me at a game of chess.

"Milo," I hailed. "How's it goin'?"

"Must be good for somebody, somewhere. Must be. But don't ask me where."

I sat down and submitted to the scrutiny of those bright eyes.

"What's wrong, Paris?"

"Who said anything was wrong?"

"Your eyes is red. Your head is hangin'. You don't have a chessboard or a book under your arm, so you must be here on bidness." Milo paused and looked a little harder. "And if it's bidness you here for, it can't be for you because if it was, you'd be in jail and callin' me on the phone. It ain't tax time, and you sure don't make enough money to need financial advice. So if it ain't you, then it must be Fearless." Milo enjoyed reading between the lines. He was good at it, I had to admit that. "But you refused to come up with his fine before, so now something must have changed. That means I was right in the first place and you are in trouble. So, what's wrong, Paris?"

"Believe me, Mr. Sweet, you don't wanna know. I got to get Fearless outta jail and I got to do it fast. Will you help me?"

"I ain't no bank."

"You're not a German insurance salesman either."

Milo didn't bother to answer that swipe. I put a stack of five one-hundred-dollar bills on the table and then placed a twenty crosswise on that.

"It's all I got," I apologized.

"You expect me to spring him for just twenty?"

"I'll pay the rest in four weeks' time."

I had done work for Milo in the past. Asked a few questions, come up with an address or two on bail jumpers, but it still burned him when he felt that he was being had.

"I can't do it, Paris," he whined. "It would set a bad example."

"I'm not tellin' anybody, Miles."

"Can you at least make it thirty?"

"They burned down my store, man," I said. "They took my money and my car and burned down my goddamn store." My voice cracked and I had to blink hard to shut down my tear ducts.

Milo began rapping his knuckles on the desktop. His look changed. It was no friendlier, but the animosity was now aimed at some unknown perpetrator.

"Your bookstore?"

"Yeah."

"Why?" There was pain in Milo's voice.

"I don't know, but if I don't do somethin' soon, they might burn me down too."

"Shit, Paris. What did you do?"

I pondered his question. I had asked it a hundred times of Fearless Jones. I couldn't believe the trouble he'd get into and all he would say is, *I didn't do nuthin', Paris. I was just mindin' my own business.* But what had I done? How could I have avoided Elana Love and Leon Douglas?

"I'on't know, man. Maybe God looked down and saw all the shit I done got away wit' an' decided to mete out my punishment just when things started to get good."

"Amen," Milo said. "Amen to that." He shook his head and smiled, then he looked at his watch. "It's too late to get him out today. I'll drop by the courthouse on my way home and make the arrangements, but we have to go get him tomorrow mornin'. Where you gonna sleep tonight?"

"I don't know."

"Loretta," Milo called across the room.

"Yes, Mr. Sweet?" she replied.

"Pull out the cot. Paris is gonna be our watchdog tonight."

"Yes sir."

AT FIVE-THIRTY, when Milo and Loretta went home, I started going through the phone books of L.A., looking for Love. I found four listings. I called the numbers, asking for Elana, but of the two that were still connected there was no clue. The two that had been disconnected were an Alvin Love in Santa Monica, which I doubted would be fruitful, and an E. E. Love on Twenty-eighth Street.

I lay back and read the newspaper after exhausting the phone book. Then I had a notion. In the phone book there was only one Tannenbaum. The first name was David, not Sol, but his address in East Los Angeles was the same one Elana had given to me the day before, on Hazzard. We'd been headed to his house when Leon and his friend tried to run us down. I considered dialing the number, but then I held back. One thing I was sure of: surviving Leon Douglas was going to take more subtlety than a call announcing how smart I was.

I turned out the lights at about nine. Milo's canvas cot was no more than a stretcher held aloft by crossed sticks of oak at either end. I lay there, the wounded soldier, the man who never asked for war and wouldn't benefit from its outcome.

Up until that moment I had been going on reflex: running and hiding. But on that stretcher, in that coffin-shaped room, with only the occasional squawk of a dreaming hen to break the silence, I decided what I needed and what I had to do. It didn't matter that I was small and weak or even that I begged for my life when that man was slapping me. None of that mattered because that bookstore was what made me somebody rather than just any-body. Burning down my store was just the same as shooting me, and somebody would have to make restitution for that crime.

LORETTA WAS in at eight o'clock exactly. I made coffee for her in the little kitchenette that they had built in the closet.

"Nine years with Mr. Sweet and he never even bought me a coffee," she said, smiling at me.

I had put away the folding cot under the kitchenette counter and returned all of the phone books. Loretta went to her desk and started working immediately. I sat at Milo's desk, thinking how lucky I was to have friends.

Milo shamed me with his generosity. Here I was trying to bail Fearless out of jail, but there was no kindness to it. I needed his protection and peculiar kind of smarts.

Fearless wasn't a bright man, at least not in straightforward thinking. He only read at a sixth-grade level even though he had finished high school. A child could beat him at checkers two times out of three. But Fearless could survive in the harshest environments. He could tell you if a man was going to pull out a gun or cry. You could fool Fearless Jones sometimes, but he always seemed to make the right choices when the chips were down. And he had eyes in the back of his head.

But the best thing about Fearless was the attribute he was named for; he didn't fear anything, not death or pain or any kind of passion. That's why women loved him unconditionally. Be-cause he wasn't afraid of their fire.

• • •

MILO CAME IN at ten-thirty, but he didn't even sit down.

"Messages?" he asked Loretta.

"Nothing to look at," she said without looking up.

"Come on, Paris," Milo said.

I followed him out the door into the strong smell of chickens.

Milo drove a green Ford Fairlane with bright chrome details. It was a fine car to ride in, but I missed my red Nash Rambler. I thought about going to the cops over the car theft, but then I worried about what they'd find and what Elana would say if she were caught.

We arrived at the county jail downtown half an hour later. Milo had set up the release by phone, so all we had to do was go to an oak-framed window that was the only opening in a huge wall facing an empty chamber on the basement floor of the county courthouse and jail building. A small white woman with gold-rimmed glasses sat on a high stool on the other side of the window ledge.

"Dorothy," Milo said in greeting.

"What is your business?" the woman asked, as if she'd never laid eyes on the ex-lawyer.

"Fine for 63J-819-PL48C." Milo handed over my money, and Dorothy counted it.

Without jotting down a note or looking up a file she said, "Have a seat. Someone will be with you in a while."

At the far left end of the huge plaster wall there was a small bench, just large enough for one big man or two smaller ones. Milo and I sat side by side. I could still see the window from where I sat. Dorothy sat there placidly staring out on the empty floor.

It was a surreal experience: the bench made to fit Milo and me, the empty room, the robot bureaucrat, and a big clock the size of a cargo plane's tire above us on the wall. Eighteen minutes after we sat down a man appeared from across the hall. He must have come out of a door, but I didn't see it open or close.

He was a white man in an all-purpose suit made from a rugged material. He wore a white shirt but no tie and carried a worn leather satchel. There was a large bunch of keys hanging from his belt.

"Mr. Sweet," the man hailed when he came within five feet of us.

"Warden Kavenaugh."

"Follow me." Mr. Kavenaugh turned and marched across the empty space.

There was a door there. I hadn't seen it because it was painted the same light green color as the wall. Even the door knob was painted. We went into a hallway with a low ceiling and walls that felt like they were closing in. The hall went for quite a long way. There were no more doors or decorations. These walls were a darker green. The floor was green too.

Finally we came to a dead end. There was a door there. This door opened onto another hallway. This underground lane had many twists and turns, but it too was doorless and without marking. At some point the hallway widened and we found ourselves in a largish room with a door on the opposite side. Warden Kavenaugh, a ruddy and unpleasant-looking man, knocked on this door. When no one answered the knock, Kavenaugh muttered something sour and then began trying the hundred keys on the lock. After about twenty, finally one fit.

We came into a hall that was all metal, like a chamber in a battleship or a submarine. It too was painted green. I felt as if we were far below ground even though we'd only gone one floor below the surface of the court building. There was another door. Kavenaugh knocked on this one, and someone did answer.

"Captain?" the unseen sentry said.

"Kavenaugh," Kavenaugh replied.

The door came open and we were in a large, sun-filled room, not in the bowels of the Earth. I was disoriented by the sunlight and high ceilings. The man who opened the door wore a dark blue uniform complete with a pistol in a leather holster. He was white, hatless, twenty, and pitifully acned. His only duty seemed to be waiting at that door. It was all very odd.

Kavenaugh pointed across the room and said, "There you are." He took a sheaf of papers from his leather satchel and handed it to Milo.

"Good luck," Kavenaugh said. And with that he turned to go back the way we had come.

On the other side of this room was a long wooden table behind which sat two uniformed men. Behind the guards was a cage that contained about a dozen men of all races and ages. Some smoked, a few hunkered down on their haunches, resting against the flat and black iron bars. There wasn't much fraternizing among these men. They were a footstep away from freedom and had no time for small talk.

"Paris!" someone shouted. I saw him then, Fearless Jones, his hands reaching out to me, his smile cut in half by a metal slat. The guard said something to him, but that didn't stop him from reaching and smiling.

When we arrived at the table Milo produced a long sheet of paper from the sheaf Kavenaugh had given him. It was covered on both sides in tiny print. There were red and black seals on the document, making it look official. He placed the paper down between the guards and said, "Tristan Jones."

One of the guards, a man with a red and chapped face, picked up the sheet and pretended to read. His partner, a handsome rake with black hair and a pencil-thin mustache, stared hard at me.

"We had to chain him hand and foot just to get him down here," the red-faced man said.

Milo did not reply.

"Waste'a money to pay his fine," Red Face continued. "He'll just be back in a week."

Milo lifted his chin an inch but gave no more recognition to the man's advice.

"Niggers always come back," the guard said in one final attempt to get a rise out of us.

Milo was quiet and so was I. For some reason these men didn't want to let Fearless go. He'd done something. Not something bad enough to be held over for, but something. If they could get Milo to blow his cool or Fearless to start ranting in his cage, then they could make a case to refuse release.

Seeing Fearless reminded me of a dozen times I'd seen him hard pressed and unbowed. In a Filmore District flophouse, bleeding and in terrible pain from the cop-inflicted knife wound, he said, "It's okay, man. Just gimme a few hours to sleep and I'll be fine."

I saw him face down three men who had gotten it into their heads to disfigure a pretty boy who had taken away a girl they all wanted. The men threatened to cut Fearless too. "Maybe you will," he said to them, "and then again, maybe you won't."

Fearless was more free in that iron cage than I was, or would ever be, on the outside.

I met Fearless in San Francisco after the war. His dress uniform was covered with medals. Around him were three young ladies, each one hoping to be his friend that night. I bought him a drink, saying that it was because I respected a soldier when really I just wanted to sit down at the table with those girls. But Fearless didn't care. He appreciated my generosity and gave me a lifetime of friendship for a single shot of scotch.

"Fuckin' four-F flat-footed fools," a snaggletoothed white man was saying to me through the bars. "They get mad when a black man's a hero 'cause they ain't shit."

The rake gave the white prisoner a stare, which was answered by a clown's grimace. When I nodded to the white con, he smiled in answer, *Nuthin' to it.*

Fearless was released from the cage. His irons were taken off. From under the table the rake brought out a gray cardboard box and handed it to Fearless.

When the guard pointed at a pen and a stack of forms, Milo spoke up.

"You should check your property before signing the release, Fearless."

"Aw, that's all right, Milo," Fearless said in that careless friendly voice of his. "Why they wanna steal my paper wallet? Wasn't no money in it in the first place."

"Check anyway, son."

6 | MILO LEFT US in front of the municipal building. I was wearing the same black slacks and loose yellow shirt I had on when Elana Love dropped in on me — the only clothes to my name since the fire. Fearless wore gray pants and a black silk shirt with two lines of blue and yellow diamonds down either side of the chest. As I said before, I'm a small man, five eight and slim. Fearless is tall, over six feet, and though he's slender, his shoulders warn you about his strength. He's also a good-looking man. A group of passing black women attested to that with their eyes. Even a couple of white women glanced more than once.

But it wasn't just a case of simple good looks. Fearless has a friendly face, a pleasant openness that makes you feel good. If you look at him, he'll nod and say good day no matter who you are.

"Fearless," I said.

"Before you say anything, Paris, I have to have me a cheddar cheese omelet, pork patty sausages, and about a gallon'a fresh orange juice. I got to have it after three months under that jail."

"Momma Tippy?" I asked.

"They ain't nobody else," Fearless said, grinning.

Momma Tippy had a canvas enclosed food stand on Temple Street not twelve blocks from where we stood. In normal times we would have driven there or at least taken the streetcar, but, finances the way they were, we walked.

Fearless limped slightly, but he could walk at a fast clip. On the way, he regaled me with tales from the county lockup. He told about the man he had to beat to be left alone and about the guards who didn't like him because he never got bothered or upset.

"I tried to tell 'em that I was a soldier," Fearless reasoned. "That I knew how to take a order if I was in the stockade. But somehow they was mad just 'cause I wasn't sour and moody. Can you believe that?"

Momma Tippy, a small nut-brown woman from Trinidad, served up seconds and thirds for Fearless at no cost because she felt bad that he had been locked up in a cell.

"M'boy didn't deserve it," she said. "Dey always be takin' 'em. N'you know it ain't right."

After commiserations and eggs, Fearless reached across the table and put his hand on my shoulder.

"I know you need me, Paris," Fearless said in an unusually somber tone. "And whatever it is I'm'onna help ya. 'Cause you know I got it."

"Got what?"

"At first I was mad that you didn't pay my fine. But then I was talkin' to Cowboy —"

"Who?"

"That white dude said about me bein' a war hero."

"The one at the courthouse?"

"Yeah. He asked me if you owed me money, and I told him no. Then he asked was we related or if I had ever pulled you outta jail. I didn't tell 'im 'bout them cops — that's between us an' them dead officers. But I started to think that over the years you done helped me again and again and I just kept on takin' like some kinda dog can't do for himself." Fearless pointed a long finger at a spot over my head. "And that's wrong, man. You don't owe me to pay my bail. Uh-uh. So from now on it's even Steven. I'm'a help you and pay you back, and the only time I'll come to you is for a good meal or a good laugh."

It wasn't true. Fearless couldn't stay out of trouble. But still, I was the one who was wrong. He proved that by forgiving me.

I told him about Elana Love and Leon Douglas.

"Damn, that's some costly lovin'," he said when I was through. "So you worried that they still gonna be after you?"

"That, yeah, but I also need to build back my store. I mean, damn, I didn't do nuthin'. Dude kick my ass then shoot at me down the street. Burn down my store. He got to pay money for that."

Fearless was looking down at his hands. He didn't nod to agree with me or say anything at all.

"What you thinkin' 'bout, Fearless?"

"Jail."

OUR FIRST STOP WAS the Bridgett Beauty Shop on LaRue. Layla Brothers, Fearless's last girlfriend before he got arrested, worked there fighting the kinks out of black women's hair. She seemed happy to see Fearless, though she hadn't even written him a card while he was in jail.

"You know, honey," she said unashamedly to my friend, "I been goin' out with Dwight Turner, and he'd'a got jealous if I started writin' letters back and forth to you."

Fearless didn't seem to care. "We need some wheels, Layla," he said. "Do you mind if we use your car?"

"'Course not. Here." She took the keys from her purse. "What you doin' after?"

"Well," Fearless hesitated, "Paris and I might need the car for a couple'a days."

"That's okay. I can use my mama's car. But you got to sleep at night, don't you?" Now that Fearless was out of jail, Dwight Turner wasn't even a consideration.

"Yeah, but . . ."

"But what?"

"Paris's place burnt down, and you know I don't have no apartment. So until we get some business done, we bound at the hip."

Layla was taller than I with skin the color of unburnished brass. Her long hair had been dyed gold. She was prettier than she made herself, buxom and thin. She looked at me with a sneer that tried to be a smile and said, "I ain't that greedy."

Fearless laughed and touched her elbow.

He said, "I understand, babe," then walked off with me and her keys.

LAYLA'S CAR WAS a big Packard. The pink sedan had a straight eight engine that guzzled gas at the rate of ten miles a gallon. We cranked down the windows and lit up Pall Mall cigarettes. Fearless had a perpetual grin on his face, and I was pretty happy too. It had been an act of will for me to leave him in that jail cell, mind over matter. I knew when we were driving that we were supposed to be together, rolling along like two carefree dogs with the wind in their faces.

The Tannenbaum house was just off Brooklyn Avenue in East L.A., the once-Jewish neighborhood that was being repopulated by Mexicans. The house was a smallish yellow job. With two floors and six windows facing the street, it had a few bushes but no trees. The lawn was lovely, however, green and manicured.

"Nice place," Fearless said as we walked up the concrete footpath to the door.

"Any place is nice if it got walls and don't smell like smoke," I said.

"Any place is nice if it ain't got bars an' it don't smell like piss an' disinfectant," Fearless corrected.

I knocked on the door, wondering what kind of lie I could use on whoever answered. I expected thirty seconds at least before anyone showed. But the door swung open immediately. A tiny woman wearing a white blouse like a man's dress shirt and a long flannel gray skirt stood there. There were spots of blood on the blouse.

When she saw our faces she was petrified. An elderly man lay on the floor behind her dressed exactly the same as she was, only the skirt was a pair of trousers instead. There was blood coming from the side of his head and also from his left shoulder.

"Leave us alone!" the woman cried, trying to push the door closed. "Don't kill us!"

"What happened?" Fearless asked. He held the door open against her feeble shove and took a step across the threshold.

"I called the police," the woman warned.

Fearless hesitated a moment, no more, but in that delay I realized that jail had hurt him.

"Go away!" the woman cried.

Fearless was already kneeling down over the man and peering into his pained face. I came to his side. I mean, I couldn't very well run when I had brought us to that door. At any rate, Fearless had the keys to Layla's car, and running on foot in L.A. is like bullfighting in a wheelchair.

"Get me something to put under his head, Paris," Fearless said.

Behind me was a parlor of some sort. I grabbed the cushion off of a couch while Fearless said to the woman, "I need a bandage, something to stop the bleeding."

"Please don't kill him," she cried.

Fearless grabbed her arm, forcing her to look down into his eyes. "I'm not gonna hurt him, but he might bleed to death if you don't bring me a bandage or sumpin' to stop the bleedin'."

"Oh," the woman uttered. "What should I do? What should I do?"

Looking around for an answer, her eyes lit upon me.

"Go get the bandages, lady," I said.

"Oh. Oh yes." She scurried along, slowed by the long skirt, through a door that swung open and back.

"Who are you?" the man was asking Fearless as I shoved the cushion under his head.

"Fearless Jones."

"Are you here to rob me?"

"No."

The man turned his head to me and asked, "What about him?"

"That's Paris," Fearless said. "He's a friend."

The pale man nodded in relief.

"What happened to you?" I asked.

"They came to take the money," the man said to Fearless. "They vanted to, but I said no."

"Here it is! Here it is!" Mrs. Tannenbaum said, rushing through the swinging door. In her hands was a small white pillowcase.

"Take it, Paris," Fearless snapped. "Put some pressure on that shoulder."

"Why did they do it? Why did they do it?" Mrs. Tannenbaum was chanting. I didn't like her color. It was way past Caucasian on the way to chalk.

"They were trying to rob you?" I asked Sol.

"They vanted the bond, the money." There was a dreamlike quality to his voice. He was going into shock.

He reached up and grabbed Fearless by the fabric of his silk shirt.

"Don't let them rob Fanny," he said.

"It's a bet," Fearless said.

"Oh God," the wife cried.

Sol shuddered and tried to rise, but the pressure I was putting on his shoulder restrained him. The pain of the exertion made him wince, then he passed out.

There was a grim look on Fearless's face. I knew from experience that that meant trouble for someone.

"He's dead," Mrs. Tannenbaum said simply and quietly. A whole lifetime of dread ending with a hush.

"Police!" a man's voice commanded.

I tried to think my way back to the bookstore when it was still standing, but there was no escaping the hand that caught me by the shoulder and flung me to the floor.

7 | "WHY DID YOU KILL Sol Tannenbaum?" Sergeant Bernard Latham asked for the fourteenth time.

"All I did was try and stop the bleedin', man," I said. Then I squinched up my face, preparing for the blow. But that time he didn't hit me.

"Tristan confessed," Latham said instead. The sergeant was a blocky-looking specimen. He was like the first draft of a drawing in one of the art lesson books I sold in my store. Block for a chest, squares for the pelvis, and cylinders for legs. A cube for a head. The only thing that humanized him was a protruding gut.

"Confessed to what?"

"He said you did the stabbing."

"Uh-huh."

"I don't think you understand, Paris," Latham said, pretending that he was my friend. "If he says that you did it and testifies to that, you get the gas chamber and he goes free. We don't believe him, so what do you have to say?"

"Whatever Fearless says," I replied.

"What?"

"Whatever Fearless says. If he said I did it, then okay, let's go to court."

Latham's backhand was in great form. He could have gone pro. His blow reopened the cut that Leon Douglas had made in my mouth the day before.

A knock came on the door of the eight-by-eight gray room that the East L.A. cops used for questioning. Another white policeman stuck his head in. I was sprawled out on the painted concrete floor. Latham was deciding between a kick or another backhand.

"They want him for the lineup, Sergeant," the head said.

When the sergeant didn't answer, the head asked, "Should I tell them you need a few more minutes?"

It had to be a nightmare. Nobody had luck this bad.

"No," Latham said. "We want him walking for the lineup. I can work on him some more after that."

With that he lifted me by the shoulder and brought me to another room where a variety of black men about my size were milling around. A couple of them registered shock when they saw my face.

"Just goin' on ugly, you the one to pick," one man in a brown T-shirt and green pants said.

We lined up against a blank wall. A severe light came on, and we stood there. A few seconds grew to a minute. One minute became three. The light went out, and we were led from the room.

Latham came up to me, and I remembered his promise to *work on me* after the lineup.

It had to be a nightmare.

"Come on," a small uniformed cop next to the sergeant said in a loud, officious voice.

"I wanted to talk to him a little more," Latham complained.

"This man is under the authority of this precinct, Sergeant. When you arrest someone in Hollywood, you can have a shot." Obviously Little Big Mouth didn't like the sergeant.

I followed him to a large room that was cut in two by a metal grate. On the other side of the grate were large metal shelves with cardboard boxes stacked in them.

A door to my left opened. A lanky police officer walked in, followed by Fearless. My friend was glowering until he saw me. Then he smiled.

"Hey hey, Paris."

I sighed in response. He knew how I felt. His jaw was lop-sided from some heavy *questions* they asked him.

I looked around for Latham, but he was nowhere to be seen.

"All right," the cop who accompanied Fearless said. "You guys can go now. But we know where you live."

I had given them my address but neglected to say that the building had burned down.

A man from behind the grate brought our confiscated belongings to the window. There wasn't much. Twenty-nine dollars in my wallet, the keys to Layla's Packard, and Fearless's empty paper wallet.

We went out through the door where Fearless had entered and then to a door that led to the street. It was a side door, so it was fortunate, or maybe unfortunate, that they saw us.

"Gentlemen," she called from down the street.

At first I didn't know who it was. I saw two white women with a big white man, that was all.

"That's the old man's wife," Fearless said. He waved at her and took me by the arm.

A thought crossed my mind: for seven dollars I could catch a bus to Frisco and get a room for two dollars a night until a dish-washing job came through. It was the thought of a job, though, that reminded me of my bookstore.

"Come on, Paris," Fearless said. "I gave my word."

The women approached us. One was indeed the old woman who cried so hard over her dead husband that she couldn't tell the arresting cops that Fearless and I were not the attackers. The other woman was taller and awkward looking, somewhere in her twenties. They were accompanied by a big, dumpy-looking guy who wore black slacks with a white shirt that wasn't tucked in very well. The pale skin around his chin was blue, though I would have bet that he had already shaved for the second time that day. He was taller than Fearless but soft looking, shaped something like a bowling pin. His big hands were worth looking at; the fingers were long and held out straight, making his hands resemble those of a stroke victim.

But he was not paralyzed. He shrank back, clutching those hands to his chest when we moved to meet them.

"I'm so sorry," the elder woman said. "I saw what they did to you. I'm sorry."

"We're sorry about your husband, ma'am," Fearless said gallantly.

"You the one who looked at me in the lineup?" I asked.

"Both of you," she said. "They kept trying to make me say that you were the ones who attacked Sol. One of them was tall like you," she said, looking at Fearless, "but he had a bigger face and dead eyes, and he wore a cowboy hat."

"A cowboy hat?" I said, thinking about the horns in my side mirror.

The old woman nodded. "When I said no, they told me that you would never be able to hurt me again. I was afraid that they were going to kill you."

"Are you all right?" the younger woman asked. Her homely face made her concern seem that much more sincere.

"We have to go," the man said, putting his discomfort into words.

"No, Morris," the older woman said. "I have to talk to these men."

"You don't know them, Aunt Hedva. The police said that this one just got out of jail."

"Didn't my Sol just get out of prison?" the diminutive woman asked.

"That was different," Morris said. "You don't know them. Why were they even at your house?"

"We were makin' the rounds," I said. "Askin' some'a the older white folks if they needed a gardener, and we stayed to try and save his life."

The younger woman said, "Hedva told us that these men helped Sol."

"Be quiet, Gella," Morris ordered. "For all you know they could all have been working together."

The sloppy man looked at us then and flinched, not, I thought,

59

because he was ashamed of treating us like we were invisible but instead because he realized that we really could have been in on it with the man who stabbed his uncle.

Morris didn't seem to fit with the women. He was right there, and scared. They were someplace else altogether, like characters from a romantic novel who found themselves in a fast-paced crime story.

It's not that the two women were cut from the same cloth. No. Gella and her aunt were as much opposites as people of the same race can be. The younger woman was tall and lean. Her ears and nose were large and so were her lips. Every movement she made was executed in two operations. If she reached out to touch her aunt's shoulder, her hand would make it half the way, stop, and then go the final distance. If she spoke, first she'd lift her head and open her mouth, then she'd lower her chin and do it all over, ending with whatever she had to say.

The older woman was short and round with small features. She had beadlike eyes and almost no lips. Her motions were quick and accurate. I had misjudged her earlier in the day. It was the shock of seeing her husband bleeding that had made her scared and confused.

"We have to go now," Morris said to the women.

It was almost as if Fearless and I weren't there on the corner. As if our dark skins somehow blended with the dusk and whisked us away.

"These men did not hurt us," Hedva said, still involved in the earlier argument. "What they say is true. They saved Solly's life."

"Saved his life?" I said. "The cops told us that he was dead."

"No." Hedva shook her head. "Not dead. He's in the hospital. They can't wake him up, but he's still alive."

"Which one of you is Fanny?" Fearless asked.

"I am," Hedva said. "That's what they called me when I was a child."

Fearless nodded, staring straight into the older woman's face. She was his charge now. Fearless would never forget that Sol, lying bleeding on the floor, had instructed him to protect Fanny from being robbed.

"Well, I'm glad it turned out all right." What I wanted was to break up our little powwow and get on with the business at hand. Sol wasn't dead, but he could still die. I wasn't dead either but, the way my luck was going, staying alive had become a long shot.

"Can I help you?" the older woman asked. "Something to make up for what they did?"

"No thank you, ma'am," Fearless said out of reflex. "But can we do anything for you?"

"Excuse me, Mrs. Tannenbaum," I interjected, "but my friend here and me don't have anything to help with. We don't even have our car. If you and your family could give us a ride back to your place, at least we could get that."

"Of course," Fanny assured me.

"There's no room," Morris, the bowling pin, said. "I have boxes in the backseat."

"You can put them in the trunk." Fanny waved her hand dismissively. I'd've bet it wasn't the first time she treated him like that.

"No," Morris said sternly. It might have been the first time that Morris stood up on his hind legs. Fanny's small eyes widened an eighth of an inch.

"I, I have a spare in the trunk," Morris said. "There's no room."

"I can take them," the younger woman said. "I drove my car from home."

"I forbid it!" Morris shrieked.

He took a step toward her. She shrank back a half step. Morris grabbed her by the arm, and Fearless tensed up. I was afraid we'd be right back in jail, but Fanny saved the day.

"Get your hands off of her," she commanded.

Morris clenched his fist hard for a moment, then he let his wife go. He locked eyes with me. I could see his rage at being forced into line by a woman. He muttered something and then stalked off down the alley.

"I'M GELLA, the younger woman said on the way to the car. "Hedva's niece."

"Paris Minton," I said. "And this here is Fearless Jones. Thanks for takin' us."

Gella smiled and looked away. She was shy and near ugly, but there was something fetching about her awkwardness, something that made your hands feel that they wanted to reach out to make sure she wouldn't fall or get lost.

Gella drove an assembly-line prewar Ford. It was painted black and didn't even have a radio installed. A spare machine, it was spotless and unadorned. Fearless and I sat in the backseat, while Fanny and her niece rode up front in silence. It was only a short ride, ten or eleven minutes. On the way we passed many white and turquoise and blue little houses, all sporting neat lawns and white cement driveways. It was around six o'clock, dinnertime for working people. Through many windows and open doors, you could see brown-skinned and some white-skinned people eating at family tables.

A few men were standing out in front watering the grass, or maybe lugging a trash can. Any man that saw us drive by stopped what he was doing and looked. That's because Los Angeles was still a small town back then, and most residents were from the country somewhere. They treated their surroundings as familiar and friendly, and they wanted to know who was driving on their street.

There I was swallowing the slow trickle of blood from the cuts inside my mouth, being driven through a blue-collar paradise. I had the irrational notion that I could just ask that gawky white woman to stop the car and I could open the door and walk out into a peaceful life, leaving the trouble I was in behind. But before I could speak up, we were pulling into the Tannenbaum drive-way. Layla's pink car was still parked at the curb. Fearless was there next to me, pressing his swollen jaw. There was no escape.

When we were all out of the Ford, Fearless went up to Fanny and shook her hand.

"I promised your husband that I wouldn't let anybody rob you, Mrs. Tannenbaum," he said. "So if you need me . . ."

Fanny looked up at Fearless with an expression that many women had for him. There was trust and hope and even faith in that gaze. Gella and I exchanged worried glances.

"Have you eaten?" Fanny asked us.

"Why no, ma'am," Fearless said.

"Hedva," said Gella.

"What, dear?"

"I have to go home."

"Go on then, I'll call you."

"But . . ." Gella let the word hang in the air, obviously meaning that Fearless and I were the reason she could not leave.

I didn't blame her. Her uncle had been stabbed, she had just
been to the police station, her husband was angry and scared
enough to have raised his hand to her. And then there we were
with our disheveled clothes and bloody faces, looking like thugs.

"Go home to your husband," Fanny said flatly. "I'm fine."

"But . . ." Gella said again.

Fanny raised her voice and fired words in a language I did not
understand. The meaning was harsh though — that was evident
by the lowering of the younger woman's gaze.

"I'm sorry, Auntie," the girl said. She looked at us and
hunched her shoulders in an apologetic sort of way. Then she
went to her car and got in.

As the engine turned over, Fanny said, "Come in, gentlemen."

We followed her through the front door we'd been to earlier
that day. This time we were ushered in with a smile.

Fanny was five feet tall, tops. Her husband had maybe an inch
on her. The house reflected their height with its low ceilings and
small chairs. The rooms were tiny, even for me.

She sat Fearless and me down at a round table in an alcove off
of the kitchen. The meal came quickly and in courses. We had
cabbage stuffed with ground beef, potato dumplings that she
called knishes, chicken soup with rice, and chopped chicken liv-
ers on white bread. It was all delicious. For me, a man who had
faced death twice in the last two days, it was a king's feast.

After she made sure that we were eating, Fanny made a call.
She wasn't on the phone very long, and when she got off she was
weepy and sad.

"That the hospital?" Fearless asked.

Fanny nodded and took a chair.

"Is he okay?"

"He came awake for a little while," Fanny replied. "They said that he's sleeping now and shouldn't have company. Not even me. Not even me."

"I'll go down there and wait with you if you want," Fearless said. "We could just sit outside and wait. If you're close family, they'll let you wait all night."

"No," she said. "I'll sleep tonight and go in the morning. But thank you."

It was kind of quiet after that. Fearless got up and served himself more soup, and I played with my fork, wishing I had a home to go to.

"Your niece didn't want to leave you alone with us," I said just to make some noise.

"You're not white and not Jewish. She's heard all kinds of stories, and she's a suggestible girl. But she has a good heart."

"But maybe she's right," I said. "You don't know us. Don't you think it's strange that two black men show up at your door after another black man tries to murder your husband?"

"Stop tryin' t'scare her, man," Fearless told me.

"No," Fanny said. "No, it's all right. I'm not afraid of you, Mr. Minton. You helped Sol even though I was screaming and yelling. You did too, Mr. Jones. If I would have come on a bleeding man and somebody yelled at me, I would have run away. You went to jail. They beat you. I'm not afraid of you. It would make more sense if you were afraid of me."

"Why we gonna be afraid of a pretty young girl like you, Fanny?" Fearless asked with a grin.

"Because all I had to do was nod my head and you would be murderers in jail."

That pulled Fearless up short a second, but then he smiled again.

"Well, I ain't ascared'a you, and you don't need to be ascared'a us," he said. "We wouldn't hurt nobody like you. It's like I said, I'm gonna make it my business that nobody else messes with you."

"How you plan to do that, man?" I said, fed up with how silly they both were. She *shouldn't* have been taking strangers into her home, and Fearless was nuts to want to protect somebody he didn't even know.

Fearless gave me his sour look. For someone else that look could have meant trouble, but it was nothing to me.

"You got a wallet with no money in it," I continued, "a borrowed car that's low on gas even when the tank is full, you don't have an apartment, and my place is burnt to the ground. You an' me lucky to keep anybody from messin' with us."

"Oh my," Fanny declared.

"It don't matter about a house, Paris. I'll find us some place to stay. And I don't need no money to stand up to some coward wanna be messin' wit' old folks. If I have to, I'll pitch a tent right here in the front yard and take a shovel for my bayonet."

"Grass salad and earthworm steak, is that what you gonna eat?" I taunted.

"Excuse me," Fanny Tannenbaum said in a small voice.

Fearless and I both turned our heads toward her. It was an odd thing to realize that we had begun to ignore her the same way that her nephew-in-law had ignored us earlier, the same way that white people had been ignoring us our entire lives.

"Yes, Fanny?" Fearless said.

"You gentlemen can stay here for a few days if you wish."

I was stunned by that. I had done some traveling in my life. Fearless had been on three continents and then some, but neither one of us had ever experienced that kind of generosity. White people didn't open their doors to questionable young black men. Hell, there weren't many black folks I knew that would be so brave, or foolish.

"It's the least I can do," Fanny said. "You saved Solly's life and . . . and . . ." — she hesitated and then drew a deep breath — ". . . and I am afraid to stay here alone."

"You got your niece and nephew a couple'a blocks away," I said. I was surprised that she offered us a place to stay, but that didn't mean I wanted to take her up on the offer.

"That putz couldn't save himself from walking down a hill," she said disdainfully.

It wasn't that funny, but Fearless laughed loud and long.

"What's that you say, Fanny?" he crooned. "He can't walk wit'out fallin' down?"

The old lady started laughing too. She laughed so hard that she doubled over in the chair with her head on her knees. She forced herself to stand, still laughing, and went to a cupboard where she located a pint bottle of peach schnapps. She poured all three of us generous shots in squat glasses. The liquor was strong, and good. We finished off the first pint and put a serious dent in a second.

I was smiling with them after a while, feeling pretty good. So when Fearless said, "Sure, Fanny, we'll stay here with you," I didn't see anything wrong with it. After all, we were already there, and it was after nine; we didn't have a home to go to, and I still had some questions to ask about Elana Love.

I made a little nod and said, "Well, if we got to go, we might as well be eatin' good and feelin' high."

FEARLESS GOT IT into his head to wash the dishes. Fanny offered to help, but he said that he missed simple chores after his twelve weeks in jail. He'd already explained to her that he'd gotten into an altercation with three mechanics that tried to cheat him. I thought that that would turn the sweet old lady against us, but instead she said, "My Sol was in jail. It's a bad place where many good men go."

SHE AND I RETIRED to the sitting room while Fearless hummed and played in the soapy water. Sol had a glass box filled with English Ovals, an imported cigarette. I smoked a few of these while we talked.

"I take it you don't like Gella's old man," I said.

She made a quizzical face that suddenly became bright. "Oh," she said, "you mean the putz."

"Yeah."

"He's a coarse man," Fanny said. "Not rude or foul-mouthed but unfinished, without manners, like a pig farmer or a policeman."

"You don't like the cops either?"

The schnapps made conversation easy.

"When I was a child," she said, "the police, the army, and the pig farmers were our enemies. Morris isn't bad, he's just stupid about things. He's always coming around offering to work on the house, to cut the grass. He's telling me that he wants to help when

Sol" — she sighed and looked to the ceiling — "when Sol was in prison. He's always telling me he wants to help, but I tell him no. He thinks I'm too old to be bothered with a checkbook or the plumber, but I'm not."

"What was that he said just before he stomped off?"

"I don't remember," Fanny said, but she did.

"Swatted?" I prodded. "Swear?"

"Svartza," she whispered.

"What's that mean?"

"It means black, but not in a nice way," she admitted.

"Oh."

"I would never be bothered with him, but Gella loves him — because he's fat."

"Huh?"

"That's true," she said, widening her eyes as much as she could. "She loves him because he's so big and fat she thinks that he can protect her."

"Protect her from what?"

"Her family was from Estonia, like us. Only they moved to Germany after the First World War. Her father, Schmoil, Solly's brother's son, was a rich man and smart." Fanny pointed at her temple to show me the degree of his intelligence. I realized then that she also had had a good share of schnapps. "We left Europe after they moved. Schmoil stayed on and did business. He owned three newspapers but sold them when he saw what was coming. He put all of his money into his art collection and moved it to Switzerland. Then he moved his wife and *kinder* to Vienna. He thought that they would be safe there."

"That don't sound too safe."

"A wife, a grandmother, three uncles, and seven children," Fanny said, "and only him and Gella survived. They were all betrayed by a Jew, but my Solly saved Schmoil and Gella."

"He did?" I said. I found it hard to believe that the little old man I'd seen could have saved anybody.

"When Schmoil and Gella ran, my Sol hired smugglers in Italy to put them in barrels and take them to Africa. Then he bought them passports and brought them here." Fanny had been whispering, and I could see why. Whatever he did, it didn't sound legal.

"Wow," I said. "Damn. That's a great thing. That why they put him in jail?"

"No. They said he was a thief," Fanny said sadly. "I don't know. He sold his tailor's shop and went to work for those goy accountants."

"Who?"

"Lawson and Widlow. He went to work for them."

"If he was a tailor, why'd they need him?"

"He did his own bookkeeping for years, and he went to work for almost nothing. He stayed late every night finishing everything they gave him. He stopped laughing with me, and then one day the police came and take him away."

"And then," I said, seeing my opening, "after he was in jail a while, a woman named Elana Love came to your door."

"You know her?" There was surprise and anger in the old woman's voice.

"You see, Fanny," I said, "Fearless an' me aren't really gardeners . . ." I related, more or less, the story of me and Elana Love.

"And this man, her boyfriend," Fanny asked when I was through, "he's the one that hurt Sol?"

"I don't think it was him in the cowboy hat, but he was probably the other one. I'd bet on it."

"But you will find out because you want the money back for your store," she said.

"I'd like my store back," I agreed. "At least I'd like a new place. But like I said, Leon is three kinds of bad. It might not be worth —"

"I will pay you." It was the kind of interruption that I didn't mind.

"What?"

"You don't have money, Mr. Minton. You will need something." She got everything right, right down to calling me mister. "Now that Solly's in the hospital, I have to do something. My nephew is a fool, and Gella is just a girl. I don't trust the police. . . . All I have is you and your friend. I heard those men shouting at Solly too. They said they wanted the money he stole."

"I thought you said he didn't steal anything?"

"He told those men that they were the thieves. He told them they were *gonif* and they worked for thieves."

"You tell the cops that?" I asked.

"I was afraid to tell them anything."

"So what can I do?"

"You said they were looking for a bond. I gave a bond to that woman. Sol had given it to me. I asked him if it was stolen, and he told me no."

"And you believe that even after those men came in here after him?"

"Solly would never lie to me," Fanny said with dignity. "He's in trouble, but he wants to protect me. I want you to help me find out what kind of trouble he's in."

"But I could tell you that right now," I said. "It's that bond."

"No," she said. "It is more than that."

"What?"

"I don't know. He told me the bond was nothing but in a way that I knew there was something he wouldn't say."

"You don't think Leon came here after the money Sol owed him?"

"He wanted money stolen," Fanny said stubbornly, "not money owed."

"How much money we talkin' about here?" I said. "I mean, what will you pay me?"

"I have one hundred dollars. I will give that to you and then, when you tell me what she says, I'll give a hundred more."

"And all you wanna know is why are they coming back after Sol?"

Fanny nodded.

"There's just one thing," I said.

"What?"

"Fearless thinks he can live on air, but we need that money. After what he told Sol, he won't let you pay us a dime."

Fanny nodded again and patted the back of my hand.

"Leave me your pants and shirt," she said.

"Say what?"

"Leave your clothes out here when you go to bed. I'll wash them and iron them in the morning and then I'll put the money in your pockets."

Fearless came in only a few moments after the deal was sealed.

"All clean and dry," he announced. "I stacked 'em in the dryin' tray though, 'cause I didn't want to put 'em away wrong."

"That's okay." Fanny was beaming. "I can do that."

I jumped up then. "But it better wait till tomorrow."

"Why?" both Fearless and Fanny asked.

"If we wanna protect Fanny, then we got to find out what they came here for," I said. "And one thing about crooks, they don't stay in one place too long."

8

WE DROPPED FANNY OFF at her niece's house, which was only three blocks away on Marianna Avenue. It made sense not to leave her at home with Leon Douglas on the loose.

Fanny gave us the keys to her house.

"We'll call you in the mornin', Mrs. Tannenbaum, 'cause you know we'll probably come in late at night," Fearless told her at the front door. Fearless was a gentleman and would never just leave a woman off at the curb. I wandered up there with him.

Morris Greenspan answered the door.

"What do you want?" he asked us.

"They're my houseguests, Morris," Fanny said.

"You can't come in my house," he said, somehow taking Fanny's explanation as a request.

"Then we'll leave you here," I said to Fanny.

"No," Fanny said. "Morris, apologize to my friends."

"You don't even know them, Aunt Fanny. They aren't family."

"We better be goin', Mrs. Tannenbaum," Fearless said. He hated seeing any man get humiliated.

"These men are my guests," Fanny repeated, looking up at her nephew-in-law.

The glower on the young man's face was the same when he was eight, I was sure. Sullen and on the verge of a pout, he might have stood there for half an hour before saying hello like a good boy.

"Mr. Minton. Mr. Jones," Gella Greenspan said as she appeared at her husband's side. The homely girl and her bearish, sullen husband made an ungainly pair. She took the big baby's arm. "Would you like to come in for coffee?"

It wasn't that Gella was any less afraid of us. She was just raised better.

"We have to go," I said. "Thanks anyway. See ya, Fanny, Morris."

The sloppy bowling pin grimaced.

"Call me if you need anything," Fanny said.

"We'll pick you up in the morning," Fearless promised.

Then we left the unmatched set of relatives to argue manners and race over coffee and rolls.

I HAD THE ADDRESS of E. E. Love written down on a scrap of paper. Fearless drove us to the Twenty-eighth Street abode. The small, single-story gray house was surrounded by sagging trellises that were heavy with vines of golden roses. There was no light on, no car in the driveway, but still we knocked at the front door.

No answer.

A big dog came strolling down the street. It was a light-colored, short-haired and meaty mutt that nearly shimmered under a granite streetlamp. I saw him before he saw us. He did an almost human double take and then started barking for all he was worth.

"We better get outta here," I said.

"We ain't even got here yet." Fearless went down on one knee and held out his hand.

The barking dog got braver and braver. Growling and gurgling murder he advanced on Fearless, who for his part looked like a modern-day African saint. The dog snapped and then he sniffed. He pushed his nose against Fearless's hand, then plopped down on the ground, turning over onto his back to show his belly.

Fearless scratched the dog and then stood up, his new best friend at his side.

There was a black, lift-top mailbox attached to the wall next to the front door. It was stuffed with mail. I pulled out an envelope wedged in at the side. By match light I read the name Miss Elana Love scrawled in purple ink.

"This is the right place," I said.

Fearless's dog growled in anticipation. Fearless pushed him by the neck toward the front walk, and the mutt seemed to understand the command. He padded his way to the curb and stood there daring some phantom intruder to try and go by.

I went around the side of the house, testing windows. On the third try I was successful. Once inside I went straight through the gloom to where the front door should have been. It was there. Fearless snaked in, closing the door behind him. I found a lamp on a table and turned it on.

After making sure that the house was empty we decided to separate to make our search. The whole front of the house was the living room. It was just a couch and two chairs with a stand-up maple bar on top of two mismatched blue throw rugs. The rugs were ugly. One had a diamond pattern, and the other was covered in small white dots.

At either end of the living room was a door. One led to the kitchen, the other to her bedroom. Between these two rooms was the toilet.

Elana's bedroom was simple enough. A single bed with pink sheets and a dresser with a mirror and chair. The window looked out on a fence cordoning off her three-foot-deep backyard. I went through the drawers of the dresser, the closet, the pockets of her clothes. I checked under the sheets and between the mattresses, on the window ledge and under the bed. There was nothing there. Nothing. She had three dresses in the closet and only one pair of shoes.

Fearless and I met in the bathroom. Two towels on a chrome rack, a half-used bar of white soap, and no floor mat. In the trash can there were a towel and a wad of cotton bandages clotted with a good deal of partially dried blood. I poked at the dressing with a handy toothbrush, but Fearless reached in and pulled out the bloody rags.

"Somebody been wounded pretty good," he said.

"No shit," I replied.

I went over the kitchen again because Fearless didn't have the patience to search for anything smaller than an elephant. There wasn't much to see there either. A jar of instant coffee, white bread, and an open can of condensed milk.

"I bet she only stays here now and then," I said. "She probably only keeps the place in case her boyfriend of the week has a change of heart."

"You think?"

"No clothes to speak of, no food," I said. "And even a blind man wouldn't have carpet like that under his feet."

Fearless laughed at that. He was slender, but he had a fat man's laugh. For a moment there I realized how much I had missed my friend.

"Come on," I said. "Let's get outta here." I led the way through the kitchen door back into the living room. We were almost out of the door when I stopped.

"What is it, Paris?"

"I didn't look under the kitchen sink. Did you?"

"No."

"I better look."

"You think she under there?" I couldn't tell if he was serious or joking.

I FOUND a tin wastebasket beneath the sink drain and dumped the contents out on the kitchen table. There were tiny bits of paper, coated with once-wet coffee grounds, torn from several notes and at least one letter. I pulled up a chair and started sifting through the mess.

I had been working for all of five minutes when Fearless started yawning. "What you doin', Paris?" he whined.

The letter was impossible to reconstruct in the time I had. It would have probably taken two or three hours, seeing that it was scrawled in small pale blue letters on both sides of at least three pages. To make it even more difficult, the words had blurred from the moisture of the coffee grounds.

The notes were written in black ink on white paper except for one that was written in pencil and another that was written on yellow paper. I concentrated on these two.

Fearless opened the front door and whistled for the dog, who came bounding in like the loyal family pet.

"Hey, boy. Hey, boy," Fearless chanted from the living room.

I didn't have to go far to see that the penciled note was a shopping list — scouring powder and Modess napkins were all I needed for that.

The yellow note had San Quentin Prison printed across the bottom. Above that, in black letters, the initials C.T. were printed slantways, along with a phone number that had an Axminster exchange.

There was a phone in Elana's bedroom, but it was dead, so we let Fearless's new pet into the backseat and drove toward a gas station on Slauson. I didn't want to bring the dog, but I didn't have the time to argue with Fearless either.

I did say, "Don't you think somebody's gonna miss his pet?"

"If he had a collar or license I'd take him home right this minute," Fearless replied. "You know a dog catcher could be givin' him cyanide tomorrow if we just let him go."

That was the end of our discussion.

When we got to the gas station I put a nickel into the slot. C.T., whoever that was, was a long shot. But it was the only shot we had.

He answered on the first ring. "Leon, is that you, man?" His voice sounded like a metal file rasping against stone.

"C.T.?" I asked, disguising my voice just in case this rough man ever heard me speak again.

"Who is?" he asked.

"It's me — Dingo," I said. I regretted the name as soon as I said it. I was scared stupid.

"Who?"

"Leon told me to call you up. He wanted me to come and get you but —"

"Get me? Man, I could hardly sit up straight."

"Leon said to come help —"

"You a doctor?"

"I can take care'a you," I said, trying to make my fake voice sound certain. "I got a brother used to be a medic in the army with me."

There was silence on the line.

"C.T.?"

"Why you callin' me that?"

"That's what Leon wrote on the paper, man. Ain't that you? I mean if —"

"When you gonna get here?" he asked, interrupting me for the third time.

"That's why I called. He wrote down your initials and phone, but I can't read the address. Clinton sumpin'."

"Clinton?" C.T. moaned. "Denker, man. Twenty-nine sixty-nine Denker. Super's apartment."

"Be right there," I said in a husky voice that would have fooled even my mother.

"YOU GOT my pistol, Paris?" Fearless asked over the loud barking in the backseat.

"I told you already, the girl stole it."

"That was my gun she took from you?"

"Yes." I took the left onto Denker.

"An' now you want me to walk unarmed into the house of a friend of a ex-con nearly killed you yesterday?"

"He don't know me, Fearless. I'll just walk in there an' tell him I'm Leon's friend." Finding that phone number and fooling C.T. had given me a sense of control.

"What if he was the one sittin' next to Leon when he was chasin' yo' ass down the street?"

"Shit." My fingers went suddenly cold.

"That's okay, man. I'll go in first. But you owe me a pistol."

THE ADDRESS C.T. had given us was a court of apartments at the corner of Horn. We left the dog in the car. The super's apartment was listed under the name of Conrad Benjamin Till. Whoever designed the court must have been a fan of Minos's maze. After every two doorways there was another turn. I lost my sense of direction almost immediately.

Most of the apartments were dark, as the next day was a workday. We went past a pair of teenagers having some kinda sex behind a skimpy rosebush. I don't know if they saw us, but they sure didn't stop.

NO ONE ANSWERED when we rang Conrad's bell. No one called out when we knocked. Fearless had brought Layla's tire iron in lieu of a pistol and used it on the door. The sound of that doorjamb being wrenched open by that twelve-pound tire iron was frightening; loud and whining with reports like small-caliber gunshots now and then. I looked around to see if anyone had turned on their lights; no one had, but that didn't mean we hadn't been heard or seen.

Fearless went in first, but I was right on his heels, running my hands along the wall. I didn't find a light switch, but Fearless snagged the overhead cord and said, "I got it."

Yellow light flooded the small sitting room as I was closing the front door.

Fearless said, "Dog."

There on a low, modern couch sat a fresh corpse.

He probably had been darker before all the blood drained out, but he'd always be a light-skinned Negro with brown freckles across his wide nose. His face seemed to belong on a fat man, but he was of normal build. He wore a light-colored jacket, blood-soaked T-shirt, and threadbare jeans. Till must've died right after we got off the phone.

I was looking at the dead man, but my mind was working overtime trying to believe that he wasn't there. I'd happened upon dead bodies before in my life: three children in a car wreck outside of Turner, Texas, the body of a sailor I saw on the shore at the Gulf of Mexico, and there's been a murdered body or two on the street. I once saw the victims of a double lynching hung from an ancient live oak not two miles from my mother's home. I've seen a good many deaths, but none of them, with the exception of those cops that Fearless killed, had anything to do with me.

I had sought out Conrad Till. And if I wasn't careful I'd end up just like him.

"The first one's always hard," Fearless said.

"Say what?"

"When me and my squad'd go out in Germany it was always the first man get killed get to us," he said in an impossibly calm voice. "Didn't matter if it was one'a us or one'a them. It's just that first dead man that reminds you that this is serious business."

With that Fearless moved to inspect the room. I moved too, his nonchalant bravery having turned my terror into mere heart-pounding fear.

Till's tan jacket had as much wet blood on it as dry. There was a lot of blood, down on his blue jeans and coagulated in the spaces between the fingers of his left hand. There was also a burned-out cigarette between those fingers. It was as if he'd been sitting there listening to music but then all of a sudden broke out in an attack of bleeding. The blood had come from a wound in the left side of his chest.

We didn't split up in the super's pad. I went with Fearless into the kitchen. I forced my eyes to look everywhere, but they didn't see much. I had forgotten that I was looking for Elana Love.

A doorway from the kitchen led to the bedroom. There was nothing there except a bloody towel in the middle of an un-made bed.

"Let's get outta here, man," I whispered to Fearless.

He nodded sagely, and we went back the way we came.

I expected to see the corpse, but not standing up in front of me.

He still looked dead, and that scared me more than his size. I don't think he expected someone to come out of the kitchen. Maybe he was going for some water to replace all the blood he'd lost.

"Hold it, man," Fearless said.

The corpse swung his heavy fist, but Fearless leaned back and then pushed the man with the flat of his hand. A variation on that dance step happened again and again. The dead man kept swinging, and Fearless kept pushing off of him as gently as possible.

"You gonna hurt yourself, man," Fearless kept saying. "Stop it."

And he was right too. The man could only swing with his right. He was holding his left hand at a high point on the left side of his chest to keep the blood in. That tactic was not working. The blood cascaded through his fingers, and as the life fluid went, the one-handed fighter started flagging. He wound down like a child's toy until he was on his knees. Finally he lunged with a roundhouse right that would have clocked Fearless on his left hip if he hadn't stepped out of the way. The man fell on his face and went back to mimicking the dead.

Fearless quickly turned him over and applied pressure to the wound.

Twice in one day. I should have been at the racetrack. Luck that consistent needed a horse to bet on.

Fearless removed Till's jacket, T-shirt, and a blood-soaked bandage. He then fashioned a new dressing from the sheet I got off the unkempt bed.

"Let's get outta here," I said when he was done.

"We got to call an ambulance," he said.

The man was on his back on the floor, bare-chested with one arm straight out to the right and the other down at his side. I knew Fearless was right. But if I had been alone, my moral responsibilities wouldn't have become apparent until I was far away and safe.

We made the call from the phone in a corner of the living room, then hurried out toward the car.

There was a siren blaring somewhere off in the night. The young lovers were gone, and we weren't far behind them.

9 | THE DAPPLED SUNLIGHT on apricot-colored walls was the most delicate thing I had seen in a very long time. The lilac-scented sheets were soft and light. Even the mosquitoes silently batting against the outside of the window were a feathery tickle in my mind. But mosquitoes led unerringly to the notion of blood, and blood would always remind me of Conrad Benjamin Till.

Someone dragged a chair across a floor downstairs, and a dog barked. The aroma of coffee blended with lilac. I sat up and looked out of the window. There I saw East L.A. with its carob and magnolia trees, its unpaved sidewalks, and tiny homes flocked with children. Pontiacs and Fords and Studebakers drove slowly toward their goals. Brown- and white-skinned people made their way.

"Hey, Paris," Fearless hailed when I came to the doorway of the kitchen. He was sitting just outside the back door in boxer shorts and a T-shirt on a chrome-and-vinyl chair, drinking coffee from a porcelain cup.

"Good morning," Fanny Tannenbaum said. She was standing at an ironing board, working the wrinkles out of my pants.

I was in my underwear like Fearless, but I wasn't embarrassed.

"What time is it?" I asked.

"Almost nine," Fearless and Fanny said together. It was like they were old friends, even family.

I walked into the room and then jumped across the floor because of the low growl to my right. It was the mongrel from the night before, chewing on a big beef bone and warning me to keep my distance.

Fearless got up from his perch and came in to join us. "Shut up, Blood," he intoned. The dog whimpered and ducked his head.

"I named him after last night," Fearless continued.

"Mr. Jones told me that I should ask questions to you, that he didn't explain things so good," Fanny said.

"He did, huh?"

"Have you found out anything?"

"You know a guy named Conrad Till?" I asked her.

"No. Who is he?"

"He's a black man, maybe one of the ones who came after you and Solly. Somebody shot him —"

"Oh my!" Fanny cried.

"But he wasn't dead. We called the ambulance. He's probably fine."

Fanny sighed with relief. It had been a while since I'd been around someone who would care about a stranger, even when that stranger might have done her wrong.

"Did you find out why they hurt my husband?" she asked.

"No," I said.

"It's all so crazy," Fanny said. She took my pants and folded them. I reached over to take them from her. It was funny, I didn't mind standing there in my drawers, but I was embarrassed to put pants on in front of her. I turned sideways, and she, sensing my embarrassment, turned to look out of the window.

It felt like there was a sock in the right front pocket, but when I put my hand in there, I discovered a large wad of what I knew was money. Small bills, I figured, that she kept in a can used for household expenses.

"When did you come in?" I asked Fanny.

"Morris brought me over at seven on his way to the bank."

"Who?"

"Gella's husband. All the way he's telling me what I should be doing. I should be careful. I should leave well enough alone. I shouldn't let whatever Solly's done get me in trouble. I should tell someone if I know something is wrong. I think he'd give Gella over to the police if he saw her walking on a red light."

"You don't like the police, Fanny?" Fearless asked.

"I have seen the soldiers. I have seen them kill. I saw what they did to you. The police are swine." The vehemence in her voice left no room for argument.

Not that I wanted to argue with her. The best cop I ever saw was the cop who wasn't there.

The doorbell was three quick high notes, a pause, and then a long tone.

Blood jumped up and started barking. Worry knitted itself in Fanny's face. I shared her emotion, but Fearless just walked to the front door in his blue boxers and opened it. I went to the kitchen door, Fanny came up behind me.

I couldn't see who it was, but Fearless knew him.

"Hello," he said, then he paused and called out, "Fanny, do you want to talk to Sergeant Latham?"

"Uh . . . um . . . oh . . . uh — what does he want?" Fanny asked.

Fearless turned and said something and then turned again. "He just wants to talk, ma'am. I think he wants to know more about what happened yesterday."

"I guess," Fanny said.

She and I came into the living room.

Big, blocky, and blond Bernard Latham walked in. He wore a light tan suit that was a bit large even on his frame, designed for quick movement. When I saw him I took a half step backward. That was the fear I'd inherited from his interrogation.

"Did you find out who attacked my husband?" Fanny asked.

"Yeah," the sergeant replied. "You and your two darkies here."

Fearless's greatest strength is also his greatest weakness; his fists had a mind of their own. Given the right circumstances Fearless could hit a man so fast that later on, when the man recovered, he couldn't remember what had happened.

Reluctantly I moved to stand between Fearless and Latham.

"If you have come to my house to insult my friends, you can leave now," Fanny said.

I liked her more every minute.

"I thought you said that you just met these boys yesterday?" Latham asked.

"They have no place to stay, they saved my husband's life, and for that you beat them. What else could I do but offer them a bed?"

Latham grinned and chortled. "Maybe they're in that bed with you."

"In what?" I asked, me, a man without a paddle or rudder.

"Her husband's a convicted embezzler," Latham told me. "He's all mixed up with the underworld. A real Jew. Good enough that he took the money and covered the trail so well that they could only get him for the tip of the iceberg. But there's millions missing. They just have to find out how he made it disappear."

Millions. My brain became a fine screen, filtering out everything but the notion of money.

"That's a lie, and you're a liar," Fanny said in that tone of hers. "Solly told me that he never stole anything, and he wouldn't lie to me."

I'd've lied to Saint Peter for just a hundred thousand dollars.

"Is that all you have to say?" the cop replied.

Fanny was too angry to speak.

"Maybe you think you can get away with it. But I'm watching you." He expanded his hands to include me and Fearless. "All of you."

"Every cop I ever seen been watchin' me, officer," Fearless offered. "I once spent three months on a Texas chain gang for spittin' on the sidewalk instead'a the street."

"If you could do that, I guess you'd kill for some good money, eh, son?" Latham asked.

"I wouldn't rob ya," Fearless replied. "But I would spit on you after you was dead."

That was the line right there, the line that should never be crossed with a cop. Once you stood straight up and looked him in the eye he had to knock you down, or the whole system would stop working.

The problem was that Latham couldn't knock Fearless down. He didn't have backup, and they were in close quarters there in the doorway. I knew from his war stories, and from that dark San Francisco night, that Fearless was trained to kill professional killers hand to hand. If Latham tried to do something, Fearless would do something back, and there was nowhere for a man to run after he'd killed an active member of the LAPD.

I was trying to think of a way to head off the inevitable when Fanny started screaming, "Get out of my house, you Cossack! Get out of here! Out of here!" She ran at Latham, and I leaned back against Fearless.

"Get off 'a me, Paris!"

"You can't help Fanny if they got you."

Fanny was pressing to get Latham out of her house, but he didn't budge.

"I could take you all down now," Latham assured us. "But I've got time. We know the crime, we know the criminals. You won't be free for long."

"And where is it you'd take us to?" I asked. The question I hoped would be a buffer between the cop's stupidity and Fearless's rage.

"What?" Latham asked.

"You gonna take us to the Hollywood jail?"

Latham's right eye twitched. That was the whole story right there, that twitch. All I had to do was figure out what it meant.

"If we are not under arrest, then go," little Fanny said.

Latham took his time staring at her and then Fearless and me in turns. The glare was intended to frighten, and I guess it worked if you consider that I was scared for his life. Finally he left. Fearless stood at the open door, watching him go.

"What do you know about this millions stuff?" I asked our host.

"He made it up," Fanny said. "He had to. We don't have that kind of money. And why steal it if not to spend? We don't have children to leave it to. Why live here?"

"Hmm. Yeah. I don't know," I said. "There was once a woman lived down the road from us when I was a kid. She was poor as corn husks, barely kept the flesh on her bones. We all thought that she couldn't have made more than a dollar a week the way she lived. But she must'a made two, because when she died at eighty-eight they found three thousand silver dollars hid up under her bed."

"You're welcome to look under my bed, Mr. Minton."

10 FANNY HAD CALLED the hospital before I woke up. They told her that Sol was being given a series of blood tests and X rays and wouldn't be able to have visitors until the afternoon.

After breakfast I spent a couple of hours on the phone trying to get a line on the Messenger of the Divine church. I called every religious group listed in twelve different counties and every soul that I knew. I wanted to ask Reverend Grove a question or two; like when had he last seen Elana Love and was she driving my red Rambler.

There was a certain urgency behind my search because I was bothered by Latham's visit. Why had he come? L.A. cops didn't make friendly visits to warn you that they were watching. They didn't come to the door unless they were serving papers or making an arrest.

So I went on thinking and calling, fretting and drinking Fanny's homemade lemonade. She spent the morning baking noodle pudding and making meals for later. She told us that cooking calmed her nerves. We didn't complain. Both Fearless and I were bachelors, and when a woman came around she did very little cooking — food, that is.

Fearless played catch with Blood. They were completely happy roughhousing and relaxing on the sunny lawn. Since he was just out of the lockup, a day in the sun was heaven for him.

At one Fearless took Fanny and Blood to pick up Gella and go for a drive down to see Sol and maybe let the dog have a run in the park. I couldn't see where they needed me, so I stayed by the telephone making useless calls.

"Hello," one man answered.

"Council for the Baptist churches of greater L.A. county?" I inquired in my pretend official tone.

"Yes."

"I was wondering if you could help me find a minister."

"A particular minister?" the soft-spoken secretary asked.

"A Reverend Grove or a Father Vincent. They're affiliated with a church called Messenger of the Divine."

"Never heard of the institution," he said with quiet distaste. "Doesn't sound like one of our congregations at all."

"No Grove or Vincent?"

"What is this concerning?"

"An exorcism," I said.

"A what?"

"I got a white man locked up in my basement and I wanna see if an old-time Holy Roller can call the devil out of him. That way maybe I can save the world from his evil . . . Uh-oh, he's trying to break out of his cage. I'll call you back." I hung up and laughed a mean laugh.

Before my venom was through, the phone rang. I had the immediate and irrational fear that somehow the Council for the Baptist churches knew the numbers of the sinners that called them. I let the ringing go on for a while before answering.

"Tannenbaum residence," I said brightly.

"May I speak to Hedva Tannenbaum, please?" a man asked. He spoke in perfect but not necessarily American English. His tone was haughty, that's really the only word for it. The words were mannered, but the voice was not.

"Who's askin'?" I said in response to the voice.

There was a moment's hesitation and then, "John Manly." The name didn't sound right on his tongue.

"Well, Mr. Manly," I said. "Mrs. Tannenbaum doesn't want to speak to anyone just now. She's had a pretty rough time of it the past few days and doesn't want to be disturbed."

I was being hard on Mr. Manly for no other reason than that his tone reminded me of the snootiness of the secretary at the Baptist Council.

"To whom am I speaking?" Manly inquired.

"To whom," I replied, "doesn't matter. What matters is that Fanny isn't gettin' on the phone, so either you gonna tell me what you want or we gonna break off the connection right here and now." For an instant the image of that bureaucrat sitting at the window of the courthouse flashed through my mind.

"Excuse me? What did you say?" Manly asked.

I realized that, in my anger, I had slipped into the fast-talking patter of my neighborhood. Manly hadn't understood my brilliant barbs.

"What do you want me to tell Fanny?" I asked, now patient.

"I must speak to her personally. It's very important."

"Maybe to you, but Fanny's got other things on her mind. Does she know you?" I asked.

"What I have to tell her is very important."

"I'll give her the message. What's your number?"

"Tell her now, while I am waiting."

"No."

There were big red-and-purple flowers, shaped like bells, clustered on a bush outside the sitting room windows. A sleek green hummingbird appeared next to one of them. From one to another that hummingbird milked five of those flowers before Manly spoke again.

"It's about business," he said. "I'm a real-estate agent. I want to know if she's interested in selling her house."

"I don't think she's movin' nowhere right now, but gimme your number and she'll call ya."

He finally relented and left a number. It was a Hollywood exchange. "Room three-two-two," he added.

I hung up and wondered about that number on the way to the window. The hummingbird fled at my approach. I could hardly blame him; when a shadow the size of a mountain looms up above you, you run first and worry about what it could be later on — from the safety of your nest. If you had a nest, that is.

FEARLESS AND FANNY RETURNED at about four. Before I could tell them about the call Fearless started in.

"Paris, it was on the car radio."

"What?"

"Conrad Till, that's what. He's dead."

"Dead?"

"Yeah. They said about him gettin' found on account of a, a what you call it, 'nonymous tip. Yeah. Then they said that they took him to Mercy Hospital, but he died in the night a'cause of the wound."

"He was shot up pretty bad."

"Yeah, he was. And maybe it killed him too. But you know, I been shot worse than that myself, an' it didn't near kill me. I mean maybe he had a weak heart or sumpin', but I don't think so. But that's not what I wanted to tell you."

"What then?"

"The cop that talked to the newsman. That there they said was Sergeant Latham."

"Damn," I said.

"That Latham gets around," Fearless said.

"What does it mean?" asked Fanny.

"Does Rya still work at Mercy?" I asked Fearless.

"Prob'ly. You know they made her head nurse in the baby section. That's the kind'a job you hold on to."

"Maybe we should talk to her."

"Okay." With that Fearless went off to the kitchen to call.

"Do you know a guy named John, um, Manly?" I asked Fanny. "Said he was a real-estate agent, but I don't know."

"No. Why?"

"He called while you and Fearless were gone."

Fanny shook her head at me.

"The only weird thing was he didn't ask for Sol. It was like he knew that he was in the hospital, at least not here. You sure you don't know his name? John Manly. Talks all proper like he learned English in another country."

"What can it all mean?" she quailed.

"He's probably just what he said," I reassured her. "He probably got your name off of a mailing list and wants to get your house to sell."

"I'm not interested," Fanny moaned. "All I want is Solly home and to get on that airplane."

"What airplane?" I asked.

"We're going to Israel," the old lady said. "We have been planning to go all the time he was in prison. We would talk about it in our letters. Now that he was home we had only to buy the tickets and make our plans."

I had a thought or two about a convicted embezzler planning to flee the country a few weeks after he got out of stir, but whatever he did, or didn't do, wasn't important to me right then. I was angry because John Manly was so rude, because Latham had threatened us. I was getting pretty mad, and anger in my small frame is almost like courage.

"How was Sol?" I asked.

"He opened his eyes. Mr. Jones told him that he was protecting me, and he smiled. But he was still too weak to talk."

"Was he happy to see you and Gella?"

"Oh yes, very much. He loves that girl as if she were his own daughter."

"What did the doctor say?"

Fanny's face clouded at that question. She didn't want to say the words. I understood. I didn't want to push her. When Fearless returned we were both relieved.

"I called her, Paris," Fearless said. "She said that we could meet her on her break at eight-fifteen tonight."

"Meet her? Didn't you ask her about Till?"

"No. You didn't say that."

"What?" For an instant I was angry, even at Fearless. But that was okay. I had to stay mad so I didn't fall prey to fear. I was in it up to my neck and scared was an anchor that would drag me down to death.

WE DROPPED FANNY OFF at her niece's house again.

"Too many people seem to know your address," I told her. "And none of them would I trust with my grandmother."

That got a smile from Fanny. She touched my wrist with her short, thick fingers.

"Where to?" Fearless asked when we were on our way.

"To where my bookstore used to be."

Fearless drove because I wanted to keep my mind free to think us out of our troubles. He stayed on main streets in mostly colored neighborhoods so there wasn't much of a chance of being stopped by the police.

The sight of the burnt-out lot still tore at my chest.

"Damn, man," Fearless said. "That's bad. Why he wanna burn you down like that?"

"I don't know. But it break my heart to see it."

We went to the convenience store next door, Antonio and Sons. It was owned by an Italian family, but five times out of six you were likely to run into Theodore Wally at the cash register. Theodore had been a neighborhood kid who used to come into Antonio's on milk-and-bread runs for his mother. Antonio liked him. He gave him a job sweeping when Theodore was twelve and increased his responsibilities over the years until he was a fixture there. I don't believe he was over twenty-five, but he looked to be forty going on sixty.

"Mr. Minton," Wally said. His fleshy face revealed deep concern over my misfortune. "They been lookin' for you."

"Who has?"

"Hey, Fearless," Theodore greeted my friend and then answered me. "The fire department investigation man and the police."

"What they want?"

"The fire might'a been because of gasoline, they said, and they wanna know if you owned that place and if you had the bookstore insured. The police was just askin', they said."

Theodore looked worried, so I asked him, "What you tell 'em?"

"I said about the man who hit you. I mean I had already told them before and I thought that they would think it was somebody tryin' to hurt you burnt down the store. That's all right, right?"

"That's okay," I said. "You right too. If they think somebody was after me, then maybe they'll blame him for the fire. Maybe they'll find the motherfucker and put him in jail."

Theodore smiled uncertainly. He wasn't a dumb man, but he was very shy, more comfortable with numbers and merchandise than he was with looking people in the eye. Antonio loved him because he was a whiz at keeping books and remembering inventory.

"You remember those Messenger of the Divine folks had the store down the street?" I asked.

99

"Uh-huh. Yeah. They used to buy two jugs'a High Mountain red wine every Thursday before their meetin'. That was the blood."

Fearless grinned at that.

"Did you know Reverend Grove or Father Vincent?"

"T'say hi."

"You know where they went when they left here?"

"Uh-uh. No. But . . ."

"But what?"

"Dorthea Williams used to go to the meetin's. She used to go on Thursdays and then some other times too."

"That's Dorthea from the beauty parlor across the street?"

"Uh-huh. Yeah."

"How much these barbecue potato chips, Theodore?" Fearless asked, holding up a big bag of chips.

"Twenty-nine cent, but you could just take 'em, Fearless. Just take 'em, okay?"

"Thanks, man."

I shook Theodore's hand, but after the usual grip he didn't let go.

"You need money, Mr. Minton?" the clerk asked me.

"Why? You wanna reach in the register and gimme some?"

"I got some savin's. I got a little money put away. If you needed to get on your feet . . ."

"Thanks, Theodore, but I need more than you got to give. But let me ask you somethin'?"

"What?"

"How come you call Fearless Fearless, but you still call me mister?"

11 | ACROSS THE STREET and down half a block was a small building with a plate-glass window for a front wall. That was The Beauty Shop, owned by Hester Grey and run by her daughter Shirley. There were three chairs set side by side before the window where a black woman could get everything from gold frosting on her hair to application of the newest skin bleaching techniques.

Shirley was smoking a cigarette, and Dorthea, her number two girl, was putting curlers in a woman's hair. They were all talking loudly.

From outside it was really nice. The three were almost yelling, you could tell by the posture they took to speak. After yelling they'd laugh hard, but you couldn't hear a sound through the thick glass. It was like experiencing the deep pleasure of music without being able to hear it.

When we opened the door, a brief moment of mirth reached us before the women clammed up. The room smelled of cigarettes and hair spray. It wasn't a pleasant odor, but it conjured the memories of many a woman I had known.

"Fearless," Shirley Grey said. "Paris."

"Afternoon, ladies," I said.

Both Shirley and Dorthea had big puffed-up hairdos. That was where the similarities ended. Shirley had a lot of flesh with no figure to speak of and a permanent scowl on her face. She thought she was a raving beauty though. She always wore tight dresses that showed more than anyone wanted to see.

Dorthea was an African beauty who had been brainwashed into thinking she was ugly by movies and magazines. She had straight blond hair puffed out like a white country singer and all kinds of costume rings and beads. Her breasts were trussed up in a brassiere that pushed them out like battering rams, and her long skirt was so tight that she walked like one of those Chinese women with the destroyed feet. Still, her face was elegant with deep brown skin and high cheekbones. Her eyes slanted up, and her teeth were as white as the enamel on a new gas stove.

She showed a lot of teeth when she saw Fearless.

"That was too bad about your store, Paris," Shirley said. "What happened?"

"I don't know, babe. I came home and it was gone."

"Where were you?"

"Out bein' a fool."

Shirley shook her head and sucked her tooth. She and her mother had lost all the men in their lives. The father ran off with the number three chair girl. Her brothers were both institutionalized, one by the prison system and the other by the armed forces.

"Shirley, can I borrow Dorthea for a moment?" Fearless asked.

We decided while approaching the beauty shop that Fearless would ask for Dorthea. Women were much more likely to say yes to him.

"Can't you see that she's workin'?" Obviously Shirley didn't see it our way.

"Oh, that's okay," Dorthea spoke up. "Mrs. Calhoun don't mind waitin'. Do ya, honey?"

Up until then I hadn't looked closely at the woman in Dorthea's chair. She was older and with a stern, strawberry-brown face. She had white-rimmed glasses and hard eyes. Her stern countenance was cause for surprise because it broke out into a big smile for Dorthea and the prospect of her talking with a good-looking man.

"Go on, honey," Mrs. Calhoun said. "Me an' Shirley can talk mess without you for a while."

Before Shirley could object, Dorthea took off her white apron and scooted toward the door. We were right after her.

Outside, the three of us convened at the curb, but I might just as well have been the fireplug as far as Dorthea was concerned.

"What you wanted, Fearless?"

"Did you know them Messenger of the Divine peoples?" he asked.

The light of love faltered in her eyes.

"Did you?" I chimed.

"What's this all about, Paris?" Now that she was angry she talked to me.

"Dorthea, honey, I don't wanna fight with you . . ."

"I ain't fightin' I just —"

"I don't wanna fight, so I'll cut this short. I need information on them Messenger people because I think it was somebody after them came and burnt down my store. You know I lost everything and somebody got to pay."

"Them's religious people, Paris," Dorthea said. "They wouldn't do nothin' like that."

"I don't think they did it," I assured her. "But somebody didn't like 'em did."

"Who?"

"Did you know Reverend Grove?" I asked.

"Why should I tell you?"

"Five dollars," I said.

Dorthea looked left and right, then she said, "You gotta car?"

"Right across the street."

"Take me around the block then."

We got into Layla's Packard. Fearless drove and I sat in the back.

"What you wanna know?" Dorthea asked.

"Do you know Grove?"

"Yeah. William. He from Arkansas. He came in as Father Vincent's head deacon, but after just a year he was so popular that he forced Vincent into semiretirement and took over the whole ministry even though they say he ain't really ordained. That man can preach. He make you feel like he's God and you the only one he care about."

"But he took the church away from the pastor was there?" Fearless asked.

Dorthea nodded. "Brought in his own deacons and everything."

"Did you know a woman around there called Elana Love?" I asked.

"What about her?" She certainly did, and she didn't like her either.

"Did you know her?"

"She was all over William. I mean, sometimes they'd go in the back while Vincent was deliverin' the sermon for him. It was just sad the way they was." Dorthea curled her lip the same way that Shirley had.

"Did they do anything but sermons there?"

"What you mean?"

"Anything illegal?" I was thinking that the church had something to do with the money or bonds or whatever and maybe Dorthea had heard about it.

She said, "No," but there was something else on her mind.

"Come on, Dorthea. Ten bucks."

"You won't tell?"

"Swear," I said, drawing an X across my heart with my finger.

"Brother Bigelow from over there sold me a pearl ring one time for fifteen dollars. It was a real nice one. He said that he got stuff like that sometimes and that if I knew ladies in the beauty shop wanted some good jewelry cheap, I should bring them to him."

"Did you?" I asked.

"Uh-uh. It's one thing just buyin' a ring, but I didn't want to be a fence."

Fearless turned to her and smiled.

"Good girl," he said.

She would have beamed at any compliment he gave.

"Why did the church move away?" I asked.

"I don't know. Really. But it was all of a sudden. One day they was just gone. Everything. You remember."

"Do you know where they went?"

Dorthea looked me in the eye. She was measuring me.

"Why should I tell you, Paris?"

Before I could think of a lie Fearless said, "You can tell me, honey."

"Well," she said. "I like you, Fearless, but I wanna see my money before I say anything else."

I counted out five wrinkled one-dollar bills followed by a five.

"They was in Compton three weeks ago, down on Alameda somewhere. At least that's what I heard."

"You know the address?"

"Uh-uh. But you could find it if you looked."

"When do they have meetings?"

"Every night they can."

Fearless pulled up in front of The Beauty Shop and parked.

"Is that it?" Dorthea asked.

"You know how we can find Elana Love?"

"That bitch? No."

She grabbed the handle and opened the door, but before she could exit, Fearless reached out for her shoulder.

"You wanna go to Rackman's tonight?"

Looking at his hand, Dorthea said, "Yeah."

"Paris and me gotta do somethin' at eight, but I could be down to get you by ten-thirty."

"You could pick me up at the Charles Diner on Eighty-ninth. I'm supposed to see my sister there."

They lingered for a moment, him looking at her and her looking at his fingers, and then she climbed out. Fearless watched her Chinese shuffle into the shop before he drove off.

"Man, don't we have enough to do without you makin' dates in the middle?" I asked.

"I been in jail for three months, Paris. You know I'm starvin' for what Dorthea can feed me."

"Oh," I said. "Oh, yeah."

"Paris?"

"Yeah?"

"Where'd you get that money?"

"What money?"

"That money you give Dorthea."

"Borrowed it from Milo."

I could see in Fearless's eyes that he knew I was lying, but he didn't press it. That's the kind of friends we were.

12 | RYA MCKENZIE WAS a stern young woman with close-cropped hair and walnut-colored eyes. Her skin was the color of forest shadows, and her judgment was swift. If she didn't like you, you knew it and stayed away, but if she was your friend, you'd never want for anything that she could provide.

She kissed Fearless and shook my hand, greeted us both with brief hellos, and then led us from the nurses' station for pediatrics to a small room furnished with a long, rickety table that supported a coffee urn, three boxes of sugar-glazed doughnuts, and a small stack of paper cups and plates next to a jumble of disposable utensils made from wood.

"When did you get out of jail?" Rya asked Fearless when we were all seated on folding chairs.

"Yesterday. Paris paid my fine."

"So what kinda trouble you in then?" she asked me.

"Conrad Till," I said, as blandly as I could manage. It was nice to see her disapproval turn into something wary.

She half rose from her squeaky chair and looked around for spies.

"What you got to do with that?"

"Conrad was a friend of a woman I need to find. His name came up when I was lookin' for her, and then I heard he'd died."

Fearless nodded, going along with my half-lie. He had a philosophy about lying. *It's okay as long as you ain't hurtin' nobody,* he told me one drunken night. *Matter'a fact a lotta times a lie is better'n the truth when the whole thing come out.*

"I don't know nuthin' 'bout no foul-mouthed murdered man," Rya said.

"You say he's foul-mouthed," I said. "But the evenin' papers said that he never regained consciousness."

"So they said. But you know you cain't believe all that you read in no papers."

"Did a lotta police come?"

"No. I mean there was cops in when they first brought him. But they left. Then that one officer, that Sergeant Latham come in. He went to talk to Till, and then, a little while later, Ginny Sidell found him dead."

"They talked?" I asked, just to be sure.

"Conrad Till was awake and cussin' two hours after they brought him in. That's when Latham come."

"What did Till die of?"

Rya looked away at a blank wall and said, "Heart failure."

"He had a heart attack?"

She shrugged.

"That's it? A man comes in shot and they say he had a heart attack?"

"Heart failure," she said, correcting me. "That's what always kill ya. That's how we know. A truck could hit ya and your spleen be in your lap, but you still ain't dead unless your heart stop."

She looked at me with her walnut eyes. Fearless checked out the clock on the wall.

"Is somebody going to investigate the death?" I asked.

"Somebody who?"

"I mean, if everybody's talking about it . . ."

"Everybody around here got a real job, Mr. Minton. Real jobs and apartments and mouths to feed. Conrad Till was just a year outta prison, an ex-con with a bullet in his chest, found after an anonymous call."

Fearless didn't have a job or an apartment or kids to feed. She wasn't talking about him though.

"Thanks, Rya," Fearless said. "We really appreciate it."

"You better watch out where you stickin' your nose, Mr. Jones," Rya warned. "Some people might get you all caught up in somethin' you can't get out of wit' a fine."

Fearless laughed.

"Baby," he said. "If I was to worry about me gettin' pulled down under the trouble I see, I'd be in my bed from mornin' to night. Man wanna kill me or put me in prison, he's welcome to try it. But, you know, I draw from a deep well, deep as a muthah-fuckah."

It was the profanity that clued me in to how serious Fearless felt. He rarely cursed, almost never in front of women. But when he did, you knew that he meant business.

• • •

"YOU KNOW we killed him, Fearless," I said on the drive back from Mercy. Blood was pacing impatiently in the backseat.

"Killed who?"

"Conrad Till."

"How the hell you figure that?"

"He was hurting but not dying when we left him. It was the report from the hospital that brought Latham into it. He probably knew that Till was Leon's buddy. And you better believe that he was the cause of Till's demise."

"Why you think?"

"I don't know. Maybe the questioning got outta hand. Maybe there's somethin' we don't know about Latham. I mean he's a Hollywood cop, so what's he doin' down near Watts and East L.A.?"

"Man, Paris, you got us into a real mess here."

"I didn't get into no mess. Mess just fell right on top'a me. I was sittin' in my store readin' a book."

"Yeah, yeah, I know. But you could'a walked away. Could'a taken that five hundred dollars you used to pay my fine and started a new store somewhere."

He was right. There I was bound up with murder and arson and even in trouble with a maybe crooked cop when I could have walked away. Could have but couldn't anymore. I was no hero but I was stubborn, and, anyway, my five hundred dollars were gone.

"Fearless."

"Yeah, Paris?"

"I'm sorry, man. Sorry I didn't get you outta jail before you went in. Sorry I got you thinkin' you gotta stay with me. I fucked up, man."

Fearless stretched out his right hand while keeping his left on the wheel. I clasped it.

"You my friend, Paris. An' this mess ain't so bad. I was in a war eight thousand miles from home with white men talkin' German in front'a me an' white men talkin' English at my back. They was all callin' me nigger. They all wanted me dead. You know I wasn't scared then, baby. This ain't no more bad than a night with a girlfriend like to bite."

THE CHARLES DINER was a night haunt. They didn't have live music, but they had waitresses and drinks. The Charles was the place you went if you didn't have the cover charge in your pocket. Fearless and I double-parked out front, and he ran in.

While waiting I tried to screw up the courage to do what I knew had to come next. I knew from experience that Fearless could be gone for a few days once he was off with a woman. He'd lose track of time, and how could I blame him? Ninety days was a long time to go without love, even for me.

I watched the blinking neon sign that lit up the old-time diner. The facade of the restaurant was made to look like a train car detailed in chrome. Now it was a place for the end of the night, when jukebox tunes would do. Thousands of people passed through those doors every week. Working people and gangsters, women looking for love or money and men looking to throw love or money away. You didn't go to the Charles to see old friends; no, the Charles was where you went to seek out somebody who wanted to help you with your problem, somebody who wanted to give you something or take what you had to give.

"Hey, Paris." Fearless opened the driver's side and leaned in.

"Dorthea got her own car an' she don't mind drivin' it. So you take Layla's, and I'll see you tomorrow afternoon at Fanny's."

"You know Dorthea ain't gonna let you go that quick."

"Cross my heart, Paris. This is just for the night, baby. Tomorrow we got ground to cover."

"Okay," I said. "But take this dog anyway. Just in case you get stuck, I don't want to have to take care'a no dog too."

I eased in behind the wheel and we shook hands.

"You better take this," I said, handing him four five-dollar bills and five ones. "Just in case you need somethin'."

"Hey, Paris. Thanks, man."

Fearless went around to the passenger door, opened it, and said, "Come on, boy."

Blood jumped out with a quick bark.

I sat behind the wheel a few minutes after Fearless and his dog were gone, wondering if I would make it through the night without getting killed. A car behind me honked its horn, and I slid away from the curb, prodded by that unknown driver, into the night.

13 I DROVE UP and down Alameda Boulevard until about twelve-thirty, finally finding the storefront by intuition instead of a sign. I'd seen the darkened windows twice on my evening reconnaissance, but both times they didn't make enough of an impression for me to look closer.

On the third pass I stopped and got out. Up close the drapes were a deep red. As soon as I saw the color I knew that it was the Messenger of the Divine. The curtains were drawn completely across the windows, but looking down past the sill I could see a thin band of light. Pressing my ear against the crack between the double doors, I could hear men talking; talking, not proselytizing, praying, or preaching.

I went around the side of the block. There was no alley behind the row of stores. That meant that whoever was in there had to come out on Alameda. I moved Layla's car down the block and sat low in the seat, not wanting some cop to nab me for loitering.

It was a long wait. There was a chill in the air, and my shirt provided little to no warmth. Whenever I got cold up north I remembered New Iberia, my home. We didn't live in the town. My mother and I were country. Our road was a dirt path only fit for feet or horses' hooves. We lived in a shack made from tin and wood, cardboard, mortar, and tar paper. There was a brick oven that burned anything and a floor paved with small stones. There were three rooms, and we fit that place like a hand in a glove. In the summertime it was as hot as you could take it. It did get cold in December, but I still remember Louisiana for the heat. I loved it. As far as I could walk in any direction there were colored people, colored people and no one else. When I was a child I knew that the white people lived somewhere, but I rarely saw one in my daily routine. Our store owners and undertakers and carpenters were all black. So were our tailors and dressmakers, our butchers, bakers, and milkmen.

Everybody was poor, but nobody starved. We partied on Saturday nights and praised the Lord for our babies on Sundays. We worked hard when we had to and took it easy when there was a chance. A lot of colored people tell me that they hate the South; Jim Crow and segregation made a heavy weight for their hearts. But I never felt like that. I mean, lynchings were a terrible thing, and some of those peckerwoods acted so stupid that they embarrassed the hell out of you sometimes. But I still loved the little shack I shared with my mother. I'd have still been there if it wasn't for one terrible event.

That event was learning to read.

I entered school at the age of six. It was a country schoolhouse with two teachers and four rooms. They broke us up among the classrooms according to size at first, and then they shuffled us around depending on ability. The fourth room was for study; children went in and out of there at the teachers' request. On the first day I heard Miss Randolph read a story, and I knew that books were my destiny, not writing or teaching or inventing spaceships, just reading and reading and reading some more. I could pick out a simple sentence based on the knowledge of a dozen words by the end of the first week. By the age of eight I was alone in the fourth classroom, reading everything I could. I read the Bible and the dictionary and every newspaper I could. I read every book in our whole neighborhood by the time I was fifteen.

There was a library in the white part of town; coloreds couldn't go inside. For a while I would go there and sit out front on the bench they had, rereading old books like *The Hinkley Reader* and *Uncle Tom's Cabin.* One day the librarian, an old battle-ax named Celestine Dowling, came out and asked me what I was doing.

"Readin'," I said proudly.

"Really," old Miss Dowling said.

"Yes'm," I replied.

"I don't believe you," she stated.

I didn't know what to reply to such a rude comment, so I sat tight and quiet.

"Read me a sentence," she ordered.

There is nothing worse than the snows of May, I read from a story called "Minnesota Snows."

Dowling frowned and said, "Go on."

I read the first page and then the second. I read all the way through the story. I had read that book many times and so did not skip or stutter hardly at all.

When I was through, Miss Dowling said, "Come on with me."

She led me through the big double doors of the library into a large room that was at least twenty feet high, lined to the ceiling with shelves that were packed with neat rows of books. I remember my heart catching. I forgot how to breathe altogether. I had no idea that there were this many books in the whole world. There was a big oak table in the center of the room with fancy chairs around it. There was a podium with a proper Webster's open to some page. The dictionary I'd read was just a small abridged thing that contained words a child might need to know.

"This is the library," the librarian said.

I nodded and gulped.

"Close your mouth, boy."

"It's beautiful," I said finally. "I never seen nuthin' like it."

"Of course you haven't," she said. "And do you know why?"

"Because I never been in here before?" I asked, not understanding the question.

"No," she said from some Olympian height. "It is because this is a white library. And no matter how much you know how to read, these books are not meant for you. These books were written by white people for white people. This is literature and art and the way our country is and should be. There will be no library card for you, so you can stop sitting out in front. You have seen as much of this building as you ever will."

The impact of her words brought tears to my eyes. I was thirteen, but, like I said, I've always been small. I looked up at Celestine Dowling, and she seemed pleased to see me cry.

"Go on now," she said.

I went home in tears. My mother asked me what was wrong, but I was too sad to say. I cried that night and all the next day. Celestine Dowling had broken my heart out of a meanness that I couldn't understand. Why would she hate me for being able to read well? I wasn't hurting her. I would have been glad to check out books from the back door or window. I wouldn't've treated those books badly.

All of the happiness flowed out of me then. For months I moped around. I made money reading contracts and warranties for my neighbors, but every time I'd read a line I'd remember the high shelves of that country library.

By the time I was seventeen I was on a train bound for San Francisco, not because I wanted to vote or was afraid of being lynched. I left because a man told me one night that in California black folks could go into any library they wanted. They could get library cards and check out books from here to Sunday.

It was cold in Frisco, but I read a book a day in the first year. Libraries still make my heart race. There is nothing like a book.

"I understand you, sir," a voice agreed.

I smiled in my doze, thinking that most people thought I was crazy when I told them that story. A door closed and I was jarred awake. Three men stood in the shadows down the street in front of the curtained church.

Some more words were spoken, but I didn't understand them. This made me think that I had given meaning to the words I heard in my sleep. Through the darkness I could tell that one of the men was white and the other two were black. One black man was well built, wearing a white suit. He laughed and slapped the white man on the shoulder. That was William Grove. I remembered him going into the church with all of the deacons shaking his hand as he went past. The other black man seemed to be older. He also wore a suit, but it was shapeless, fitting the man like the everyday uniform of a night watchman or usher.

The white man was powerfully built too. That's really all I could tell about him, except that he seemed to have some kind of foreign accent. They talked briefly, and then a dark-colored sedan drove up. The white man got in, and the sedan drove off.

I crouched down as the sedan went past. When I rose partway up again, the black men were still talking.

They talked for a while more, and then Grove walked away down the street. The older man used a key in the front door to the church and went in.

I had brought myself to the edge of that minefield by asking a couple of good questions and by perseverance. But every step from then on was laid out for a better man than I was. So I sat there trying to will myself up the evolutionary ladder from man to superman. But when I got out of that car, there was no cape dragging behind me, only a tail between my legs.

14

I NEEDED TO RELIEVE my bladder, but I was scared. In a car I was an even match for Leon Douglas; on foot gawky Gella Greenspan had about equal odds to kick my ass.

I knocked on the church door, braced by the cold air and the possibility of finding a toilet. I was standing there for quite a while before a baritone voice asked, "William?"

"It's Tyrell Lockwood," I said, loud and clear.

"What you want?"

"I came to speak to Reverend Grove."

"It's three in the morning," the opera voice informed me.

"It's very important," I said. "About a woman named Elana Love."

There was a moment of silence, and then the lock snicked and cracked. The door came open and a frosty-headed older gentleman looked at me with a deeply furrowed brow.

"What about Sister Love?" he asked.

"She hired me to find you, said it was somethin' important she had to say."

"What?" His features were African Negro with very little other racial influence. Based on his facial structure you would have expected his skin to be dark, very dark, but instead it was fifty-fifty, coffee and cream.

"I'm sorry, sir," I said. "But my business is with Reverend Grove. I spent the whole night driving around trying to find this place and I got to go."

"I'm Vincent," the man said warily. "Father Vincent la Trieste. At one time I was the minister of this congregation."

"May I use your facilities, Father Vincent?"

There was a moment when he might have refused me, but then he stepped back, allowing me in.

I had only seen the Messenger of the Divine church once, about a half year before. The landlord brought me around because I was making noises about renting a place and the Messenger was behind on the rent for the second month in a row. Mr. Anderson, the landlord, brought me in on a Tuesday afternoon when there was no one in the place. The room I entered with Father Vincent was exactly the same as I remembered. Plush red drapes on all four walls. Folding walnut chairs set in rows before an oak podium that was edged in gold and jet. There were hymn books with cardboard covers lined with royal blue felt on each seat and a huge, rough-hewn cross propped on its side and leaning against the draperies behind the podium. It was almost an exact replica of the room I had seen on Central. I would have taken the place after Anderson showed it to me, but the church came up with the rent, and I ended up taking the storefront down the street.

In the corner there were three chairs set at a wobbly pine table with three glasses, each one almost empty of red wine, and a tin ashtray full of butts set in the center.

"Through there," Vincent said, gesturing at the wall.

"What?" I asked.

"Through that door," he said in an exasperated tone. "The toilet."

There was a short hallway that led to an old-fashioned toilet that had a pull handle connected to a tank on the wall above. As nervous as I was, urinating afforded me great relief and pleasure. I leaned a hand against the wall while I did my business, exhausted from the past few days of pressure.

I poked my head out of the john, noticing a half-open door a little farther on in the back. In that room I spied a table strewn with watches, jewelry, and 35-millimeter cameras. There were two console televisions with round screens against the far wall and a fur coat of some kind hanging on a nail in the back door.

I snaked my way back to the bathroom, flushed the toilet, and then returned to my host.

"You look familiar," he said when I returned.

"I used to work part-time for the bookstore near to your church when it was on Central."

"Where is she?" Vincent asked me.

I pulled out a chair from the rickety table and sat.

"Kidnapped."

"What?"

"She came to me looking for Grove. Like I said, I worked near to where you used to be. She come in there askin' 'bout where she could find the reverend."

"You said she was kidnapped?"

"She told me that if I could find Grove, she'd give me five hundred dollars. So I said I'd help out. Only when I started drivin' her, a man attacked us and took her away. He chased us. Big motherfucker. You know, I fought him, but he laid me out. Before he did though, she screamed at him, called him Leon."

"Leon Douglas?" he whispered.

"She didn't yell his full name."

Vincent took a chair for himself. He was staring hard at me. I wasn't scared though. He was an old guy, sixty or more, and I always felt comfortable if given the time to roll out a lie. I'm good at lying. My mother always said that it was because of all those lying books I read.

"You lyin'," Vincent said.

"Why you say that?"

"Why would she trust you? Why she gonna offer you good money like that to find William?"

"She didn't trust me completely, that's why I don't know why she wanted you guys. You know, I've done some findin'-people work for Milo Sweet, the bail bondsman."

"Why you believe her? Did she pay you anything?"

"Man, the curves on that woman and the way she moved 'em, damn, five hundred dollars was the least she had to offer."

"You go to the law?"

"No." I made eye contact with the holy man as I said so.

"Why not?"

I shrugged, looked at him again, and then said, "If she offered me five, there had to be more, and if I went to the cops, there was no chance of being paid a dime. What I figured was that I'd find the reverend and see what was what."

Vincent held out his hands in a show of helplessness. "I haven't heard from Sister Love in more than two months, and I don't know anything about any money. All I do is God's work. I spread His word."

Like a boxer getting on his bicycle and putting out the jab, that was Vincent. I had staggered him with my information, and all he could fall back on was his everyday con.

"Well, if you can't help me . . ." I stood up.

"But I could ask Brother Grove," Vincent offered.

"Maybe I should ask him."

"Maybe," the canny man of God replied. "If you got here five minutes earlier, you would'a seen him. But he's gone now, won't be back for a few weeks."

"Where'd he go?"

"Church business, in Tulsa."

"Oh. Well I guess that's that."

"But he's gonna call me. When he gets there he said he'd call. I could ask him then."

"I don't know," I said. "Maybe you're right. Maybe I should just go to the police."

"Better no," he said.

"Why?"

"Let me ask William first. Maybe he could shed some light on it. I'll tell you what, you go home and get some sleep, and when I talk to William sometime tomorrow night, next mornin' at the latest, I'll call you."

I thought about sleeping in that lilac-scented, apricot-colored room. It sounded pretty good. I mused on that for a few seconds, pretending that I was thinking about Vincent's selfless offer.

"Call you by ten day after tomorrow," he added.

"All right," I said, nodding. "All right. But I'll have to call the cops if you don't call me by then. You know it's a crime not to report a crime."

Vincent was scanning the tabletop until he located a short pencil and a paper matchbook. He took the nub and said, "Tell me your number."

I gave him the Tannenbaum phone number.

"What's the address?"

"Why you need my address?"

"Well, uh, we might have to run over there or somethin'."

"No, uh-uh. You just call me. Call me by ten day after tomorrow." I stood up.

"We could use the address too," he said with no apology or excuse.

"I'll give you what you need after I talk to Grove."

I had a question in mind, and it must've shown on my face.

"Something else?" he asked.

"Why did you pull up your red skirts and run from the old church so fast?"

Father Vincent blinked twice but said nothing.

"I mean," I continued, "you ran outta there in the middle'a the night. The landlord came around askin' everybody if they knew where you'd gone."

"A misunderstanding about the rent," the elder Holy Roller said. "Anderson made some promises about work that he was gonna do to the buildin'. After a year we told him that we wouldn't pay, you know, the rent until, uh, he did what he said he would."

"Hmm." I pondered his lie. "Only time I ever seen people pull up stakes that fast they were either runnin' from the law or from a loaded gun."

"Nuthin' like that," Vincent assured me. "Just a misunderstanding is all."

"All right," I said, still leery. "You call me when you've talked to Grove."

I turned and walked out of there, feeling in charge for the first time since Elana Love walked in the door. I didn't look back at Father Vincent. I was sure that he'd be on the phone to Grove as soon as I was gone. But that was okay. I wanted them upset. I wanted them to feel like I felt.

JOHN-JOHN'S ALL-NIGHT HAMBURGER STAND on Slauson was the right place for me. Their hamburgers came with beefsteak tomatoes, Bermuda onions, sour pickles, mustard, mayonnaise, and homemade chili. You had the choice of cheese. My fries always had chili and cheese on them. A strawberry malted for my milk and I was on cloud nine.

The only two things that I was proud of consistently were that I could eat anything and never gain an ounce and that I'm extremely well endowed in the sexual organ sort of way. My manhood was questionable as far as courage or strength, but once in the bed I could out-joust the best of them.

I once thought that all I had to be was slender and sexually imposing and women would love me for that alone. But I realized as time went on that women, though they were often excited by my size, got used to it pretty quickly and were willing to leave me for what I thought were lesser men.

I guess I was thinking about Fearless. He was with a woman right then, and there I was eating a chili burger at four-thirty in the morning.

Sal Grimaldi, the night manager of John-John's, liked to play chess. He pulled out his small wooden board and sat across from me in the courtyard space that they covered with canvas on a cold night like that. He said that I looked tired and maybe he could beat me.

He couldn't. Grimaldi was a white guy from outside of Barre, Vermont. He always loved telling me that he had never even seen a Negro until after his twenty-first birthday.

"I mean," he said more than once, "I knew you guys existed in theory, but seeing a real black man shocked the shit out of me the first time."

I believed him. Over the years I had come to realize that people who had no experience with each other rarely hated with the vehemence that I had experienced from some southerners. Sal didn't have any preconceptions about blacks. Because of that he was critical in ways that other people weren't. He loved to talk to me about how he didn't understand why Negroes didn't make more out of themselves.

"I mean, why don't you guys just go to school and buy the businesses and take over your own communities like the Catholics and the Jews?" he'd ask.

He didn't believe that racism existed except in the southern fraternities. He was a nice guy, but just like the libraries of the North and South, he had very little information about me.

• • •

I BEAT SAL seven games straight. It took until just after nine. He stayed to play out the last game when the breakfast man came in. He wasn't perturbed at losing to a Negro, and so I felt friendly toward him. Sometimes it's just a little something that makes a man feel good.

I was exhausted, but I never liked to sleep in the daytime. And even if I'd wanted to take a nap, the only options for a bed I had were the backseat of Layla's car or the upstairs bedroom at Fanny Tannenbaum's house. Both of those choices had serious disadvantages. If the police found me curled up in the backseat of a car I didn't own, they could take me to jail for vagrancy or worse. Fanny's was no safer; Leon Douglas or at least one of his friends had already been there once.

I went over to a small shoeshine-and-magazine stand on Florence. I hung around there a couple of hours reading *Jet* magazine and shooting the breeze with a few other men like me, men who were between here and there. For a couple of hours I loitered, joking with those young men. I was free of bookstores and killers and ladies so beautiful that they could make you bleed. It was another world, where there were good laughs and no immediate danger, where nothing was different from yesterday and tomorrow promised the same.

15 │ WHEN I PULLED UP in front of the Greenspan
house it was almost eleven o'clock. My intention
was to take Fanny back home and spend the rest of
the afternoon in bed. I was so tired that I wasn't even afraid of
running into Leon Douglas.

Gella came to the door all awkward and timid, ready to run.

"Mr. Minton?" she said.

"I came by for Fanny," I told the girl. She wore a medium gray
dress cut from coarse material with dark gray buttons up the
middle. The sagging hem came down to her shins. It was a
dowdy dress without style or promise. I couldn't understand who
would make such an ugly piece of clothing, who would sell it,
much less walk into some store and decide that this was the rag
they wanted to hang on their shoulders.

"She went home early this morning," Gella said, half grinning, half looking away.

"She walk?"

"Morris drove her when he went to work." She couldn't help but smile and puff up a little when saying her lard-bottomed husband's name. "I'm going over there now myself. We're going to visit Uncle Sol."

"I'll follow you," I said. "Maybe Fearless is over there too."

"He wasn't when I called."

"When was that?"

"About seven-fifteen. I called to make sure that everything was okay."

Fanny's husband was just out of prison and in the hospital with knife wounds inflicted by a criminal who was still on the loose — and her niece calls to ask is everything okay. I could see why that old woman turned to Fearless and me for help.

GELLA PARKED in the driveway, and I pulled up to the curb. By the time I got to the front door, she'd had enough time to ring the bell and knock.

"Nice day," I said while we waited for Fanny to answer.

"What? Oh yes. Yes it *is* nice." She pressed the doorbell again.

I could hear the three short notes, then the long tone — then an even longer silence. Gella looked at me, and I tried to look unconcerned.

"She probably in the bathtub or something," I said.

"Aunt Hedva never bathes in the daytime," Gella pronounced with all the weight of a hanging judge.

I took out the key Fanny had given me and used it in the lock. When I pushed the door open the girl ran in.

"Hedva! Fanny!" She ran up the stairs in great galloping bounds.

I wandered into the den. For some reason I expected her to be there.

Her foot, half in a blue canvas shoe, was visible from around the cushioned chair.

"She's here," I said loudly enough for Gella to hear.

I didn't move. Gella's heavy feet hurried quickly to the stairs and down. When she got to my side she froze.

The wail from Fanny's niece was enough to break anybody's heart. She threw the chair aside and fell in a heap next to the corpse. There was no question about Fanny being dead. Her small face was a dark blue, and her tongue protruded. She looked like some demented soul from an old Bosch painting.

I moved backward and lowered myself toward the chair. But the chair wasn't where I remembered it, so I fell to the floor. It didn't bother me to sit there, flat on my ass.

As I said before, I've been around hard times, but the death of that tiny woman who had taken me in without the slightest hesitation hit me hard. It was like I was groggy or something. I crawled over to Gella and put my hands on her shoulders. She rose and we held each other, her for a shoulder to cry on and me so I didn't fall again.

"What can we do?" she wailed.

"Cops," I said. "Call 'em."

She went to use the phone in the kitchen while I remained, silent witness to an old woman's death. From various windows sunlight poured into the rooms. Blobs of light and hard-lined shadows were everywhere. Birds were singing. Cars going up and down the street made the sounds of rushing wind. There was a mambo band playing on a radio somewhere down the block. I wouldn't have heard any of it if it weren't for the silence imposed by death.

Gella came back into the room. When she saw Fanny she fell to her knees again.

"There's nothing we can do until they get here," I told her.

"Why?" she asked me.

I was looking at her, trying to think if there was an answer in the world to fit that question. My mouth opened and I was about to say something, but I had no idea what.

Just then the phone rang. I went into the kitchen as much to get away from the body as to answer the phone.

"Yeah?"

"Mr. Lockwood?"

"Who?"

"Tyrell Lockwood?"

"Who is this?"

"William Grove."

"I thought you was on your way to Tulsa." Though my mind was still numb from the grisly death, my tongue was on automatic.

"I had a change of plans," the reverend said.

"I bet you did."

"I want to get together and talk to you about our friend."

"Elana Love?"

"That's right."

"You know the Charles Diner?"

"On Eighty-ninth?"

"That's the place. Meet ya there at nine tonight."

"I'm in a little bit of a hurry, Tyrell," Grove said.

"I'm jammed up right now myself, brother," I said. "It's nine or nuthin'." Looking around I saw pieces of glass on the floor near the back door. The little window had been broken in.

"Maybe I could come to your place," he suggested.

"Not a chance," I said, thinking that he might never know the favor I was doing him.

There was silence and then, "Nine."

Grove hung up, but I didn't. I just stood there with the phone in my hand. I couldn't believe all the trouble that had followed that woman into my bookstore.

"Was that the police?" Gella asked me. She was so pale that it was frightening to look at her.

"No, Fearless," I lied as a reflex.

Gella sank into a chair in the dinette.

"When did she come back?" I asked.

"I told you, this morning. Morris brought her."

"What time was that?"

"Morris was on the way to work at the bank. It was about seven."

"Did he come in?" I asked.

"No. I called five minutes later. Hedva said that Morris was gone and that she was going to make kugel for you. She sounded upset."

"About what?"

"I don't know. I didn't ask because I knew I was going to see her for lunch . . ." She sat there on the verge of tears.

"So that was seven-fifteen?"

"Maybe. About then. What does it matter what time it was?"

The doorbell rang, and I realized that I was about to be arrested for murder. I was so shocked by the death that I had forgotten to run. A dead white woman, and there I was, a black man already suspected in an attack on her husband. I should have run out the back door at that moment, but I didn't. I didn't have the strength in my legs.

Gella went to the door. I trailed in behind her. Seven uniformed cops came in and spread out through the lower floor.

"Who are you?" the lead cop, a sergeant, asked me.

"Paris Minton," I said.

"What are you doing here?"

I tried to think of a reason but failed.

"He was my aunt's boarder," Gella said, neatly explaining what for me was inexplicable.

"Where were you when this happened?"

"I wasn't here last night," I said. "This morning I was playing chess with a friend over on Slauson, at John-John's."

"The chili burger place?" a corporal asked.

"Yeah," I said. "I was playing chess with the night guy. After that I went over to the shoeshine stand on Florence near Central. I got here about eleven."

"Gino, right?" the corporal asked.

"Say what?"

"The night guy at John-John's."

"Salvatore," I said.

"You found her?" the sergeant asked.

I told him the events as they occurred. I guess I was pretty broken up. Not blubbering or even crying but still deeply hurt and sad.

They questioned me, but there was no edge or threat involved.

They got my name and looked at my license. They probably called into the station to make sure that there weren't any warrants out on me. I wondered why Bernard Latham wasn't with them, but I didn't ask.

"Why are you living here?" the sergeant asked me. He didn't need to add *a black man with two old Jews.*

"My place had a fire."

"And they just happened to have a room?"

"Fearless, my friend, did Fanny a favor, and so she did us one in return. Anyway, she was scared after her husband was attacked, and she wanted us around to protect her."

"Her husband was attacked?" The sergeant had four dark brown moles on his face. They made him ugly. "He dead too?"

I gave him a brief version of Sol's attack, leaving out Elana Love and adding the lie that Fearless and I were gardeners.

"For protection, huh?" the sergeant sneered. "You did a helluva job, didn't you?"

The questions switched over to Gella after that. She told them that Fanny had stayed at her house the night before, that her husband brought her over early.

"Why was she at your house?" a policeman in a suit asked. "Why didn't she stay at home?"

Gella said that it was because of the stabbing.

"Then why leave her here when there was no one else around?" the detective asked reasonably.

"She wanted to come," Gella said weakly. "She would have walked if Morris didn't take her."

They asked her about the night before and the early-morning ride to Fanny's house. They were asking the questions again and again in different ways. That's the way the cops work; they try and trip you up, make you say something and then say it wrong from another viewpoint.

But because of the shock Gella answered every question mechanically and exactly the same. Her husband, Morris, took Fanny to her house sometime around seven. At seven-fifteen or thereabouts Gella called to see that Fanny was safe. Morris was already gone off to work, and Fanny was making noodle pudding for me and Fearless.

"Where is this Fearless?" the sergeant asked me.

"He spent the night with his girlfriend," I said. "Dorthea."

"Where can I find her?" he asked me.

"I don't know, officer," I said. "She's his girlfriend and all, but I don't know her."

It was a lie but not that bad. I didn't want the cops coming down on Fearless before I got to talk to him. That is, if I could keep out of jail myself.

The ambulance arrived soon after that. The attendants came running in, but they slowed down after they saw the body. No mouth-to-mouth or injection was going to save this patient's life.

A police doctor came and checked out the corpse. After he did that the cops all stood around me. They wanted to see my hands. The doctor looked at my fingers and then measured the length of my hand.

Finally he turned to the sergeant and said, "I don't think so, no."

The police moved around the house looking for clues or something. They checked the doors and windows for signs of break-in.

They found the broken glass and fussed around but never took fingerprints that I saw.

"Are you staying here?" the sergeant asked me.

"I guess. Nowhere else to go," I said.

"Lay off anything around the back door," he said. "Crime scene."

They asked me more questions without aggression or anger. They seemed more interested in Gella. They kept asking why Fanny left so early. They wondered why she was so frightened when Fanny didn't answer on the first ring of the doorbell.

She had good reason to be nervous. Those cops had just as much reason to be suspicious. But I knew that Gella would never have harmed Fanny. I saw her fall apart; nobody could fake that. And I could tell by the way they talked to each other that there was a deep love between those women.

Gella went with the ambulance, and the police finished their searches.

16

I PACED the somber house, taking inventory of the tokens of the Tannenbaums' life. On their bedroom dresser were more than a dozen photographs in little stand-up frames. Old black-and-whites, and even older sepia-and-whites showing stern-faced, soft-skinned people in dark clothes. Even the children put on frowns for the camera. I didn't know which one was Sol Tannenbaum, but I recognized Fanny sitting in a high-backed chair, holding a bouquet of lilies. Her face was so sour in that picture that I had to laugh. I knew her well enough that I could see past the pose into the woman who was now dead.

Her rings and bracelets were in a jewelry box. Perfume was a single bottle. One scent was enough at her age. On matching night tables on either side of the bed there were pictures of Gella. Fanny's photo was a more sedate one of the girl becoming a woman with someone else's baby in her arms. Sol had one of her in a flaring summer dress, smiling and impatient. I imagined the plain girl was feeling beautiful that night, and she wanted to run away to dance.

Sol's top drawer had about sixty dollars in bills and change in it. I took the money without feeling like a thief. The money Fanny had given me wouldn't last long, and I needed cash to keep me and Fearless afloat.

There were papers of many sorts in Sol's drawers. Mixed in among them were cuff links and thick rings, keys, and a pocket-knife. Many of the papers were letters in foreign languages. I made out postmarks from Israel, Germany, and Argentina. There were old newspaper clippings of many things, including a recital that Gella had performed on the violin at a Jewish temple not far away. There was one article, clipped and circled in red, about Lawson and Widlow, the accounting company Sol had worked for. The firm was acting as broker for a French company that was selling an antique collection of jewelers' tools to a museum in New York. The Cuthbert and Rothstein Museum of the Jeweler's Art had purchased the eighty-seven instruments that were used to create the crowns of French royalty in the sixteenth and seventeenth centuries. The article was a few years old and yellowing. I put it in my pocket and opened the bottom drawer.

There was a clip-loading .38 in its original box down there. The maker's name was Belson-Teeg. The gun was made from dark metal, and it was well cared for. I checked it out. It was open for business. The safety was off, and there was a bullet in the chamber.

I spent the longest moment thinking about that gun. Should I take it? I wasn't a good shot, but I knew how to pull a trigger.

Since Elana Love had taken Fearless's piece I felt vulnerable. But if I took Sol's fancy pistol and the cops found it on me, I'd be in trouble.

Would you rather be in trouble or be dead? The voice that came into my head was that of Lonnie "two-hand" Samuels, my pretend uncle and the number one troublemaker of Avery Island at one time. In his youth he had been on the chain gang twice. The sheriff of our sleepy community always braced Lonnie when a crime had been committed. But Lonnie didn't do crimes by the time I was twelve. He just spoke out loud about what a man had to do if he wanted to keep his dignity and his life.

Remembering Lonnie's advice usually made me do the opposite of what he said, because even though I loved my uncle, I knew he had a head harder than cast iron and he never worried about consequence.

"Hello?" a man's voice called from downstairs. "Is anybody home?"

That made up my mind for me. I put the pistol in the belt under my loose shirt and went cautiously out of the bedroom.

The man I found standing at the foot of the stairs was smaller than I by a head, and that's short. I could also tell that he was slight of frame in spite of the heavy overcoat he wore. But I didn't regret my pistol. Even a little man can carry a gun. The visitor's hands were in plain sight, so I went the rest of the way down to meet him.

"Hello," he said, looking up at me with an expression too mild to be honest. I mean, here I was a black man in elderly white folks' house with the door obviously left unlocked, and he didn't so much as frown. Instead, all he did was ask, "Is Fanny or Sol here?"

"He's in the hospital and she's dead," I said casually.

It's hard to tell from a man's face how he responds to terrible news. Sometimes tears are a blind for guilt. But the little man in the big coat didn't cry. His eyebrows knitted a quarter inch. His lips pressed ever so slightly tighter.

"What happened? What, what happened?"

"Somebody came over here two days ago and put the hurt to Sol. This morning somebody broke in and choked Fanny till she was dead."

"That's terrible. My old friend. My old friends." The little man took the opportunity to sit upon the bottom stair.

"Who are you?" I asked.

"Minor," he said. "Zev Minor. I'm from Estonia. Like Sol and Fanny's families." He looked down at the floor and shook his head. Then he looked up and asked, "Could I have some water or something?"

"Yeah, come on." I gave him my hand to help him stand and led him into the kitchen.

There was an unopened pint of peach schnapps in the spice cabinet. I poured a shot into the bottom of a water glass. Mr. Zev Minor took the glass gratefully. With both hands he poured the pink liquor down his throat. He closed his eyes against the burn and then opened them again to look at me.

"Excuse me," he said, "but who are you?"

The right question at last.

I put the bottle down next to his glass and said, "My name's Paris. I'm a friend'a the family's. They asked me to come stay with Fanny after Sol got hurt."

"But you say she's dead?" Zev asked in a mildly accusatory tone. Again the right thing to say. "And where are Morris and Gella?"

"She's with the police, helping them to find out what happened to Fanny after her husband dropped her off here," I said, answering both his question and his accusation at the same time.

"Sol is alive though?"

"He got stabbed. He's in the hospital."

"Stabbed, choked," Minor said, rolling his eyes from side to side. "This does not happen to good Jewish people. How can it happen?"

"I know what you mean. They were both good people as far as I knew them. Real people, you know? I mean if Fanny said it, then it was true, no lie to that."

A light shone in Zev Minor's eyes. A light that told me he knew what I meant. It brought us together in lamentation.

"I don't understand. Why did they attack Sol?"

"I don't know," I said, only partway lying.

"Didn't he say? Didn't he tell you?"

"He was stabbed. Bad. Unconscious in his hospital bed."

"Coma?"

"I don't know about all that. His eyes are closed, at least that's what Fanny said, and he ain't talkin'."

"I would like to see him," Zev said. He took the bottle and poured another small shot. "Maybe I can do something."

I saw no reason to keep Sol's hospital a secret from a family friend. He was a mild old man who didn't push or seem worried about hidden bonds. And so I felt bad when saying, "They had him at Temple, but then they said that he was transferred. I don't know if it was because of his wound or for safety."

Zev's eyebrows knitted a fraction of an inch again. He stared at me long enough to ask himself a question and answer it, and then he nodded. He downed his drink and then stood up.

"If you see Morris, tell him to call me," he said. "Tell Morris and Gella both how sorry I am. It's so sad. It's more than sad."

He walked heavily toward the front door. I followed him, feeling guilty, like I had knocked somebody down and then kicked him for no good reason.

At the front door I said, "Mr. Minor."

"Yes, Mr. Paris?" I could tell by his voice and his eyes that he was expecting me to give him a way to call Sol.

"Do you have a number I could give Gella and Morris?"

The expectations died in Zev Minor's eyes, but he didn't seem bitter.

"Morris knows my number by heart," Minor said. "Don't forget to tell him that I called and how sorry I am. Tell him that I will do whatever I can."

"Where'd you say you knew Sol from?" I asked in a bushwhack sort of way.

"We were from the same town, like I told you," he said in a whispery tone, "but that was long ago."

"And he introduced you to Morris?"

"No," Zev said. "That's what's funny. I met Morris only in the last year. We were doing business together, and while we were talking I found out that he was married to Sol's niece."

"I thought that Morris worked for a bank?" I asked.

"That's right." The tiny man reached out for my hand.

His skin was dry and papery, a little cool.

A few minutes after he left I shuddered, recalling the feel of his onionskin hand on my fingers.

17 | ZEV MINOR'S VISIT faded quickly from my thoughts. I felt sluggish once alone again. The death of Fanny Tannenbaum had hit me hard. She was just an old white woman, that's what I thought, but she reminded me of the women in my own family. She was strong and brave in the face of people much more powerful than she. She was sweet and comfortable in the company of strange men. Maybe she even sparkled a little while cooking for us and ironing our clothes.

I knew that I should be doing something, but I didn't remember what.

I went through the library in the den, finally resting my eyes on a book, the title of which I had never seen before. *Dead Souls,* by Nikolay Gogol. The preface said that it was a Russian masterpiece. I had read Tolstoy and Dostoyevsky but never Gogol. The preface went on to say that he wrote about the travesty of serfdom in old Russia. It seemed like those old white people used to own each other at the same time that whites owned blacks in America.

For a moment or so I forgot about my problems and started to read the words of the long-dead Russian.

I suppose that the lock on the front door had been wedged open by the cops, because he just walked on in without rousing me from my reverie. When I sensed a shadow passing somewhere at the edge of my peripheral vision I jumped, screamed, and threw my book all at the same time. Luckily my aim was bad and Fearless had stayed back, knowing how jumpy I could be sometimes.

"Hey, Paris," he said, holding his hands up in mock surrender. "I give."

He wore black jeans and a denim jacket of the same color over a gray shirt. There was a watch with a gold band on his wrist and a pair of sunglasses stuffed in the breast pocket of his new jacket.

I wanted to crack wise about his new wardrobe, but the fear that made me jump was deeper than just edginess.

"What's wrong, Paris?"

"They killed Fanny."

Fearless and I hadn't met until we were both full-grown men, but I felt that I knew him as a child, because every once in a while the boy would come out in his face. Loss and disbelief erased any swagger from the sex he had had with Dorthea the night before.

"No."

Blood padded in from the doorway and regarded his new-found master.

"Somebody came in and choked her."

"Where were you, Paris?"

"I was out lookin' for them Messenger people. Didn't come in till about eleven. I went over her niece's house to get her, but Fanny'd already come here."

Fearless hunkered down on the floor, elbows on his knees, hands propped on either side of his face. Blood licked a hand, but Fearless pushed him away.

"Who did it, man?"

He wasn't looking at me, but still I only shook my head.

Fearless stood up all at once.

"Muthahfuckah," he said, and then he grabbed me by the front of my shirt and lifted me from the floor.

He raised his fist, but I didn't resist. Fearless was one of the kindest men I ever met, but the devil lived in him too. In a rage he was capable of murder. But he had never killed any friend that I knew of.

His eyes could have belonged to a dead man, they were so fixed. He didn't seem to be breathing. I hovered there an inch or so over the floor.

Even though I'm often frightened, I have never been afraid of Fearless. I felt such a deep kinship with him that he never scared me.

When he let me go I stumbled but remained on my feet.

"Where is she?" he asked.

"Ambulance took her," I said. "Gella went with them."

"What you got?"

I considered my words carefully then. I knew he was close to killing, and I was taught never to point a loaded weapon at somebody unless I intended to shoot.

"Grove called me. He's gonna meet us at the Charles Diner at nine."

"He do this?"

"Naw. Naw, I don't think so."

"He know who did it?"

Before I could answer, Blood started barking and Morris Greenspan rushed in.

"Blood!" Fearless commanded, and the dog, still growling, stood down.

"Where?" Morris Greenspan asked. He was looking around the room. His eyes stopped on the floor of the den. "Gella said it was in there."

The big, sloppy man was nearly in shock. His eyes were wide and his voice was strained to cracking. He lurched into the den and looked around, twisting from side to side.

"What happened?" he shouted, and then he fell to the floor just like a two-year-old throwing a tantrum. "What happened?"

He jerked and flailed around on the carpet for a while, but I didn't mind. At least the spectacle distracted Fearless. After a minute or so we helped Morris back to his feet and sat him down in a chair.

"Why would anyone . . . how could they?" he said, and then he cried in earnest.

It was a deep, mournful wailing with no modesty or shame. He cried from his eyes and nose and mouth. He bent forward in the chair and called out for his Fanny, his Hedva. It was more like a pagan priest who had witnessed the death of his patron deity than a man who'd lost an in-law.

It was a full ten minutes before the lament subsided.

"How did you hear about it?" I asked.

"Gella called me at work from the hospital. She said that they were taking her to the police station to talk."

"What did she tell you?"

"That Hedva was dead!" he declared.

"Did she want you to pick her up or meet her?"

"She, she . . . I guess."

"Then why did you come here?"

"I thought I could do something. I hoped I could do something. I wanted to help."

"But she's dead, man," I said. The anger probably came from my own frustration. "She's dead, and your wife needs help down at the cops."

"Leave him alone, Paris," Fearless said.

Blood growled to back up his new master's command, but he wasn't sure if he was growling at me or Morris.

"No," Morris said. "He's right. I should go."

"You better not drive," Fearless said. "We'll take you."

GELLA WASN'T too much better off than her husband. She was sitting at the far end of the long bench in the entrance room of the Boyleston Heights precinct. There were a few others seated here and there. Mostly Mexicans. Mostly women. Waiting for their men, I guess. Nobody seemed happy.

One young woman, she couldn't have been twenty-five, had four small children running around, a toddler holding on to her skirts, and a baby in her arms. The children laughed and played on the hard floor, explored the area in front of the sergeant's desk, and watched as three brown men were brought in in chains.

Them chirren is where they gonna be, I could hear my mother say. *Ain't nobody even care 'cept her. An' look at her. What could she do?*

When Gella saw us she went straight to her husband and put her arms around him. He brought his arms around her, but it was more a hopeless gesture than it was a hug. Fearless and I waited for the pitiful embrace to be over, and then I suggested we make tracks.

But before we could get out of there a ranking officer in uniform came up to us.

"Mrs. Greenspan," the tallish, portly man said. His smile was an amenity, like a blindfold offered before the firing squad. "Is this your husband?"

"Yes. This is Lieutenant Binder," she said to our assembly.

Binder shook Morris's hand and looked into his eyes. "Sorry for your loss."

Morris mumbled something.

"Which one of you boys is Paris Minton?" the policeman asked.

I hesitated and then lifted a finger to indicate myself.

His eyes were peacock blue, his skin tended toward gray.

I was trying to keep my mind on freedom.

"Would you spare me a few minutes?" Lieutenant Binder asked.

He didn't wait for an answer. Instead he touched my arm and steered me to a small room behind the admitting sergeant's desk.

It wasn't a room really, but just a space behind a frosted glass door. Inside were a wooden table and chair. It was a place where the desk sergeant could eat his meal or take a cigarette break.

"Mrs. Greenspan tells me that you happened on her great-aunt and -uncle after they were attacked two days ago," the lieutenant said.

"Yeah, yeah. We were lookin' for a gardenin' job, and then there the old man was, stabbed."

"Then the old woman invited you to stay at their home?" He had the satisfied grin of a crocodile.

"We needed a place to stay," I said.

"Because of a fire, I believe the young lady said."

"Uh-huh."

"Sit down, Mr. Minton," Binder said.

"No, thank you."

"Sit, please."

"No," I replied.

That was the test. If I were close to arrest he would have made me bend. That's how it worked: a cop pushed you to the limit but never more unless he could turn a key on you.

"Okay," Binder said. "Have it your way. I just wanted to ask you a few more questions."

"Shoot."

He didn't jump right off. First he gauged me with those shiny blue eyes of his. His orbs were so bright that it was hard for me to imagine that there was intelligence behind them.

"What do you think of these Jews?" he asked. He twisted his lips on the last word as if it was a lemon peel in his mouth.

"Like you say, I've only been there two days. That whole time the old man's been unconscious in the hospital. Fanny's okay, though."

"Did she get along with her niece and her nephew-in-law?"

"Yeh. Sure. I mean, she thought Morris was kind of a fool. But I guess he kinda is."

"Do you think that either one of them might have wanted the old Jews harmed?"

Jew turned to *nigger* in my ears, and I started disliking the cop.

"No," I said. "No. The girl and Fanny really loved each other. And Morris is more broke up than Gella over Fanny bein' dead."

Binder wasn't really listening. He didn't really care about the people in this case. But he seemed to want something. He regarded me again with those beautiful but stupid eyes.

"What about Bernard Latham?" he asked.

At first I thought we were experiencing an earthquake. The ground seemed to swell under my feet. I regretted my decision to stand.

"What about 'im?"

"What did he ask you?"

"He wrote it down, man." I got dodgy, hoping to figure out where these questions came from — and where they were going.

"Don't get wise, son," the uniform said.

"He wanted to know why we were at Fanny's house. He thought maybe we were the ones who stabbed Sol." I decided to skim the truth off a little at a time.

"Who's we?"

"Me an' Fearless."

"Fearless the other boy outside?"

"Latham brought us here," I said.

"Who was he riding with?" Binder asked.

I tried to remember. I was handcuffed and in the backseat next to Fearless.

"He was in uniform," I ventured. "White guy. Pink really."

"Billings?" Binder asked. "Pullman? Nazareth?"

It's a mess, Naz, I remembered Latham saying to the cop next to him in the front seat. At the time it meant nothing to me.

"I think I heard him call somebody Naz," I said.

Binder considered me then. He could have delved deeper into my story, or he could let me go.

"And...," I said.

"And what?"

"I seen where Sergeant Latham been all over town. I mean I saw in the newspapers that he was interrogatin' that guy who got shot down in Watts and died over in Mercy Hospital. I just figured that he was on some kinda citywide police unit to be showin' up all over." I was hoping that Binder didn't read all the papers. He probably didn't. He probably didn't know any more about that crime than any other citizen.

"What paper did you read that in?"

"I forget. Either the *Times* or the *Examiner*. It was just on the counter in a coffee shop I was at. You know I was surprised to see Latham's name over south when I knew he was a Hollywood cop and I had just seen 'im in East L.A."

Again those eyes considered me. They probed so deep that I began to wonder what he could have on me. I hadn't done anything wrong except maybe to take that money from Sol's drawer. That's when I remembered the pistol I had hitched up in my belt. They wouldn't frisk me unless I was going to be arrested, but if they found an illegal, and stolen, concealed weapon on me, prison was right around the corner.

I cursed Elana Love in silence.

"Anything else?" he asked.

"Like what?"

He stuck out his lower lip and raised his right shoulder an inch or two. "I don't know. Maybe something Latham asked you. Something the Jews might have said."

I counted three breaths and considered my situation. I wanted the policeman to trust me, to think that I was too scared to be anywhere but on his side.

"Latham said that the old man stole some money," I said. "A lot of it. And they never recovered it even though they caught him and had him in jail."

"Did the sergeant say that he was investigating the case?"

"He didn't say, but I guessed he was."

"Did you find out anything?"

"I asked Fanny about it, but she said that her husband would never steal a thing."

Binder snorted his contempt and then asked, "What about the niece and her husband?"

I shook my head. "I ain't really talked to them at all. Morris didn't like us much, and Gella's kinda scared."

Binder frowned, and then he smiled. He offered me his hand, but when I took it he pressed down hard with his thumb.

"If you're in this, it's gonna hurt," Binder said.

"The way you mashin' on my hand it hurts right now."

"It could get worse," he said and then let me go.

"I don't know nuthin' more, man," I said.

The lieutenant smiled and then gestured, telling me that I could go.

I left the police station, thinking again about the Greyhound Bus Company. This time I thought maybe I'd return to Louisiana. A white man would have to look pretty hard down around the colored parishes of southern swamps to find a little black man like me.

18

THE FIRST THING I did when I got back to the car was to slip Sol's pistol from under my shirt and shove it beneath the driver's seat. The Greenspans sat in the backseat on the ride to their home. Morris laid his meaty head against the window, and Gella was wound so tight that she shook slightly, like a palsied old woman. Half the way there Fearless turned around and took her two slender hands into his one big one.

"You gonna make it through this, girl," he said. "You gonna make it."

I don't know how she responded because I was looking in the rearview mirror at Morris to make sure he wasn't going to start swinging because another man, a black man, was holding his wife by the hand. But Morris didn't even budge. He was more shattered than my grandfather had been when his wife of sixty-three years had passed.

When we stopped in front of their house Morris stumbled out of his side and fell on the lawn. He got to his feet and strode up to the door like a toddler whose gait changes every three steps. Fearless walked Gella slowly to the door, still holding her by one hand. Morris had worked his key on the lock and blundered in by the time they reached the single stair. Fearless lifted Gella's chin and kissed her on the lips. When he whispered something, she leaned into him for another osculation and an embrace. He ushered her through the door and closed it behind her.

Back next to me he took the posture of someone waiting for the car to begin moving. I didn't engage the gears.

"Somethin' wrong with the car, Paris?"

I didn't answer.

Fearless turned to me.

"Something wrong?"

"What was that?" I asked.

"What?"

"With that white girl. Jail so hard on you that you got to take a woman right out from under her husband?"

"What?" Fearless complained. "Naw, man. I ain't interested in that crooked-nosed girl."

"You could'a fooled me and about half the neighborhood too."

"She needed a kiss, Paris. That's all. A kiss and a kind word. She just lost her family, man. That big bum of a husband don't care. I just kissed her and told her that I was there. That's all."

"And if she still felt bad," I taunted, "you'd take her up in the bed but still that wouldn't be nuthin'?"

"Maybe. Sometimes you got to give, Paris. Sometimes a man or a woman needs the opposite sex to say, hey it's okay. But she don't mean nuthin' t'me. Neither do that dumb husband. If he was holdin' her, then she wouldn't'a needed me to do it."

I shifted into first and drove off.

Fearless had a smart heart. He had a brave heart too. When he talked to me like he did about Gella, I never understood, not really, a word.

WE MADE IT to the Charles Diner by nine-fifteen. The place was alive. The girls couldn't help but move their butts, even if it was just in their chairs, when Big Joe Turner was playing on the jukebox, and the men couldn't help but watch. At the Charles men dressed as differently as the women did. From T-shirts to tuxedos the fashions ranged. The women sat in groups at the small tables in the great round room while solitary men smelling anywhere from Classic Gent to hard-earned sweat came up and made their offers for a little wiggle on the dance floor in back.

"At the table over next to the plastic palm tree," the bartender told Fearless when he asked if anyone was looking for Tyrell Lockwood.

A woman was sitting next to him, leaning toward him like a sailboat under a squall.

"Reverend Grove?" I said in greeting. There was only a faint light of recognition in his eyes for me, but I knew him. The minister was the cock of the walk down around Central and 101 when the Messenger had its doors open.

"Get yourself another fizz and park it at the bar, babe. I'll be there in a minute," the reverend told the girl.

He handed her a two-dollar bill. She kissed his fingers before taking the money with her teeth. I think she was a pretty girl. She might have been a knockout. But I couldn't tell. My mind was going over and over the lies and questions I had for the holy man.

His suit was three-button, maroon, and silk. He was a hair shorter than Fearless and more substantial but not portly or fat. He had a full face that was medium brown and diabolical in a mild way. Everything turned up: the almond eyes, the slightly receding hairline, the corners of his smile; all like small horns on a masquerade devil or, more likely, a minister who had studied sin for too long and who was finally overwhelmed by its beauty. The left side of his jaw was a little larger than the right, and that eye was bloodshot, and not from lack of sleep.

"Tyrell Lockwood?" the devil inquired of either of us.

"Me," I said. "This is my friend."

Grove motioned for us to join him. A waitress wearing a black T-shirt and a tight white skirt came up. There was a nasty-looking scar that came from the bottom of her chin to the middle of her generous lower lip. On that lip the scar took a left turn and went all the way to the corner of her mouth. It made her look vulnerable, so I looked away.

"Drinks?" the waitress asked in a husky voice.

Fearless looked to Grove, who shook his head slightly. Fearless showed two fingers and said, "Beers." The waitress went off.

"Where is she?" Grove asked.

"Didn't Vincent tell you what I said?"

"He said some nonsense about her paying you to find me."

"Well I found you now, didn't I?"

The waitress came back. She tried to look me in the eye while serving the drinks, but I looked away again. Fearless gave her something and then tapped the table for her to bring more when the time came. She said thanks, so I supposed he had tipped her nicely.

When the waitress had gone Grove lowered his voice and said, "Don't try and fool with me, niggah."

"Don't fool yourself," Fearless interjected, his cool certainty bringing doubt to the reverend's eye.

He gazed over toward the door. Maybe he thought it was foolish to come alone to meet two strangers in that dangerous business. Maybe he recognized that his arrogance didn't carry any weight outside of his red-draped storefront church.

"You lookin' for Elana. Elana lookin' for you. Why?" I asked.

Grove didn't respond. He was trying to figure out what to do. He spent as much time looking at the door as he did at us. Louis Armstrong was singing duets with Billie Holiday on the box. Fearless stretched out on his chair like a cat. I think he was just enjoying being free.

"She promised me five hundred dollars," I told Grove. "I already put in my time."

"I don't believe you," the Holy Roller replied.

Fearless straightened up in his chair.

"Leon Douglas." I spoke Elana's ex-con boyfriend's name as if it were a complete sentence. "And a bearer bond. How about that?"

"Do you know where she is?" Grove asked, no longer looking for a way out.

"I might know how to find her," I said. "But I wanna know what I'm gettin' into before I take another step."

"Tell me where she is."

"No, uh-uh. I put my money on the table, man," I said. "Now it's your turn. If you got somethin' I could use, then maybe we could do somethin' together."

"The bond," he said, his voice changing this time to a breath of air. "It's worth a lot more than she said."

"She lied?"

"Sister Love was made to lie. Prob'ly half'a everything she told you was a lie," Grove said. "But she didn't lie about the bond. She just don't know. It's worth ten times what she thinks."

Using gangster logic I figured he meant a hundred times what she said.

"How's that?" I asked.

"That's for me to know."

"Well how's this?" I added. "Elana told me that you were the one had the bond. She said that she left it with you, but that —"

"It's all a lie," the preacher said. There was the musical note of a sermon in his voice.

"There ain't no bond?"

"Oh yeah. There's a bond all right. Damn sure enough. But I don't have it. I *did* have it but not no more."

"All you're sayin' is what isn't and what's lies and what didn't happen. What me and my friend here need to know is what is." I felt confident when Fearless was at my back, smart too.

Grove took me in for a moment or two.

"I remember you now," he said. "At the bookstore. Vincent told me you worked there, but I didn't remember the name."

I nodded and waited.

"Leon," he said, "sent Elana a letter askin' her to come see him in prison. She was stayin' with me at that time but still had her own place."

"And you didn't mind her gettin' mail from an old boyfriend?"

"I saw my fortieth birthday two years ago, son. I know that women go to the bathroom and everything. I wasn't her first man. I wasn't her best man. Leon mentioned a thousand dollars in the letter, and so she took a day trip. Three days later we had the note."

"Tell me about the note," I said.

"What about it?"

"What country it come from? What's the face value?"

"Ten thousand Swiss francs," he said.

I was happy because at least one thing Elana said might be true.

"And she give it to you?" Fearless asked.

"It was new love. She saw in me what a woman wants to see in a man when they first start out." Grove spoke from experience. "I could do anything at first. But then, when the bank told me on the phone that I had to have proof that I was David Tannenbaum, she saw a little tarnish here and there. I wanted to keep on the good side of a woman like that, so I go down to see the wife — Fanny."

"You went to the Tannenbaum house?" I asked.

Fearless tensed up and then began his descent into a crouch.

"Yeah," Grove said.

"When?"

"That was maybe four months ago," he replied. "I went there to find out why her husband was in jail, the particulars."

"Why she wanna talk to you?" Fearless asked.

"I said that I was the visiting chaplain at the prison. I said that her husband wanted me to tell her that he was okay."

"Why she gonna believe that shit?" Fearless had no love lost for this messenger.

"Her husband forbade her to go up to the prison. That's why Elana had to go up, to get a letter from the Jew to give to his wife. So all I did was say that he was doing okay and that he was safe and missing her."

"And what she give you in return?" I asked.

That was the heart of our talk — what Fanny told Grove. He knew it and he knew I knew it. I was riding high on the powerful presence of Fearless and the fact that Grove was a little shy.

"It wasn't nuthin'," he said. "She didn't know a thing."

"That's why you ran out on Elana? That's why the Messenger packed up its drapes and ran?"

Grove took a deep breath, reaching for strength and conviction.

"Elana got the bond. No matter what she told you, she got it. You find her, you find the bond. You do that, and you come to me. I can make ten times ten thousand."

"How?"

Grove shook his head while looking me in the eye.

"So now what?" I asked.

"I know how to make the money. You bring me the bond."

"Maybe I should go to the cops," I speculated.

Grove decided on that moment to stand up.

"Messenger of the Divine is where you could get in touch with me. I might be a little bit scarce the next week or so, but Vincent knows how to get to me," he said. "Going to the cops might get me in trouble, but it'll get you boys killed."

Fearless blew Grove a kiss in reply. I wasn't feeling so cocky.

The self-proclaimed minister walked away from the table and to the woman who was waiting for him at the bar. Together they went out the front door. I sat there wondering, was there a dollar amount worth my life?

FEARLESS AND I FINISHED our drinks in silence. Then we went toward the door. He was the first one through, and I was just about to follow when someone grabbed me, roughly, by the shoulder. It was the waitress with the scarred lip.

"Excuse me," she said.

"Uh-huh?"

"Why cain't you look at me? I'm so ugly that you got to be rude?"

I looked at her then. I saw a lovely female face, except for that scar, on a woman not over twenty. Her expression was petulant but sweet; that face had seen some life.

"It ain't that, sugar," I said.

"Then what?"

I brought a finger to her face, tracing the scar up to her lip. She didn't move away.

"I wanna kiss that streak. I wanna bite it. But you know I don't even have a roof or rent for a room. That scar meant that somebody hurt you, so I looked away. I wanted to say somethin' nice, but what use is a man smooth talkin' when he ain't got two nickels to rub together?"

The woman didn't believe me, but she wanted to. One brow was knitted in anger, but the other one was wide with hope.

"I'm Charlotte," she said.

"Paris. Paris Minton. You be workin' here in two nights, Charlotte?"

"Uh-huh."

"I'll drop by."

"Sure. I bet."

"You got a pencil?" I asked her.

She took out her yellow number two and her bill pad. I gave her Milo Sweet's phone number and said, "You can call there if I don't show, but don't worry, I'm comin' back around."

"HEY, PARIS," Fearless said in a shy tone. We were in the car driving toward Milo's office.

"What?"

"I just remembered somethin'."

"Yeah?"

"I know Leon Douglas."

"Say what?"

"I know 'im, Paris. He went in for armed robbery. But he was in the city jail 'cause he got a fancy new lawyer and a retrial. His cell was just down the hall from me."

I pulled the car to the curb and turned off the ignition. I put my head on the steering wheel and closed my eyes. The darkness called me toward sleep, but I sat up again and asked, "Why the hell you wait till now to tell me this?"

"I just didn't think of it. In the can they called him Big Bama 'cause he was from Alabama an' he was big. I hardly even knew him."

"So? What do you know about him?"

"Nuthin'. He was smug about bein' down at the jail. He did a payroll robbery and shot two men. They had him for thirty at San Quentin, but the evidence wasn't hard. The gun they found on him when he was arrested was the wrong caliber.

He did it, but this new lawyer was trying to get the case thrown out."

"Who's the lawyer?"

Fearless shrugged his shoulders.

"What kinda dude is he?" I asked.

"Armed robbery, single-handed, two men shot. Three-quarters bad if he can blindside ya. Half bad face-to-face."

Fearless considered himself and maybe three other people he'd ever met to be *full bad:* Jacob Trench, Doolen Waters, and, of course, Raymond Alexander. But three-quarters was plenty scary enough for me.

19 | LORETTA WAS SHUFFLING papers on her desk before Fearless and I awoke the next morning. We had decided that sleeping at the Tannenbaum house was too much for either of us, and I still had Milo's key.

"Morning, Mr. Jones, Mr. Minton." Our presence held no surprise for her.

"Mornin'," we said together.

I had let Fearless have the couch because he was just out of jail, and I was still feeling guilty for not helping him sooner.

"When's Milo due in?" I asked the Japanese passe-partout.

"Soon, I think," she said. "He has a problem with a client who has to show up for sentencing at three. A friend of yours."

"Who's that?"

"Lucas North."

"Luke?" Fearless smiled. "What's that boy up to?"

"He was with some friends in a stolen car. He wasn't driving. He didn't even know the driver. They had gotten drunk together and were taking some high school girls for a ride. The judge had seen Lucas before and decided to scare him, I guess. He found him guilty but postponed the sentencing. Milo thinks it was just to make Lucas sweat, but if he doesn't show up, there's six hundred dollars on the bond."

Fearless scratched his head. I stifled a yawn. It wasn't our problem.

MILO CAME IN at around nine. Fearless was taking his dog over to Dorthea to keep for the day. I was reading about Chichikov, the con man protagonist of *Dead Souls*.

"Hey, Paris," Milo said. "You gonna have to start payin' rent you keep warmin' my couch."

"I got a problem, Milo."

"One shot to the temple and problems just go away," the bailbondsman replied. Then he turned to Loretta. "We hear from Mr. North?"

"No sir, not yet."

"Shoot."

"Milo."

"What, Paris?"

"I got a problem, man."

The china whites of Milo's eyes flashed out from his coalblack face. "I'm out six hundred dollars at three o'clock, and you want me to worry about you?"

"Lucas North," I said. "Fearless and I will look for him if you do somethin' for us."

• • •

LUCAS'S MOTHER, Inez North, was in her late thirties. Lucas was maybe twenty-one, at least in years. He was an immature boy who got into trouble as a kind of hobby. He worked at that pursuit twenty-four hours a day because he couldn't hold a job for over a week.

I first met Lucas when he was only fifteen. His mother and Fearless had a thing going for a while. In the middle of it Lucas got arrested for knocking down an ex-girlfriend's fence with his mother's new used car.

The girlfriend's father wanted to press charges, and as much as Fearless tried to argue with him, old Landry Lamming wasn't buying. Fearless came to me because he was on the verge of coming to blows with Landry and he knew that that would have been wrong.

I asked around about Landry and found that he was from Guyana originally and was so conceited about his lineage and education that most of the people in the neighborhood were happy to run him down.

"He jes' fulla himself, that's all," Lana Rudd confided in me. "Always away on business and comin' home like he was king'a the hill."

"What kinda business?" I asked. Lana wasn't the first to talk about Landry's out-of-town business.

"Don't ask me," she replied, waving her hands as if deflecting fists. "He got a job with the city but he down there in San Diego every other week, seems like."

Fearless needed me to save Lucas from prosecution because he had grown tired of Inez and he believed that saving her son would lessen the sting of their breakup. So I broke into Lamming's car one night when all the hardworking people were in their beds dreaming about money. I found four bills addressed to a Laval and Kyla Biendieu, on a 24th Street address in San Diego.

I spent the next few days watching Landry. When he threw a small suitcase in his trunk and kissed his daughter and wife good-bye, I followed him down the coast highway toward the city in the sun.

I was stopped on the way by an overzealous highway patrolman. He needed to check my tires and brake lights, my spare in the trunk, and my license, license plate, the contents of my lunch bag, and what destination I had that day.

"The zoo, officer," I said with a smile. "My auntie and sister, her husband and kids, they went down earlier, but I just got off work. I heard that they got a two-headed snake in the snake house. You know I'd pay money to see anything with two heads."

"Where do you work?" the young white behemoth asked. He had blue eyes and broad shoulders and he didn't like me one bit.

"At a beauty parlor on Slauson," I said. "I do hair and nails for men and women."

That made the motorcycle cop wince.

"It's called Charlene's," I added. "Do you ever come up to L.A.?"

"Make sure you check the pressure in those tires," he replied.

I drove off glad that I had had the foresight to break into Landry's car.

Landry's new turquoise Bel Air was parked in front of Laval Biendieu's home address. I walked up to the front door and read the name on the iron mailbox that was nailed to the wall: Laval and Kyla Biendieu.

"Yes?" Landry Lamming asked, answering the door in his bathrobe. He was a small man. His English-like accent seemed incongruent with his dark Negro features. I never have gotten used to black men who don't speak in the dialect of the American South.

"Mr. Beendoo?" I asked, mauling the pronunciation terribly.

"What do you want?"

"Are you Mr. Laval Beendoo?" I insisted.

"Yes," he said reluctantly.

"Because I fount somethin'a yours and I wanted to give it back."

"What do you have of mine? How would you know something was mine? I haven't lost my wallet." Even as he spoke he reached for his back pocket to make sure, but, since he was in his robe, there was no back pocket to be found.

"My sister's kids is nine an' eleven," I said, as if those facts should have cleared up everything.

"So?"

"They fount some bills and was playin' with 'em like they was money." I've found that talking in a way that sounds ignorant makes arrogant people like Landry feel like they are in charge.

"Let me see," he commanded, opening the door three inches.

I handed him the envelopes I had stolen from his glove compartment.

"Where did your nephews find these?"

"Niece and nephew," I corrected.

"Where did they find them?" he asked with greater volume.

A light-skinned young woman with a baby in her arms appeared behind Landry/Laval.

"Somethin' wrong, Lal?" she asked.

"Go back in the other room, Kyla. Go on now."

The baby started yowling and Kyla faded beyond the range of the screen.

"Now will you answer my question?" *Lal* asked.

"They just said that they fount 'em in the street," I said.

He wanted their address, and I made up a 23rd Street location. He wanted to go over there right then, but I told him that they were at church.

"On Wednesday?" he asked.

"God don't take no days off, Mr. Beendoo," I replied piously.

After that he said thanks, that he would go talk to the parents later that day.

I didn't leave when he said good-bye.

"Is there something else?" he asked.

"Well," I hesitated. "Wasn't there some kind of reward?"

Laval/Landry regarded me with disgust. He looked around and reached for a coin that was on a lamp stand next to the door. Fifty cents! He deserved the trouble I represented.

Fearless told Landry to drop the charges or else he'd have to tell somebody about the bigamy. Milo got involved, leading Landry through how he could make sure that Lucas wasn't charged with a crime.

Some months later Fearless told me that Landry had offered him a thousand dollars to keep quiet.

"And you didn't take it?" I said.

"That would'a been wrong, Paris," Fearless told me. "You know I just wanted to do right by the boy."

• • •

FEARLESS AND I DROVE over to a small house on Ninety-second Place. That was Elbert's house. I knew that all the comic book kids congregated there when they weren't at my bookstore. I knocked on the front door, but no one answered. We went around the side driveway. In the back was a red garage. The carport door was pulled down, but there was a side door that was open. We walked in on seven little boys and a full-grown man handing comic books back and forth.

"Hey, Mr. Minton, Fearless," one of the boys droned.

The man stood up and looked at us angrily.

"Hey, Elbert," I said to the lanky eight-year-old who had greeted us.

The man squatted back down and started putting his comic books into a brown paper bag.

"Where you goin', Luke?" one of the boys asked.

"Home," the man said petulantly.

He was a beautiful young man, tall and muscular with large eyes and lips that belonged on a sculpture entitled *Negro Perfection*. Even his white T-shirt and torn jeans didn't take away from the image. Lucas North was made for trouble. But that wasn't my problem.

"You got to go with us, Luke," Fearless said.

The young man's face broke into tears.

"Why?"

"'Cause if you don't go to court, then Milo's gonna have to get the cops after your momma for the bail money."

The little boys started snickering. I could hardly blame them.

"I don't want my momma to go to jail," Lucas whimpered.

"Then come with us," I said.

Lucas was just one of the kids when it came to the comic books at my store. He dropped by as much as the little ones, wanting to trade old ones for ones he hadn't read yet.

Most of those comics were torn and tattered. But the ones on the floor were brand-new.

"Where'd you boys get new comics?" I asked Elbert.

"Mr. Wally from the market give 'em 'cause he said he was sorry that our store burned down," the gawky, fish-eyed boy said.

"Maybe he buy you a new store," Fearless said.

"Yeah," I said. "Yeah, when his boss giv 'im a little raise."

20 | WE MADE the courthouse before Milo. When he came up to us sitting there with Lucas, he didn't even give the boy a glance.

"Officer of the court been here?" he asked me.

"Yeah."

"He sign the boy in?"

"Uh-huh."

"Then let's get outta here."

I got up off the bench.

"Wait up," Fearless complained. "I wanna know what's gonna happen with Lucas."

Milo took a mangled cigarette from his breast pocket and a match from his vest. He lit the cigarette with deliberation. Then he said, "We don't have the time for that."

"You go on then," Fearless said. "I brought Luke down here and I'm gonna stand by 'im."

I would have left Fearless, but Milo was not so inclined. A few minutes later the boy's court-appointed lawyer, a white man named Todd, shuffled in and took the boy in for the sentencing. Fearless followed, but Milo and I stayed out.

Milo led me up five flights of stairs to a large and empty, granite-floored hall. We sat together on a polished mahogany bench, and Milo moved close to me like a man who was just about to get serious on a date.

"What you boys into?" he whispered. His breath was so rank that I had to swallow twice before speaking.

"What did you find?"

"Waverly, Brightwater, and Hoffman," he replied.

"Who are they?"

"People you don't wanna know. Lawyers that spend all their time with the mob. The kinda lawyers know where the bodies are buried."

"So?"

Milo peered into my face. He took a deep breath and I leaned back before he could exhale. He put a hand on my neck and squeezed slightly.

"What, Milo?"

"I went down to the state courthouse and fount out that the bailbondsman for your boy is Les Haverford, a white guy work outta Santa Monica."

I didn't ask him anything because I wasn't sure that I wanted to hear the answer.

"I asked him about Leon Douglas like you asked me to," he said at last. "Had to lie and tell him that I had a man runnin' around with Leon and that he just jumped his bond. Give him fifty bucks for an address, but that can come outta your ten percent for Lucas."

"Is that why you brought me up here? To talk about my fee?"

"Douglas was in jail for robbery and attempted murder. He was guilty but he was railroaded too. He did it all right, but they never got the right goods."

"That's what Fearless said," I said, to fill in Milo's suspicious silence.

"He the one told me about the mob lawyer and whatnot." Milo stalled again, giving me that questioning stare.

"Come on, Milo. Finish what you got to say or let's go. This ain't no interrogation."

"No?"

"Did you find out where Douglas lives?"

"Yeah."

"That's all I want."

"No it ain't. Least it better not be."

"What, Milo?"

"Waverly and them are bad news. And they're your boy Douglas's lawyers. They don't walk into court without ten thousand dollars in their pockets. They the kind if you a witness against 'em, you might just end up dead. I never heard'a Waverly comin' in on no colored case. They do the Jewish mob and the old money when they cross the line. Niggahs don't mean a thing to them."

I was clenching my hands together. My nails were biting into the skin, but I couldn't let go.

"What you an' Fearless into, Paris?" Milo Sweet asked.

"I don't know, Milo," I said. "I don't know. I was just sittin' in my bookstore, that's all."

"That innocent act ain't gonna save you, boy. You got to know where you steppin' on somethin' like this."

I told Milo everything I knew. About Fanny and Sol, about Elana Love and Reverend Grove. I told him about the car chase where they were shooting at me and about them burning down my bookstore. Some of it he already knew, but I laid out everything so he'd know exactly where I stood.

"So you see," I explained. "I didn't start nuthin'. I mean, a man got to seek out some justice if he been done wrong, right?"

"Not if justice gonna be your own hangin'."

The words bore down into my mind. I pulled my hands apart and rubbed them down my chest. It wasn't that Milo had let me know something so much more terrible than I already knew. But his point of view let me stand back and see how frightening my situation was.

"But there is one thing," Milo suggested.

"What's that?"

"If Waverly's in it, then there's a whole lotta money involved for sure. I ain't talkin' 'bout no colored money now, Paris. I ain't talkin' 'bout six months' rent or new-car kinda money. I'm talkin' Swiss ski chalet. I'm talkin' luxury for life."

Or death, I thought.

"So what you sayin', Miles?"

"Let's work together. Let's find out where the money's comin' from. Let's skim a little luxury off 'a the top."

"I thought you was so scared 'a these boys?" I asked.

"I am," he agreed vigorously. "Them boys scare me. They should scare you too. Shit. These boys is serious."

"But you still want in with me an' Fearless?"

"Just 'cause I'm scared don't make me no coward," Milo

claimed. "I don't want them white boys feelin' that just 'cause they walk in the room that I'm'a scurry out like I'm some kinda rat or cockroach. Naw, baby, scared keep ya sharp."

FEARLESS, LUCAS, AND INEZ were waiting out in front of the courthouse when Milo and I came down. Inez was grinning at Fearless, holding his hand. He took it all in good spirit, but I could tell that Inez wanted something more tangible.

"Thank you, Mr. Minton," Lucas said. "They makin' me do community service with the county park department, but you know that's good. The judge said that if I learned somethin' they might just give me a real job there."

"Thank you, Paris," Inez said. "And thank you for believing in us, Mr. Sweet."

"Uh-huh," the ex-lawyer grunted. "Fearless, you, me, an' Paris gotta talk."

"Okay, Milo," the war hero said.

Inez didn't want to let go at first. But Fearless finally managed to disentangle himself.

"You gonna call me, Fearless?" she asked.

"Just as soon as I get me a phone, baby. Just as soon as I get me a phone."

"WE WORK IT together and split whatever profit three ways," Milo said to us at his office after sending Loretta out for sandwiches.

"Not that I wanna insult you, Milo," Fearless said, "but what you gonna do for us to deserve a third?"

"I found out about Douglas and his lawyers, didn't I?" Milo whined.

"We agreed to find Lucas in trade," I said.

"I let you sleep in my office."

"That's about two percent," I said. "Where's the other thirty-one and a third?"

"You'll definitely need professional help if it comes to making bonds into money," Milo suggested.

"That could work on a percentage," I replied. "And not nowhere near the kind you want. I mean, you can't even practice law, Miles. If we needed someone in a courtroom, we'd have to hire somebody else."

It was a ritual dance. The conclusion was foregone. Fearless and I wanted Milo in it with us. He was smart and he knew things we didn't, and he was less likely to turn us over than some other men we knew. But the problem we had — the problem we always had — was money.

"How much?" Milo asked.

"The same amount you was gonna lose on Lucas," I said.

"Six hundred dollars!"

"That's it," Fearless chimed.

"In cash, in our hands, right now," I added.

"This come back on the other end," Milo amended.

"Uh-uh," I said. "Our blood, your money, that's the fuel and the investment."

When Mr. Sweet put those thirty twenty-dollar bills on the desk I knew that he believed in us. I was a young man then. His faith would only mean something to a young fool.

21 | THE FIRST THING Fearless and I did was to drive over to Merrydale Circle, a single-story court of apartments on Ninety-fifth Street. Fontanelle Roberts was the superintendent of the nine units there. She rented to tenants by the week and paid the owners based on a monthly rent schedule. Monthly rent was forty dollars, but she charged eleven bucks a week.

Fontanelle was also a bookie, a fence, and a go-between when somebody needed the services of a criminal or a shady doctor or lawyer, all of whom she held in the same low esteem. She was a small woman with dark red skin, Negro features, and black eyes. She always wore a dress and hat. She carried a purse too. In that purse was a dull gray .45. I knew about the gun because she once showed it to me and said that she celebrated every January 1 by firing off the old bullets and then reloading with fresh ammunition for the new year.

"Hi, Fearless," the older woman cried, honestly happy to see my friend. "Paris."

"Hey, Fell," I said. Fearless echoed my greeting.

"What happent to yo bookstore, Paris? I seen it all burned down. They was clearin' off the lot."

"Who was?"

"Workmen. Had a fancy truck with writin' on it, but I didn't stop to read."

I wanted to know more about the lot I'd left behind, but there was no time for nostalgia with the tasks before me and Fearless Jones.

"You got a place for us?" Fearless asked.

"How long you boys wanna stay?"

"We'll pay for the month," I said, knowing that the price went up if you didn't pay four and a half weeks in advance.

"You got furniture?" the ebony-eyed businesswoman wanted to know.

We didn't answer.

"I had Florence Landis move out real quick last week. She left one adult bed and another one for her boy. There's a table and chairs and some kitchen supplies. Two dollars more a week and you can have it."

"Okay," I said, going for my pocket.

Fontanelle reached out to stay my hand.

"Is this just livin', or is it bidness?" she asked.

"Livin'," I said.

Fontanelle didn't have anything against me. We had done

bidness in the past and I never gave her any reason to question me, but she turned to Fearless, the same question in her glance.

"Livin'," Fearless repeated.

Fontanelle smiled, took our money, and went to find the keys.

WE DIDN'T SPEND more than an hour in our new home. Two seven-minute baths, canned soup heated on the gas range, and we were out of the door.

Milo had found out from the white bailbondsman that Leon Douglas had taken a place on Orchard Street just a little south of Vernon Avenue. It was on a small half-lot, but that didn't matter much because the house was no larger than a shack. The paint was so faded and worn that it was hard to tell if the place had been white or tan or blue.

"Ain't that your car parked on the lawn, Paris?" Fearless asked.

It was. I wondered if Elana went along with the wheels. Had he killed her? I doubted it.

"Paris?"

"What?"

"What you wanna do?"

On my own I watched or lied or misrepresented. I never took danger head-on if there was a second choice. Fearless was the opposite of me; he moved ahead as a rule. He might use a back entrance or even surprise, but no matter what, he was always going forward.

I considered going up to the front door, but then Leon Douglas returned to my mind. He was an engine of destruction, a stick of dynamite ready to explode.

"Let's watch for a while, Fearless."

"How come?"

"Maybe he's got some accomplices in there. These are desperate men. If we walk in and find ourselves outnumbered, they ain't gonna let us stroll."

Fearless didn't look convinced, but he sat tight. We had a good relationship in the field. He would call me the intelligence officer, while he was the man with the heavy artillery.

We moved down to the end of the block to watch the house from a distance. That street was populated by black people from the South. Almost everyone in that neighborhood was from someplace down in the western South. Texans, Louisianans, some from Arkansas. Southern neighborhoods, even in the North, were friendly in the extreme.

Small children were drawn to us first.

"Mister, why you sittin' in your car?" a boy no more than three asked Fearless. He was wearing a T-shirt with horizontal rainbow stripes but no pants or underwear.

"Waitin' for somebody," Fearless replied.

"He waitin' for somebody!" the boy yelled at a gang of kids who were standing in the driveway of a nearby house.

The children then wandered down to the patch of grass at the curb next to our car. One girl, probably the boy's older sister, brought down a small pair of blue pants for the brave scout.

"He don't like his clothes," the shy six-year-old told us while tussling with her brother.

They asked us a few more questions and then set up camp there next to the car, playing games and shouting. I was nervous having them there, but Fearless calmed me.

"It's like camouflage, Paris," he said. "Nobody gonna be suspicious of kids tearin' and rippin' around."

After the little kids the older ones came by. First it was the twelve-year-old boys on their bicycles and then their older sisters. The girls were young and budding nicely. They were part children and part women, leaning up on Fearless's side of the car.

"Could you take us to the store?" one fifteen-year-old asked.

"Not my car, honey," my friend said easily.

"But if your friend wanted to, would you take us?"

I was beginning to get nervous because there was a definite logic to that line of guests. First the babies, then the children, next the boys on bicycles that they dream can fly, after that the young girls who feel the stirrings of womanhood — wary mothers and angry fathers wouldn't be too far behind.

"That him, Paris?" Fearless asked.

The tree trunk of a man was now wearing yellow pants and a loose-fitting, striped red shirt. He also wore a straw hat, for a disguise I guess. He walked leisurely to my car, dropped into the driver's seat, and released the emergency brake. By the time he'd rolled down to the curb, the door was shut and the engine turned over. It was a poor way to treat an automobile, but I had no desire to tell him that.

"Follow him?" Fearless asked.

"No. No," I said. "Let's go check out the house."

"I thought you said he might have some friends in there?"

"They don't know us."

"What about the girl?" Fearless asked sensibly.

"That girl ain't nobody's friend."

I started the car and rolled away from the curb.

"Where y'all goin'?" the little scout shouted.

• • •

TAKING FEARLESS'S QUESTION into account, the first thing we did was knock on the front door. I didn't think that there was anybody there, but it was always good to be certain.

To my surprise the door swung open.

Elana Love looked better every time I saw her. She was wearing a short brown bathrobe that barely covered the tops of her brown thighs. Her hair was wrapped in a towel. That lovely flat face considered us a moment and then smiled.

"Hi, Paris. Who's your friend?"

I walked past her into the house. Fearless followed my lead, closing the door behind him.

"Elana," I said. "We got to talk."

"Do you mind if I put on some clothes first?"

"Go right ahead," I said. "It ain't nuthin' I ain't already seen, and I don't think it'll come as any surprise to my friend neither."

Elana put on a petulant look for a second, but she didn't really care. She dropped the bathrobe and squatted down to pull a floral-patterned dress out of a satchel next to the couch. She stepped into the brightly colored shift and buttoned up the front. I stole a glance at Fearless while she was dressing. He didn't seem to be concerned at all. As long as I had known Fearless he proved at least once every day that he was a better man than I.

The room we had entered was almost the entire house. There was one door at the back, which I suspected was to the toilet. That was the only thing missing. There was a stove, a couch, a bed, and a bathtub in the room where we stood, making the house reminiscent of many a country home I had seen. We were standing near a table covered with dirty dishes, crumbs, newspapers, and other, less recognizable, trash. A line of tiny black ants had crossed the floor and then scattered across the table, foraging among the treasures they found there.

"How'd you find me?" Elana asked.

"We didn't," I said.

At first she was confused by my answer, but then a little twinkle told me she understood.

"You found Leon," she said.

Her intelligence did not set my mind at ease.

"I came back to see you the same day I took your car, you know," she said with a smile that made me wish it were true.

"What for? You tasted my gold fillin' when you was kissin' me and you wanted that too?"

"Don't be like that, Paris. I came back to give you your car and say I was sorry, but the store was burned down and nobody knew where you were."

There was something easy about Elana Love. All you had to do was talk to her a minute or two and a whole new life appeared before you. *Maybe everything could be different,* I thought. But then I remembered that Leon might be back any minute.

"We want the bond, Elana," I said.

She sighed and went to the couch, seating herself squarely in the middle.

"You got a cigarette, honey?" she asked Fearless.

He just stared at her, a soldier on reconnaissance duty.

I gave her a cigarette and lit it.

"You were lookin' for me and found Leon instead?" I asked.

"Yeah," she said, crossing the right leg over the left.

I sat down on the wooden arm of the calico couch and nodded for her to continue.

"Leon came back around your place just before I did. He thought you an' me were together and figured if he waited long enough, one or the other of us'd show up. It was just about the only smart thing he ever did in his life, and that was just a stupid mistake."

"Was he with Conrad Till then?" I asked.

"Naw, he had already taken Conrad to my apartment, lookin' for me. I guess I must'a shot Conrad when they was comin' after you and me in your car —"

Fearless grunted at that. I couldn't tell if it was admiration or commiseration with the dumb luck of the dead man.

"Conrad was afraid to go to his own house at first because he was on parole. He thought he could get cleaned up enough so that he could say he was sick without bleedin' all over whoever came to the door."

"So then you took Conrad to his place . . . ," I prompted.

"They made me. They said they was gonna kill me if I didn't do what they said. At first it was just to take care'a Conrad's wound."

"They didn't mind that you were the one who shot him?"

"I told 'em that it was you shootin' out the windah," she said.

"So now Douglas thinks it was me killed his friend?"

"I'ont know what he's thinkin'," Elana protested. "Anyways, I worked on Conrad's wounds, and then Leon forgot how mad he was and started lookin' at me like a man looks at a woman."

"Yeah, I know," I said.

"You cain't blame me," Elana said as if we had a relationship that had gone bad. "I'm alone out here. Men all gruff and mean, lookin' at me like I'm a piece'a meat."

"Look how you dressed," I said.

"Look how you just pushed your way into my house," was her retort.

I didn't have anything to say to that.

"You see," Elana said. "There's people out there kill me in a second. Sure I took your money and your car. But I left the five dollars in your shoe. And if you weren't out after me now, you'd be safe while my life is still on the line."

"I wouldn't be here if your boyfriend didn't burn down my motherfuckin' store," I said, getting hot.

"Leon didn't burn down your store."

"If he didn't, then who did?"

"I don't know. But he asked me the same question when he grabbed me off the street."

"That could just be a lie," I said.

"Why he wanna lie about that? Why he wanna burn your place down anyway?"

"So what happened with you and Leon?" I asked.

"We went to see William. Leon fount out where he was through a fence he knew."

"Leon the one messed up his face like that?"

"What are you, a cop?"

"Just talk, sister," Fearless said.

The timbre of his voice drew a strange stare from Elana.

"Yeah," she said, answering my question. "Leon slapped him around a little but —"

"But then he realized that the good William was tellin' the

truth and you still had the bond," I said to cut off whatever lie she was going to tell.

"If you know so fuckin' much, then why you askin' me?"

"Does Leon have the bond?"

Elana's nod was as subtle as a first kiss.

"What's he plan to do with it?" I asked.

"I don't know," she lied.

"Is the bond here?"

"No," she said. "He like me, but he don't trust me."

"Smart kid," I said.

"So we got to get the bond from this Douglas," Fearless said to me.

Elana Love was beautiful, but she had an ugly laugh, cruel and cold. "You're pretty, Paris's friend, but you don't have the stuff to take Leon Douglas down."

Fearless gave her a smile and a salute.

"What did you do after you braced Grove?" I wanted to get the conversation back to business.

"We went to my place, but the cops were there. I guess somebody found somethin'a mines at Conrad's."

"Why did your boyfriend kill Fanny Tannenbaum?" Fearless asked.

For the first time Elana lost her poise. "What?"

"Don't act like you don't know what he's talkin' about," I said. "Somebody killed her. I'm almost sure that Leon and his friend the cowboy went to Fanny's house after we got away. He stabbed Sol and ran. Cowboy or Leon just went back to finish the job."

"I don't know about Tricks, but I been wit' Leon almost every minute," Elana said uncertainly. "An' why go after her if we already had the bond?"

"Maybe he wanted more," Fearless suggested.

"No," she said.

"Why not?"

"Because. Because Leon knows a man who'll pay a lotta money for just one bond. He thinks that if he can follow down one, then all the rest'a the money that the old Jew stole will be easy to find."

"I don't get it," I said.

"Sol took money from somebody he worked for."

"Who?" I asked, just to see what she would say.

"I don't know. Leon says that there's this guy wanna get that bond 'cause he thinks that the serial numbers will lead them to a lot more money."

"When does this guy pay off?" I wanted to know.

"Leon's the only one who knows him. We have to wait for Leon to make the deal." Elana didn't sound satisfied with Leon having control.

"You know Leon might remember how you tricked him and tried to cheat him after he gets his hands on all that money," I suggested.

Elana thought over the possibility.

"But he's the only one could get the money," she said.

"No," I said. "Your friend Grove knows how too. He'd be a lot easier to deal with."

I was sure that Elana was thinking of how to get the bond and go to her old lover. If Fearless and I had walked out right then, Leon would have been bondless and dead by sunset.

"You wanna throw in with me and Fearless?" I asked.

Elana was wondering about the offer when I heard a familiar-sounding motor drive up almost to the front door. A car door slammed. Four seconds later the front door flew open. Leon Douglas, gaudy as a butterfly and ugly as a stump, filled the doorway with an instantaneous murderous rage.

22

ELANA LOVE MOVED to a neutral corner where she could wait to see which side would win. I could hardly blame her.

Leon scanned the room quickly. He registered Elana, now in a dress, passed over me without a pause, and then looked at Fearless. He may have recognized his former cell-block neighbor, or maybe not.

The fireplug gangster moved even faster than the first time I saw him. He went straight at Fearless and clocked him on the jaw with a blow that sounded like a twenty-pound hammer on stone. Fearless almost flew backward, hit the wall, and slid to the ground. Douglas turned toward me then.

"I remember you," he said.

I reached for Sol's pistol, then remembered that I'd left it under the front seat of Layla's car.

Leon Douglas saw my futile gesture and smiled a smile as cruel as Elana Love's laugh.

Elana gasped. I looked at her, and so did Douglas.

She was looking toward the wall where Fearless had regained his feet.

The grunt of amazement that issued from Douglas's deep chest was probably the closest thing to a compliment that he ever gave. He closed on Fearless again and connected with a left hook that even Rocky Marciano would have feared. Fearless went down halfway, but this time he was up before Douglas regained his balance.

Again Douglas lunged, but this time it was with the intention of catching Fearless in a bear hug. Before the thug could get his arms into position Fearless connected with a one-two to the head. The gangster leapt again. This time he got his arms around Fearless and squeezed. He would have certainly broken Fearless's back except that my friend had his left hand free. With that mighty mace he landed body blows to Douglas's right side. One, two, three — and there was no effect — four, five, six — Leon went down on one knee. By seven and eight Douglas let go and fell back with his fists up but his speed greatly diminished.

Fearless smiled.

That was the exact moment of the greatest elation that I had ever experienced. Leon Douglas had already beaten me. He had defeated my heart and my spirit. I couldn't imagine anyone standing up to his murderous brutality.

And then Fearless smiled.

Leon came at Fearless again. But Fearless was connecting with his own hands of steel. He hit Douglas again and again. You

could see the ugly man's body shake under the power of the war
hero's blows. In a final act of courage Douglas raised both arms
and came after Fearless. The latter opened up with a barrage of
blows to the rib cage. Douglas crumbled, tried to rise, fell to the
floor again, and began to shake as if he were entering the throes
of death.

"Where he got the bond?" Fearless demanded of Elana as he
flipped Leon over on his back.

The loser had his arms clenched tightly around his ribs and
he was talking to himself, though I couldn't understand what he
was saying.

"In his, in the back of his pants," Elana stuttered.

Fearless tossed Douglas back over on his stomach and pulled
up his gaudy shirt. There was a brown envelope stuffed halfway
down the back of his pants.

Fearless took the envelope, jammed his hand into Leon's
pocket and came out with my key ring, and said, "Let's go."

"Hold up," I said. I took the envelope from Fearless and
ripped it open.

The bond was no larger than a dollar bill. It was printed on
high-quality paper in blue ink. On the left side of the bill there
was the image of a hatless, bearded, and mustachioed man who
wore a monocle and some kind of jacket that was buttoned up to
his throat. On the right side was the denomination — 2500 Fr.
With a lot of blue curlicues around it. The opposite side of the
bond was written all over in German. All I could make out was
Wetterling Bank and the name David Tannenbaum, which had
been written by hand. It didn't look like it was worth killing over
or dying for.

"Okay," I said. "Let's get outta here." I handed the bond and its envelope back to Fearless. I figured that if it needed protecting, he was a better guard than I.

"Take me," Elana cried.

Fearless and I looked at each other then. He gave no inkling of what he felt, but I guess I seemed unsure.

"Let's take her if you want, man," Fearless said. "But hurry. 'Cause if he get up again, I'm'a have to kill 'im."

Fearless took Elana in my car, and I followed in Layla's pink Packard.

WE DECIDED ON the lawn to make it to Milo's office, but as soon as Fearless took the lead, I knew it was a mistake. He cut over to Central, which was a cruising street at that time. Everybody you knew turned up on Central sooner or later. There were churches, nightclubs, liquor stores, and open-lot bazaars up and down the street. Fearless had been in jail and he had just bested a warrior in battle. He was feeling cocky and sure of himself. And even though he showed no interest in Love, she was still a beautiful woman that he could show off. The flowery dress she'd put on was revealing and festive.

Now and then Fearless would toot the horn at someone he'd recognize. People waved and said hello. I followed along, worried about something going wrong, not knowing what that wrong might be, and helpless, at any rate, to make any difference in the outcome.

After a mile or two on Central, Elana Love looked back at me and then said something to Fearless. Two blocks past Gage, Fearless took a left. I was going to follow, but a car sped up on my right, hitting its siren as it did. Automatically I hit the brakes. The police car was joined by a second one that veered and bounced over the curb on my right side.

The cruisers cut Fearless off on the side street. Four cops raced out with their guns drawn, yelling and moving toward the car. I drove past the turn and pulled to the curb just beyond the street's line of sight. I jumped out and crossed over to the other side of the street just in time to see Fearless thrown over the hood of my car and Elana being relieved of her purse.

I had been so concerned that trouble was coming that I didn't look out for it. The police came up behind me using my car to hide from Fearless. I wanted to curse out loud, but instead I bit my tongue and moved behind a group of three men who had witnessed the arrest from the street.

They searched Fearless and then they searched the car. They cuffed Fearless and put him in the backseat of one cruiser and Elana in the front seat of the other. That was strange right there. Elana was being treated differently.

I walked back and forth, up and down the avenue, putting on a baseball cap that was in the backseat of Layla's car. I took the hat off, turned up a collar. I don't know if my disguises were working or if the police weren't worried about anybody watching them in broad daylight while they made an arrest. That was still a time when white policemen handled blacks in public with impunity. They were, after all, the law.

I had crossed the street maybe a dozen times when Bernard Latham pulled around the corner. He drove right past me.

He got out of his deep blue Chevrolet and sauntered over to

the cops who had been waiting. He looked into the backseat that contained Fearless. He asked Fearless a question, then moved toward Elana Love.

Something was wrong, I was sure of that. I ran to my car and started it up, then did a U-turn on Central and came back to turn down the street. I drove past the cops, my best friend, and that woman, pretending to be a commuter coming home from work. None of them registered my passage, so I picked an empty-looking house halfway down the block and backed deep into the driveway.

By the time I was crouched down into position Elana was walking toward Latham's car. Fearless was out too, his hands free. Latham put Elana in the front seat and then leisurely walked around to his side. He drove down past my hiding place.

I had to make a decision then. Actually I had to make three decisions. The first was whether or not to leave Fearless in the hands of the cops. It didn't look like they were about to arrest him, and it was unlikely that they'd shoot him in broad daylight. And even if they were going to shoot him, there was little I could do to stop it. The second decision was whether or not to follow Latham. He was a cop and there was something crooked about him; even his fellow cop Lieutenant Binder thought so. A gun license for a policeman was like a permit to kill Negroes, and for a crooked cop that permit was just a formality.

The first two decisions were simple. Of course I had to leave Fearless and follow the girl. Latham might have taken the bond. If he was dirty, maybe there was still a chance to steal it back. But the final resolve, to actually drive the car out of that driveway, that was the hardest decision of all.

When Latham's car drove by me I decided to count to eight before following, telling myself it was to keep from being seen. I had gotten to fifteen before I got the courage to move. Down in the street I was panting, driving not more than ten miles an hour. My car sped up and then slowed. There was a lump in my throat and spots before my eyes. I had faced death earlier that day in the shape of Leon Douglas, but Leon didn't scare me nearly as much as Latham's taillights.

I've never respected law enforcement, merely feared it. I'm an honest man as far as it goes, meaning that I'd rather make my own money than take somebody else's. I'm almost always on the right side of the law, but lawmen scare me anyway, they terrify me. I have always believed that more black folks have been killed by those claiming to be enforcing the law than by those who were breaking it. So following that man I felt like a deer stalking a tiger, or a leaf pretending that it was driving the wind.

LATHAM DOUBLED BACK to Central and cruised toward downtown. I couldn't tell if he and Elana were talking, much less sharing secrets. There wasn't much movement between them. Of course I couldn't see them very well because I lagged pretty far behind most of the time.

When we hit the outskirts of downtown, Latham headed north toward the swankier districts. We went up through the center of the city and then west on Beverly. We finally ended up on Shatto, a street that looked almost residential. Four blocks up we came upon a small hotel, the Pine Grove. A man in a partial uniform rushed out and opened Elana's door. Even though the valet was colored, you could see that he was surprised to see Elana's hue. But he swallowed that and ushered the cop and his prisoner in through the cast-iron front doors.

The valet took Latham's car to park it, so I knew where to wait for his return. But I was worried about Fearless. Had they taken him to jail?

I was afraid for my friend and feeling guilty too. What good was it for me to bail Fearless out of jail if it was just to get him thrown into prison?

I watched the front of the hotel for a minute, a minute that felt like the first sixty seconds of a twenty-year term at Alcatraz. There was no pay phone in sight and I knew that the hotel staff would be unlikely to let me make a call from the desk; and even if they were feeling generous, I didn't want to take the chance of running across Latham and Elana.

I knew that the longer I waited, the more likely Latham was to come out and drive off, so I made my decision. I walked over to the valet who had returned from parking the cop's car.

"Hey, brother," I hailed.

The man's coat was a conservative dark red and the buttons were metal but not shiny. His features were large for his face. The big eyes and expressive mouth added a startled tinge to his distrust of me. He was my size, that is to say small and slender, and suspicious of any man who claimed a relation.

"What?"

"My car broke down," I said, pointing across and partway down the street to Layla's gaudy Packard.

The valet, whose name tag said George, looked suspiciously at the car and back at me.

"This ain't no garage," he said.

"Even if it was it wouldn't help me, 'cause I ain't got no money for a mechanic," I said, filling my mouth with words and self-deprecation.

"So what you want from me?" George asked sensibly.

"I wanna call my cousin," I replied. "He come over and gimme a jump or whatever."

"There ain't no phone here for you," he said. "Phone for guests or people who work here."

"I know you got a phone at your station, man. I'll give you a dollar and you can dial the number yourself."

Dollar was the magic word in porter/valet/waiter language. A dollar was ten tips. A dollar bought six packs of cigarettes, enough to last a week if you didn't have any broke friends.

George snuck me into a little cubby where he had a chair, a desk, and a phone. I fed him Milo Sweet's number. He dialed and then handed me the receiver.

"Sweet's," Loretta Kuroko said pleasantly.

"You sayin' that in my ear almost makes everything else okay," I said.

"Hold on." Her reply was cold and curt. I wondered if she was insulted somehow by my friendliness. I knew they didn't have another line that she needed to answer.

"Paris," Fearless said into the phone.

"You okay, Fearless?"

"Yeah, yeah. When the detective took off, the other cops just let me walk. I looked for you and then figured that you came here, so I did too. I'm sorry, Paris, I really am."

"About what?"

"The bond."

"They took it?"

"Naw. The girl saw the cops behind you. She told me an' I saw 'em too. She said that she could hide the bond in the linin'a her purse and so I give it to her —"

"I know what happened after that," I said.

George tapped on the door, indicating that my time was up.

"Listen, Fearless," I whispered. "I'm at a hotel called the Pine Grove up on Shatto. I don't know how long I'll be here, so you sit tight until I call back."

"You got it."

I cut the connection with my finger and said in a slightly louder tone, "Well when is she comin' in? . . . No? . . . Shit!" Then I hung up the phone.

I opened the door, looked at George, and said, "Never let one'a your relations marry a woman think she's a beauty queen." I gave him the dollar and went back across the street.

23 | I PUT UP the hood on Layla's pink Packard and stood behind it, pretending to be working on the engine. From there I could watch the front of the hotel without causing too much concern in the staff or the chance police cruiser. I had to wait about an hour before Latham and Love came out. They were escorted by a tall white man in a gray suit.

They all spoke at the curb while the valet ran to retrieve Latham's car. Latham and the man clasped hands, then the man took both of Elana's hands in his and said something that was meant to be sincere. It was odd to see a black woman so well treated at a fancy Hollywood hotel. I didn't even think that a police detective had the clout to make a place like that serve a Negro. That made me wonder about the man they were talking to. But there was no time for thinking. I jumped in my car and made a U-turn. By the time Latham and Elana were ready to go, I was too.

The ride wasn't very far. They drove toward the south side of downtown; a rougher neighborhood with motels instead of hotels, hot dog stands instead of fine restaurants.

They pulled into a motel call Las Palmas on Adams. Latham and Elana went into the main office together. He didn't want to let her out of his reach. I wondered if he knew about the bond in her purse.

After they took room 12B on the second floor of the open-air two-tiered motel, I went to call Fearless at a pay phone next to a pop machine in the parking lot.

"Paris?" Fearless said, answering Milo's phone.

I gave him the address.

"Milo wants to know what's happenin'."

"Tell 'im that we're looking for the money. That should make him happy."

"See you soon," Fearless said.

THERE WAS an all-night coffee shop down the block where I loaded up on pork sandwiches and beer. Milo sent Fearless down with a pint of rye whiskey. It was the friendly gesture of an insecure business partner. I think he knew that if Fearless took the gift, he wouldn't let me cut the ex-lawyer out. He was right about that.

We watched the motel from my car parked across the street. I was in the front seat, and Fearless was in back. We sat low so as not to be seen if the cops cruised by.

"Paris?" Fearless said at a little after one.

"What?"

"You think she in there lovin' him?"

"How should I know?"

"I didn't ask if you knew," Fearless pointed out. "I just won-dered what you thought."

"Why?"

"It ain't like she's your girlfriend or nuthin'. Damn, she just laid you so she could get your money and your car."

"Thank you, Fearless. I didn't know that until you told me."

"You don't have to get all mad, Paris. It's just that I been thinkin' about her."

"Thinkin' what?"

"She's definitely smart. Smart like you, you know? And she's in deep. Now what's she gonna do? Woman cain't run around like a man. I mean, I know she shot Conrad Till, but more times than not she be in a situation where the man has the more muscle. So she got to use bein' a woman to fight her way through, like she said at that shack."

"This the first time you ever thought that a woman use sex to get what she want?" I said.

"'Course not. But I never thought of it like fightin'. I never thought that a kiss could be like a loaded gun."

I had never thought of that either.

BY FOUR A.M. Fearless had fallen asleep in the backseat. It was cold again, and I could see the steam of my breath in the darkness. I closed my eyes, trying not to think about what Elana and Latham were up to.

In the dream I was standing at a corner flirting with a woman, Elana Love. I had a long key chain, and I was twirling it while telling her lies about my riches and exploits. There were children playing on the street and a fat man sitting on a wooden crate. The man was winded and asking for help. I thought that he might have been having a heart attack, but I kept talking to Elana anyway. In mid-swing of my key chain I felt something like a nibble on the bait of a fishing line. I looked and saw three of the children from the day before running away. They were rounding the corner into an alley.

"Stop him!" the fat man yelled. "Stop!"

I realized that the smallest boy had taken my keys. I took off after them. It was the opposite of the dream I usually have. Usually I'm running hard trying to get away from some attacker; I'm running hard but I make no progress. In this dream I was running at full speed unable to close the gap. The children were scurrying like little kids do while I barreled down on them, getting no closer. The fat man was laboring behind me, yelling, "Stop! Stop!"

"Paris!" Fearless said.

I was just gaining on the kids, but then someone grabbed my shoulder. Three loud gunshots blasted through my dream.

I opened my eyes. Fearless was rushing out of the passenger's door from the backseat.

"What?" I said, and then there was a fourth report.

Fearless was running toward an alley down the block from the motel. I turned the engine over and nosed the car to follow. Before I reached the alley I heard a car screeching in the motel lot. I looked back and saw Latham's sedan race off in the opposite direction.

Under the neon glow of the motel sign I caught a glimpse of Elana Love at the wheel. I couldn't follow though, because Fearless needed me. It was just like old times, times that I wished were over and forgotten.

Lights were coming on in the windows of an apartment building that bordered the alley. Two men were down. Fearless was moving from the first body and going to the second. I jumped out of the car.

"We got to go, man!" I shouted through a whisper.

The soldier ignored me. The second body was still moving. The first man, who was sprawled out on his belly, was Reverend Grove. His left temple was gone, and grim dark liquid had leaked out next to his amazed eye.

The other man was Latham. Fearless squatted down next to him. The wound in his chest looked bad even in that weak light. His breathing was labored and liquid. There was no mistaking his gurgling. The rest of his life would be measured in seconds.

He said something, and then he said something else that resembled the first sound but was even less comprehensible.

"Come on, man," I said to Fearless.

Latham faded out then. I think that was the moment he died, but the final end might have come a moment or two later.

Fearless stood. He nodded and said, "There was somebody else."

"What?"

"When I got here, there was somebody way up the alley — runnin'."

"Come on, Fearless. We gotta get outta here."

"What about the runner?"

I noticed a purse on the ground a few feet farther down the alley. Fearless saw it too.

As he went to pick it up, I said, "Probably some tramp didn't wanna get his ass shot off."

Fearless picked up the purse, and then we were both running for my car. I backed into the street and drove away from the motel. Through the rearview mirror I could see that there were people standing outside of the windowed office, talking and pointing toward my car.

After a block or two Fearless began laughing. He laughed full out.

"What's wrong with you, fool?" I said, afraid that he had cracked under the strain.

"Nuthin'," was all Fearless could say for a moment. He had to take a deep breath to keep the mirth down.

"Nuthin'? Have you gone crazy?"

"Naw, Paris. Naw, man. It's you."

"Me what?"

"You know I promised myself a long time ago that I wasn't gonna put myself back in a war for nuthin', not even America."

"So?"

"This right here is war, baby," he said, suddenly serious. "And where my own country couldn't make me — you did."

He made another short bark, but this time there was no humor behind it.

24 IT WASN'T UNTIL I was parking down the street from Arthur's Pet Shop and Animal Grooming that my hands stopped shaking. The side door to Arthur's led to three rooms that made up an after-hours club that a few dozen regulars kept in business. In order to get to Arthur's you had to come in the back alley and park at least a block away. It wasn't a party place or a music hall; there wasn't any dance floor. All it was was a jukebox and Nathan Wellman, an insomniac tailor who ran the place to make a few extra dollars while having people to talk to between midnight and dawn.

Nathan brought two generous shots of whiskey to our table.

"You boys look serious," Nathan said as a conversation opener.

"I need to use the phone, Nate," I replied.

He gave me a sour look and went over to the mahogany bar,

returning with a baseball bat that had a hole drilled in the handle. Through the hole was knotted a string that held a single brass key.

Nathan's place was a dive. The wood floor wasn't sealed or waxed, the walls were devoid of paint. The tables and chairs were mismatched and wobbly. But for all that it was primitive, Nathan's had something that even the Waldorf Astoria in New York City couldn't brag about; he had a telephone *room*. It was rustic and spare, but it was a whole room, six feet square with a pay phone on the wall and a table and chair. There was a phone book too.

I dialed a number.

"Las Palmas," a woman said, after answering on the sixth ring.

"Certainly," I said, doing my best to mimic the snooty Landry Lamming. "Helen Huggins," I continued, cursing myself for making up such dumb names, "in room twelve B, if you please."

"Uh . . . well . . . hold on," the night clerk said.

There was silence and then a series a clicks and bangs. A man's voice finally said, "Who is this?"

"Excuse me," I said primly, "but I asked for Miss Huggins in twelve B. They must have connected me with the wrong room."

"Who is this?" the man repeated. "Are you the one who called twelve B earlier tonight?"

"Who, may I ask, are you, sir?"

"Police Sergeant Bryant," he said. "Did you call earlier tonight?"

"I was looking for my friend," I said. "Miss Huggins."

"Did you ask for a man named Latham?"

"No. Who is he?"

"He was with the woman in twelve B."

"Oh my," I said in a fey tone.

"What's your name, sir?"

"Is Miss Huggins in trouble, Officer Bryant?"

"I'm asking the questions, Mr. . . ?"

"Is Miss Huggins there, Sergeant?"

"Two men have been shot," Bryant said, trying the frank approach. After all, maybe I really was a foreigner, far from home and unfamiliar with the legal customs of America.

"And Miss Huggins?" I asked, all aflutter.

"There was a woman. She fled the scene. You say her name is Huggins?"

I chose that moment to hang up.

Nathan and Fearless were having a good old time talking about Fearless's experience in the county lockup. I came back and downed my drink. Fearless took that as a cue to stand.

"See you later, Nathan," Fearless said.

"But you didn't finish your story."

"Save it for the next time."

Fearless clapped Nathan on the shoulder, and we left.

WE MADE IT back to Fontanelle's court near five. I let Fearless have the mother's bedroom. I took the child's bed, just a urine-stained mattress on the floor, because I was the smaller of us two. As scared as I was, I needed sleep. We had nothing to go on. Elana's purse was ripped open and the bond was gone. The bond was gone and we didn't know who had it. I had a pretty good idea that it was in Elana's possession, but at five in the morning I hardly even cared.

I slept soundly until I felt a tongue on my face. I opened my eyes and saw Blood, Fearless's adopted dog. I sat up and pushed him away. Fearless was drinking some hot liquid out of a cup and relaxing, slouched back in his chair. From his demeanor you would have thought that we were on vacation.

"What time is it?" I asked.

"'Bout twelve-thirty."

"Where'd this dog come from? I thought you left him with Dorthea."

"I called her, and she told me to come get 'im."

"What you think Fell gonna say when we got pets in her court?"

"That's three questions wit'out you sayin' good mornin'," Fearless said.

"Good morning," I said.

Fearless's face broke out into a friendly smile. "Fontanelle said it was okay. She said that she might even want a good watchdog to protect her garage when she holdin' stuff fo' people."

I got up and pulled on my pants. After using the toilet and washing up, I was almost ready for the day. Fearless was sitting in the blue chair, so that left me the red one. They were both wooden and badly painted. My chair wobbled whenever I shifted.

"Tea?" Fearless asked me.

"Since when do you drink tea?"

"My auntie Leigh Lenore used to drink tea with lemon every mornin'."

"What's that got to do with you?" I asked.

"In that jail cell I used to think how much I missed Leigh. I really loved her, and that made me think about tea. You want some?"

I took the tea but turned down the lemon.

"I bought milk," Fearless said.

"What did Latham say?" I asked.

"I think it was Man. Jam. Manjam," Fearless said. "Jamman. It was the name of somebody or something, I'm pretty sure."

"You really think so? All it sounded like was a cough to me."

"I listened to a lotta dyin' men, Paris. The trick is you got to keep your heart open. You got to listen wit' your heart. That's the trick."

The tea, from the cracked pottery crock that Fearless had found on some shelf, was hot and made me feel good. I let my eyes close for a moment, which was a mistake because William Grove's death stare came up in my mind.

I sat up quickly and said, "Let's get over to Milo's."

"SO WHAT YOU THINK we got here, Paris?" Milo Sweet asked me.

We were sitting in his office, listening to the gentle clucking of hens through the heating vents. Loretta was there and so was Fearless, but the discussion was between me and Milo.

"I don't know, man," I said. "I mean really — I don't know."

"One always knows something," the bailbondsman replied. "It's just that we don't know it all. What is it that we *do* know?"

I got his meaning and so tried to think. Sometimes I find thinking out loud is the best way to solve a problem. Of course, I've also found that thinking out loud is the best way to get yourself into trouble too.

"Well," I said. "We know that there are people, white people, looking for a bond that Sol Tannenbaum gave to Leon through Fanny and Elana for protection in the joint."

Milo nodded. Fearless sat back and laced his fingers behind his neck. Loretta let her eyes run up and down his long, strong body.

"We know there's a real bond because we saw it."

Again Milo nodded.

"We know that Leon was after Elana, but then they were together, that there was a white man at the Pine Grove Hotel who met with Latham and Elana probably about the bond. Maybe he even has the bond now. Maybe he's the one with the money. If that's true, then Elana's long gone. There's another white man, John Manly, he said, who knew that Sol wasn't home. He wanted to talk to Fanny in the worst way, but he was probably just a real-estate agent who heard about Sol somehow and thought he might find someone who needed to sell off their house for hospital bills. And then there's the little old white man named Zev Minor, who came to their house and opened the front door without ringing the bell. Latham is dead. William Grove is dead. Fanny Tannenbaum is dead. My bookstore done burned, and Sol is in the hospital — and it's him probably that stole the money in the first place. And, oh yeah, whatever money there is, it's between ten thousand francs and ten million dollars."

"Shouldn't you just drop it?" Loretta Kuroko said.

"What's that, Loretta?" Milo asked. He didn't sound angry or brusque at his secretary for interrupting our talk. He was sincerely interested in her opinion.

"A policeman is dead, Mr. Sweet. A cop. They can come and take you away over that, take you away for good."

Fearless sat up. I began drumming my fingers on Milo's desk.

"But he was a crooked cop," Milo said. "The newspaper didn't even identify him as an officer. You know somebody's hidin' somethin' behind that. And this is real money too."

"Anyway," Fearless added. "We didn't shoot him."

"Why would any'a these people burn down your store, Paris?" Milo asked. He blew out a thick cloud of cigar smoke.

"Man as mean as Leon Douglas, he might burn the muthah-fuckah down just outta spite," I said.

"Maybe it was an accident," the ex-lawyer suggested.

"I don't think so," I said. "Theodore said that the police thought it was started with gasoline. But I should probably check that out anyway. I mean, maybe somebody saw something."

Milo nodded.

"But what I wanna know," I continued, "is why should we even be talkin' 'bout this? I mean, the bond is gone, and we don't even know who has it. It could be Elana, it could be the man Fearless saw running down the alley. And whoever that was, it might be somebody in on it or just some bum got scared when he heard shots."

"It wasn't no bum," Fearless added.

"How you know that?" Milo asked.

"'Cause Latham was farther up the alley. He was runnin' an' I don't see Latham runnin' from one man. He was tough. There was two men after him, and the one who got away was the one who kilt the cop and tore open the purse."

"You don't know that," I said, but I wasn't sure that he was wrong.

"If Grove's partner has the bond, then it's over," Milo said.

"We don't know if that was his partner," I said. "And we don't know if he got the bond. Elana took off in Latham's car. She lit outta there wit'out lookin' back. Maybe she got it."

"Maybe," Milo said. "But that's an *if* even in the best light. The real way to the money is this Tannenbaum man. Maybe if we went to him and told him what happened, he'd give us somethin'."

We turned to Fearless then.

"What?" he complained.

"You the one he likes," I said.

"I told him that I'd protect his wife, and you see what that did?"

"You couldn't help that, son," the suddenly paternal Milo Sweet said.

"He's right, Fearless," I added. "Sol'd want you to tell him about what's happenin'. He would. You don't have to tell him about Fanny."

"You think he don't know? You think he don't know that his wife for forty-some years ain't comin' to the hospital t'see 'im? He knows. But you right, I should go there. I should go there an' make sure nobody else come into that room."

"You'll ask him about the bond?" Milo suggested.

"I'll tell 'im what I know," Fearless said. "And then he can tell me what he wants."

"I'll go back over to the bookstore," I said. "Maybe somebody knows about the fire, if it was set like the cops and the firemen suspected."

"Okay," Milo said. "Okay, you guys go out and do what you think is right, what you think is gonna get somethin'. But remember, this is money here. Money. Don't go out there actin' like this is everyday goin' to work or throwin' some dice. This is the big time. You go out there and your life is on the line. So try an' bring somethin' back wichya."

I was moved by Milo's pep talk, but I doubt if Fearless was. From the few political books I had read I knew Fearless was a natural-born anarchist. If he had what he needed, he thought of himself as a rich man; if he had less, well, that would have to do.

"What you gonna do, Milo?" I asked our partner.

"Ask a few questions. Get a few lies. Ask somethin' else and then see what don't jibe." He was a poet of the lawyer's caste.

25

FEARLESS, MILO, AND I WERE all set to go, Fearless to ride shotgun on Sol's hospital bed, and Milo to gather information in his own secret ways.

Milo's gas tank ran on schemes. He was into clandestine real-estate deals, small-business investments, and some more shady enterprises. He was serious about everything he did, and most projects he got involved with, I felt, had a good chance of making it. But Milo was impatient. He wanted to see the money. He wanted a Cadillac and a fat Cuban cigar. After a few months he'd always start pushing. He'd expand before the business showed a profit or sell out for another, more promising scheme before the one he was into had a chance to grow.

When I first met Milo I wanted to do business with him. I was always asking his advice and suggesting that he take me in as a partner. But as time passed and I saw how he never got past the first stages, I was happy that he was too jealous to let anybody else in on his deals.

So when Milo left for one of his *clandestine* negotiations, I didn't expect much. I had business of my own, business in which failure was not an easy pill to swallow.

"Paris," Loretta said to me as I was following her boss out the door.

"Yeah?"

"Hold on a minute, will you?"

The door shut behind Milo, and I went back to Miss Kuroko's desk.

"I didn't want to say anything in front of Milo," she said hesitantly. "You know how he gets when he thinks that he's being taken advantage of."

"What'd I do now?" I asked.

"It's the phone calls."

"What calls?"

"The women."

"Oh shit," I said. "Here we go. Women got a whiff that Fearless is over here?"

"They're calling for you too, Paris," Loretta said, as if I knew it all along. "And you know how Milo feels about using his office for personal affairs."

"Women? What women? Ain't no women callin' on me."

"Charlotte Bingham," Loretta said.

"Who?"

"She said you knew her from the Charles Diner."

"The Charles . . ." I stopped when I remembered the young woman with the scar. "Oh. Uh, did she leave a number?"

Loretta handed me a small orange slip of paper with the waitress's information.

"And what about this Gella Greenspan calling for Fearless?" the secretary asked.

"Who? Oh."

"You don't have to pretend, Paris."

"I'm not pretendin', Loretta. I can't remember all these names. Gella is the woman whose aunt got killed."

"Oh." An urgency entered the woman's tone. "She said that it was important to get in touch with Fearless, but I thought . . ."

"I'm sure it's okay. Just gimme that number too."

I went to Milo's desk and dialed Gella Greenspan's number.

"Hello," a timid voice said upon answering the phone.

"Gella?"

"Mr. Jones?"

"No, it's Paris. Paris Minton — the one who was with Fearless."

"Oh. Is he with you now?"

"No. No, he went out to visit your uncle. He was worried after what happened to Fanny and decided to make sure Sol is safe."

"Oh. Yes. Yes, I guess that's more important."

"More important than what?" I figured that the distraught young woman wanted to see what came after the first two kisses. I hoped to head her off before we got sidetracked into some kind of domestic mess. *A kiss could be like a loaded gun,* Fearless's words came back to me.

"It's Morris."

"What's wrong with him?"

"He's gone."

"Gone where?"

"I don't know. The police came to ask questions about Fanny

and the black man who stabbed Sol, and Morris yelled at them that they had to find him and put him in jail. I never saw him so upset."

"We're all upset. Damn, I haven't been this worried since the bogeyman used to live under my bed."

"I know," she said. "I know. But it was more than that with Mo."

"What do you mean?"

"He stayed in bed a whole day. He just lay there in the dark, looking up at the ceiling. He wouldn't talk to me."

"He wouldn't eat or anything?"

"When he went for water, he didn't turn off the faucet, he didn't even flush the toilet. And then I was in the kitchen, and I heard his car start in the driveway. When I got to the front door he was already going down the street. I called for him, but he didn't hear me." The desolation in Gella's voice reminded me of her lost European family.

"Was he that close to your aunt?"

"He liked her, but she didn't have much use for him. Uncle Sol and Aunt Fanny liked people with more of a sense of humor. But Morris always wanted to do things for them. When Sol was in prison, he would go over and take care of things. If something broke, he fixed it, and if there was some problem with the bills, he took care of it." She paused and then said, "Do you think Fearless might come over and help me look for him after he sees to Uncle Sol?"

The thought of Fearless holding that awkward girl and then Morris stumbling in was like a train wreck in my mind.

"I don't know," I said. "Maybe I could come by if he's too busy. Maybe, yeah, I could come over."

"Okay," she said, accepting second best.

"But first I got to look into a couple'a things. First that, and then I'll come by."

"Okay. But please hurry."

"If Morris comes back, you go up and sit with him when you can, okay?" I said. "I know it doesn't seem like he notices you, but he does. He knows you're there, but he's just too sad to say it."

"Thank you," Gella said, sighing. "Thank you for that."

We hung up on that high note, but I knew that she was still scared.

"Is she okay?" Loretta asked.

"Oh yeah. She just needed to talk to somebody."

MILO HAD AGREED to take Fearless to retrieve Layla's car from the street in front of the Las Palmas, where we'd left it when we took off after Latham and Grove were shot. Fearless had called Layla to apologize for keeping the car for so long. She was mad at first, but after a few minutes of Fearless saying he was sorry, she let him keep it a while longer. I left Milo's place in my own car. That felt pretty good, me sitting behind the wheel, not on anybody's tail and nobody on mine. That was fine. I drove over to the burnt-out lot that had been my bookstore only a few days before. Fontanelle was right. The few standing timbers of the frame had been torn down and dragged off. The lot had been raked so clean that it almost looked as if it had been swept.

I went inside expecting to see Theodore Wally in his blue T-shirt and green apron standing behind the candy-crowded counter. But instead, an older white man stood there. It was Antonio, the owner. Antonio had a bulbous face with a pencil-thin mustache that didn't fit at all. You got the idea that he grew the lip hair when he was a younger, thinner man.

"Can I help you?" he asked in a tone that was anything but helpful. Antonio had seen me a few dozen times since I had been his neighbor. He took my money, gave me change. But he never recognized me, never learned my name.

"Where's Theodore?"

"He doesn't work here anymore."

"Say what?"

He looked away from me instead of answering.

"Excuse me," I said.

"What?"

"I'm lookin' for Wally."

"I told you —"

"Listen, man. Theodore has been workin' in this store for more than ten years. He worked here four days ago. Now I know he didn't just disappear."

"He does not work here anymore," the store owner said as if he were talking to an idiot. "He quit his job this morning. Just wrote a note and locked the door behind him. He didn't even call. So now I have to come here every day because there is nobody else. If you know him so well, then you must know where he lives, so why don't you go there and leave me in peace?"

I thought, *Oh my achin' back,* but I said, "My name's Paris Minton."

Antonio gave me that blank look that said, *Don't know you and don't care to.*

"I had the bookstore next door."

"Oh," he said, nodding. "So it was you. You're the reason I don't have my insurance."

"What?"

"I got damage," he said, the hint of an Italian accent coming through. "I called the insurance company and they send a man down here. He finds violations. Violations and he says that they won't pay and that my insurance is canceled."

"I didn't make your violations, man. I lost my whole store."

"But you were illegal. You slept there. You had a hot plate, maybe. Because you were careless, they punish me, a real businessman."

It was the *real businessman* crack that got to me. I mean, what did he think? Didn't he realize that I was in business too? Maybe I wasn't making big money or anything like that, but I had regular hours and customers and fair prices. I was in business just like him. But that wasn't the time for a philosophical discussion on the nature of business.

"Did somebody say that the fire was caused by a hot plate?" I asked.

"They don't know. Maybe a cigarette, they said. Or maybe something with the wires. One man said something about gasoline."

"Are they investigating?"

Antonio had small eyes. Between the bulge of his forehead and the chubbiness of his cheeks, they seemed gleeful in an evil sort of way. He homed those eyes in on me and said, "It wasn't no more than an empty room. Why they want to investigate?"

I didn't like what I was hearing. But I heard something even worse, something he didn't mean to say. I didn't like that either.

"Who cleaned off the lot next door?" I asked.

"How should I know? They were workmen. The landlords

over there had insurance too. But their insurance agents couldn't see the violations you had."

It was my turn to stare. I looked hard at the store owner. He took out a small green rag with which he began to wipe the small space of the glass counter before him.

"Did the fire investigators come over here to talk to you?" I asked.

"Why would they?" he said, more defensive than angry.

26

I GOT BACK in my car, uncertain whether I should go find Theodore or wait and take care of the business at hand. Finally I decided that my worries over the store had to wait.

MESSENGER OF THE DIVINE looked a lot different in daylight. The stucco bungalow it inhabited was pathetic and gray around the edges. The red velvet curtains that had covered the picture window were now drawn back to reveal dozens of black men, women, and children crowded together, dressed in their Easter best. The men wore black suits with white flowers in their lapels. The women wore dark dress suits with fancy hats.

Recorded organ music issued through the open doors. I spied the coffin that stood up front. Before the coffin stood the elderly

African-featured man I had met a few nights before, Father Vincent la Trieste.

Father Vincent was in the middle of his baritone sermon when I entered.

". . . they won't let us have his body," Vincent was saying. "No. They say they're keepin' it for the coroner to examine. But we don't care about them or their laws, do we, brothers and sisters?"

"No, Father. No," was said by more than one.

"We know that the Lord called on Brother Grove. The Lord in his wisdom laid down his iron hand!"

"Preach," someone said.

"Tell it," another agreed.

"He laid down his iron hand for the mighty to tremble and the vermin to scurry away. But we are not afraid. No, no. We are not afraid of bullets and knives, of policemen who bar our way or of doctors fool enough to believe that they hold the answers of life and death in their hands. Only the Almighty has the power of life and death. Only the Almighty can reach out and snuff out the flame of life as if it was no more than a matchstick." Vincent held out his left hand, slowly closing it against a powerful though unseen force. While he did this, he looked into the eyes of each man, woman, and child in the room. He was God, and they were witnessing the miracle and the majesty of His terrible strength. The older man's eyes were potent even from the back of the room where I stood. They were potent, that is, until they lit on me. And then, for only a moment, they switched to fear. He glanced quickly from side to side, and three large men turned their heads in my direction.

These men were dressed darkly like everyone else, but they were wearing white gloves. These were the deacons, the faithful, the sergeants at arms. I wondered if it was Vincent and these men who had routed the tough detective Latham and snuffed his life like Vincent's mimed God did to that imagined flame.

I turned away, a mourner who, after registering his regrets, heads off to the bar for a final toast to the dearly departed. I didn't turn my whole body, just my head and torso. Another deacon stood directly behind me. From the look on his walnut-colored face I knew that he had gotten the high sign from somewhere.

I resumed my listening position.

". . . Brother Grove is free . . . ," I remember Vincent saying. It struck me that he was calling the dead man brother and not minister or reverend. He said a lot of things. None of them made much sense, but they were moving. Or at least they would have been moving if I hadn't been thinking that that shiny black coffin up front might soon be my home.

The sermon went on for quite a while afterward. I don't know how much time passed. All I know is that I was wishing for a few more minutes when it was over. I hadn't been able to think my way out of the trouble I was in in the time allowed.

I felt a walnut-hard hand on my shoulder.

"The Father would like to see you in back," a meaty voice said.

"I'd like to, but I got to get home," I replied.

The hand turned into a vise. I followed the pressure toward the doorway to the back room.

One or two of the pained parishioners noticed the strong-arm move, but they didn't interfere. There was party mix and clam dip, fruit punch and sandwiches for the mourners. They were hungry, and I was a stranger in shabby clothes.

The deacon pushed me through the same side door I'd used to

go to the toilet a few nights before. Then he led me into the room I had spied upon. That room was now empty of contraband.

Empty of stolen merchandise but full of life. Vincent and four of his deacons were in there with me.

The deacon who had waylaid me let go and shut the door, casting the room into a particularly frightening darkness. There was only one light source, and a featureless deacon stood in front of that.

"Why are you here, Mr. Lockwood?" Father Vincent asked, using the name I had given him when we met.

"I heard about Reverend Grove. I heard about Grove." I wondered if I would ever get beyond those words. "And . . . and I wanted to find out what had happened."

"What does that have to do with you?" a big deacon standing behind Vincent asked. It was less a question than it was a threat.

"Quiet, Brother Bigelow," Vincent said sternly. I got the feeling that the elder reverend was struggling to maintain order among Grove's deacons.

The big man was of the same size and disposition as Leon Douglas, but there was less wear and tear on his face. He grumbled something and shifted restlessly.

"Why did you come, Mr. Lockwood?" Vincent asked again. His tone told me that he only intended to ask a certain number of times before something else happened.

I looked around at the deacons. All of them were rough men. Their suits satisfied the appearance of Sunday school, but on a closer look the fabric was cheap, and one or two jackets were ill-fitting. These were men who had lived with Satan before coming to God, and they were still willing to venture over to the wrong side of holiness if the situation demanded it.

"This man," Vincent said, addressing his rough-hewn hench-men, "came asking about Brother Grove a few days ago, and now William is dead."

I could feel the room turn colder.

"Have you come to kill somebody else, Mr. Lockwood?"

"I didn't kill William Grove," I said in a surprisingly calm voice. I mean, I doubt if my voice surprised any of those men, but it astonished me. "I came here to wonder why he was dead. Him and that police sergeant."

The mention of a policeman sent a wave of anxiety through the room.

"I walked in here," I continued, "with no gun, nobody to back me up. All I have is a little information about a government bond and about a white man I saw talking to Grove right out in front of this church three nights ago."

"What white man?" Brother Bigelow wanted to know.

I moved my head upward, prepared to answer the question, but Father Vincent cut me off before I had the chance.

"Wait a minute," the elder said hastily. "I need to talk to this man alone."

This caused bewilderment among the deacons.

"Let us alone for a few minutes," Vincent said. "Let me talk with him."

"But, Father —" one deep-voiced deacon said. The rough men hesitated.

"Not now, Brother Noble. Not now. Go on, leave us, I want to question this man alone before he damages William's name."

The deacons moved slowly at first as if they were a tangle of logs gradually giving way to a strong river flow. Each one committed my face to memory as he walked around me toward the door.

The last man out closed the door behind him.

"This is —" I began, but Vincent put his hand up for silence.

We sat there quietly for over a minute. Then Vincent walked over to the door. He turned the knob and pushed it open quickly. It hit something, a head I'd bet, and Vincent looked at someone on the other side without saying anything that I could hear.

"Come with me," he said to me.

He led me from the storage room through the hall to the back of the building. We went through a small yard and into a building that had probably been the garage of the house behind. This was Vincent's office. There was a green metal desk in the center of the concrete floor with throw rugs and folding wooden chairs here and there. The ceiling was cross-hatched with unpainted rafter beams and decorated with spider webs.

"This is all I wanted to start with, Father Vincent. I don't want any trouble."

"What's this about a policeman?"

"There was a cop killed with Grove."

"How do you know that?"

"It's in the late edition of the *Examiner*," I lied. But it was late enough for me to have seen an afternoon article. "Where'd you find out?"

"The police came. They told me what happent. They didn't say nuthin' 'bout no policeman gettin' killed."

I hunched my shoulders.

"What do you want, Mr. Lockwood?"

"I wanna know what that white man had to say to you."

"What white man?"

"The one who you talked to the night that I came knockin' at your door."

"You were spying on me?" The Holy Roller's voice rose, promising righteous retribution to follow, but I wasn't impressed.

"There's a lotta money in this, Vincent. And at least four dead people —"

"Four?"

"A woman was murdered too. And a man, an associate of Leon Douglas, died of gunshot wounds in a hospital a few days ago."

The mention of Douglas hit Vincent like a slap.

"What does any of this have to do with me?" he asked.

"To begin with," I said. "You don't want the people who killed Grove to kill you. And to end with, you might be concerned at the worth of that bearer bond."

"Do you have it?"

"Have what?"

Vincent pinched his lower lip and tugged at it.

"You know what," he said.

"Who was that white man?" I asked again.

"You aren't the one in power here, Lockwood," the minister said, seeking strength in his own words. "This is my stronghold. Those men outside answer to me now that William is gone. At just a word I can bring a terrible wrath down on you."

I took my time before answering, allowing the air to seep out of his hollow threat. "Yeah, yeah," I said. "Bigelow breathes on me hard and I tell 'im that there's a bond somebody wanna buy for a hundred thousand dollars and then he kills me. And then he grabs you and says, 'We all get a taste'a this pie.' And if you're lucky, you see a few bucks. That is, if one of the deacons don't off you, or if they don't do somethin' stupid and get you arrested."

"You should be careful what accusations you make, boy."

"I'm not the one who has to be careful, Reverend. It's you who's got to watch out. 'Cause the man you set up with Grove might figure out that it was you called the crooked cop and told him they were comin'."

"What kinda stupidity are you talkin'?" Vincent's eyes grew wider with each syllable.

"A man called Latham at the motel he was at," I said, holding up a finger as if I were the elder's teacher. "Right after that, Latham tore outta there. Grove was already outside, though, Grove and a partner. The way I see it, Elana put Latham to sleep with a special wiggle she got, and then she called you, because she heard somewhere that Grove could turn that bond into gold. You called Grove, and him and a friend went over there. But then you called Latham to warn him. That's the way I see it."

"Th-th-that's crazy," he said. "Crazy."

"No, it ain't. Not crazy, it's evil." Those words broke down the minister's defenses. "And if somebody find out about it, retribution gonna belong to them."

"I ain't sayin' that anyone called me," he said. "But even if they did, and even if I did send William down there, why would I turn around and warn the cop that I sent him?"

"Because Grove stole your congregation," I said. "Because he brought in those goons callin' themselves deacons, because they were using your church to sell stolen merchandise. But mostly just because you saw the opportunity and you took it."

It could have happened differently, but Vincent's frightened eyes told me that I was right.

"It had to be that white man with him," I said. "'Cause Grove was afraid of Leon, and, anyway, Sol didn't take no millions from some Negro."

My voice was strong, but my knees were weak. I swore to myself that if I got out of the building and into my car, I would drive to Chicago, change my name, and end my days as a dishwasher on the southside.

"You cain't prove that," Vincent said.

"I don't need to," I replied. "You're the one gonna be in trouble if anyone hears that Latham was warned. All I have to do is cast blame, and your goose is cooked."

"What do you want from me, Lockwood?"

"I want you to answer my questions. No bullshit."

"What you wanna know?"

"First of all, why did you run from your place on Central?"

Father Vincent glared at me with something close to hatred in his eyes.

"William's girlfriend, Elana Love, got hold of a bond," he said. "Through her old boyfriend, who was in prison. William decided that he was going to cash it in. He went to a bank, but they told him that they could only cash it for the man it was signed to. He should have let it alone right there, but William was a greedy man, he had to have everything he saw.

"The man the bond was made out to was a Jew in jail with Elana's boyfriend. William went to the Jew's wife with some lie and got her to tell him who it was the old man stole from."

"So what?" I asked. "What good would that do?"

"He goes to 'em —"

"To who?"

"Lawson and Widlow, the accountants. He goes to 'em and says he got their money in a bond. They tell him that they're all so interested and make a meeting at the church to see the bond —"

"He didn't show it to 'em?"

"William was greedy to a fault but wasn't stupid. He kept the bond safe in case they tried to use muscle or the law on 'im. Anyway, the next thing we knew, they had three white hoodlums down there knockin' at our door. Real thugs. Me and William could see through the curtains that they didn't come to negotiate, so we made it out the back and had the deacons move us out overnight."

"That's it?" I asked.

Father Vincent looked in my eyes and saw that he had to give more to be let off the hook.

"Elana got mad 'cause William wouldn't tell her why we were runnin' or who was after him."

"She didn't know about the accountants?"

Vincent shook his head. "William didn't trust that girl. He just wanted to be on her good side."

"Did he stay there?"

"No. Elana took the bond back and left him."

I realized that Elana had known where Grove was the whole time she was crying in my bookstore.

"Good riddance to bad garbage," Vincent said. "Everything was okay for a couple'a months. We moved out here, and William kept a low profile. He still did some fencin', but not so much as before. But then that Leon Douglas, Elana's old boyfriend, got outta jail. Douglas beat William somethin' terrible. He beat him so bad that he realized that Elana had to be lyin' about him havin' the bond, so they left — leavin' William to bleed.

"After that, William called the accountants again. He told them that he was in hidin', that they couldn't find him, but maybe he could still get their bond."

"Why he say that?" I asked.

"'Cause he was a fool," Vincent declared. "The only thing he got outta that beatin' was that the bond must'a been worth somethin' more than what Elana said. Two days later the accountants sent over the man, and we had a meetin'."

"What was that about?"

"It was a man named Holderlin," the minister said. He sat back against a shelf, weak himself from the strain of our bluffs. "He told us that Leon had been working for him to get the bond but that Leon lost the girl, so he needed our help to find her. Holderlin said that he was working for the Jewish government, that money was stole from them by this Tannenbaum guy. He said that the bond was probably one of many, that they were probably printed in sequence. He said one bond would lead to the rest and that there would be a finder's fee."

"He said that he worked for Israel?" I asked.

"Yuh."

"How much did he say it was worth?"

Vincent gave me a suspicious look.

"I heard millions," I said, trying to head off his misgivings. "But I don't know exactly."

"I want outta this, Lockwood. I don't need to get killed over somethin' like this."

I remember thinking that he was giving better advice than when he stood in front of his transient congregation.

"Was this Holderlin a young man?" I asked, adding my description of the man I saw with Latham and Elana out in front of the Pine Grove Hotel.

"No, no. He was in his forties, big dude. Grove's age, maybe a little more. He had a partner too. I didn't get a good look at him 'cause he drove the car."

"Did this Holderlin tell you how you could get in touch with him?"

"No. He got our number, but we never had his."

"What are you gonna do now?" I asked.

"The congregation needs me now that Brother Grove has passed on," the pastor said. "They need me more than ever."

"That may be," I said. "But I suggest you change your address again, Reverend, and maybe the name of your congregation."

Father Vincent considered my words as I considered him. He was a killer like Leon Douglas, but he didn't use his hands. Instead he had used stealth and lies, along with good timing, to manage the murder of his nemesis, William Grove. He was a murderer, but I couldn't do anything about it. I doubted if any court would convict him. It put a sour taste in my mouth.

I swallowed deeply and then left the minister to his God. But I wasn't breathing easy. Brother Bigelow and two other deacons were waiting for me in the small yard.

"What you doin' here, man?" Bigelow demanded.

"Reverend Grove had been seeing my cousin." Lies came out of me like shit from a pig, as my Aunt Calais used to say. "She went missin' behind all kindsa crazy stories. I wanted to find out where she was."

"Who's this cousin?" an unnamed deacon asked.

"Elana Love," I said. A feeling of triumph snaked down my spine. Let them make the connections, that was the only way out.

"Elana," another deacon said.

"Yeah," I said. "She came to me talkin' 'bout how Grove had stolen her stuff and now her boyfriend out of jail, Leon, was comin' after them. Now Grove is dead, and I want to know about my cousin. She haven't called or nuthin'."

I was trying to keep my breathing from going crazy. I knew that if I showed the panic I felt, they would think I was lying — and if they thought that, they might not let me go.

It seemed like a long time before Bigelow said, "Get the hell outta here."

They let me go but didn't stand out of the way. I had to walk around them on the recently watered soggy lawn. But I did so happily.

In the storefront church, the congregation was still mourning the empty coffin. They were drinking wine and eating sandwiches. I half-expected someone else to grab me, to interrogate me, to threaten my life, but no one even noticed. I slipped through the throng, no more remarkable than a shadow.

27

I WAS SWEATING, but it wasn't hot. My heart was throbbing instead of beating, and my legs couldn't seem to coordinate to keep a steady stride. When I got in the car my fingers went numb, and I couldn't seem to hold the key right. It took me four or five tries before I realized that I was trying to fit my new apartment key into the ignition.

I started the car and drove off. Three blocks away I pulled to the curb. There I took in great gulps of air, trying to bring my spirit back into alignment with my body — because that's how it felt, as if my soul were somehow trying to flee the flesh, as if I had been so close to death so often in the past few days that the ghost was ready to bolt. That's how it goes with me. I face danger and survive it, acting just fine, but as soon as it's over and I'm alone, I break down.

There was a World-Wide gas station just up the block. There I found a phone booth.

"Hello," a woman answered flatly.

"Charlotte?"

"Hold on."

The phone rumbled from being set down on a hard surface.

"Hello?" a much sweeter voice asked.

"Charlotte?"

"Who is this?"

"It's Paris."

"Oh, hi," she said. "I thought that number you gave me was just sumpin' you thought up when I called it. It sounded like a law office or sumpin'."

"Can we get some coffee or something?" I asked.

"Yeah. Why'ont you come on ovah?" She gave me her address.

CHARLOTTE'S APARTMENT COMPLEX was a series of big brick-and-plaster affairs on 109. The buildings were long and thin looking, like army barracks, separated by green lawns. She was in building K on the third floor.

The hallway was lit by the setting sun through a window at the far end. The walls were white and pretty except for a mark here and there. You could tell that the place was new. I hoped that it would maintain its beauty, but I had my doubts. The suffering of a people often showed up in their material surroundings. Like a broken heart leaving a forlorn lover a physical mess, the weight of racism and poverty often made colored neighborhoods downtrodden and marred.

Charlotte answered the door. She was wearing a close-fitting but not tight black dress with no hose and no makeup.

"Hi." She smiled and looked me in the eye, but then she saw something and asked, "What's wrong?"

"Can I come in?"

She stepped back, and I stumbled a little crossing the threshold. There was a low couch with chrome legs and orange vinyl cushions. Beyond that was a glass door that led out onto a tiny landing. The sun was shining in on a large rubber plant in a terra-cotta pot. The living room and kitchen were one. But the couch was placed so that it marked the line between the two.

"This is very modern," I said, sitting down.

Charlotte beamed with pleasure.

There was a console record player/radio across from the couch. She lifted the reddish brown lid and started the stack of records. I remember the first song was by Ella Fitzgerald, but I forget the tune.

"You want that coffee?" she asked.

"Where's your roommate?"

"She went to see her sister. I'm'a call her later on."

Charlotte lit on the couch next to me.

"I didn't think you'd call," she said.

"I shouldn't have."

"Why not?"

"'Cause I'm in trouble," I said. "'Cause I'm in trouble, and I hardly know you to come over here and burden you."

"I'm from outside Galveston," she said. "Where you from?"

"Near New Iberia."

"Where's that?"

"Louisiana."

She put a hand on my knee, "You see?"

"See what?"

"We're both from the South. People from the South is just nicer. We don't get all cold and push people away when they in need."

"How long you been here?" I asked.

"Where?" She leaned forward and I slid a little in her direction.

"In L.A.?"

"Two months."

I kissed her chin right in the middle of that scar. She shuddered and moved her hand up on my erection. She didn't gasp or make any declaration about my size. That was fine by me. I didn't want any big expectations. I just wanted someone close and caring.

"Bite it," she said.

I knew what she meant and nipped her chin and lip.

"Li'l harder, baby," she said and her hand tightened on my erection to show me how much harder she meant.

I groaned and bit harder.

"Oh, that's it," she whispered. "I wanted that ever since you said it. It's like you caught me, just sayin' you'd bite my lip."

She shuddered again, and I grabbed her head with both hands to steady it as I ran my tongue slowly from her chin up across her lip. I spent many minutes on that scar. It drove her wild. She used those moments to take off our clothes and lead us to the bed.

Again it was a new kind of lovemaking for me. Usually there was a game I played with women. They adored my big thing and ignored my skinny chest. I pretended that I was a wild animal, furious and feral in my passion. It led all too quickly to something explosive and not quite real. But with Charlotte it was different. There were some explosions, but at other times there was a settling in. Like when we lay on our sides, me deep inside her, facing each other.

"A man cut me on the face, and when it healed I headed for L.A.," she said in a strained whisper.

I stroked her cheek in reply.

"Would you do somethin' like that?" she asked.

"Neither," I said.

Her face framed the question that a moment of passion would not allow into words.

"Not cut you or run," I said.

She twisted my ear pretty hard, and I came so violently that I lost consciousness for a while.

I awoke to the smell of coffee, disoriented because I didn't know where I was. I had to look around the bare room a couple of times before I remembered Charlotte. The floor was finished pine with no rug. The open closet was a door-size indentation with three dresses hanging on wire hangers. The single bed I was on was the only furniture in the room. I realized that the furniture in the living room must belong to the flat-voiced roommate; that Charlotte had nothing; that she was just a refugee from the violence of her recent past.

I tried to get up, but the bed was too comfortable. The pillow had the sweet smell of some kind of hair product, the sheets were clean. My bed back at Fontanelle's was a six-year-old's smelly mattress with no sheet on a gritty, pitted floor. I had the urge to get married right then. I could get married to Charlotte, get a job with the city, move out toward Compton — maybe even change my name.

"Paris, you 'wake?" She was standing at the door.

"Uh," I admitted.

"I got coffee on the deck."

IT WAS CROWDED on the deck, and the kitchen chairs we used rocked a little on the metal grating that stood for a floor. But the early evening was pretty, and Charlotte's conversation was just what I needed.

"What kinda trouble you in?" she asked after her second cup of coffee.

"I don't really know," I said.

"How could you not know? Is somebody after you?"

"Maybe. They have been. One or two. One of 'em burnt down my little bookstore over on Eighty-nine and Central."

"You worked there?"

"I owned it," I said with faded pride.

"I used to go by there. I mean when it wasn't burned. I always wanted to go in, but I was scared."

"Scared'a what?"

"I don't know. Things out here scare me. People don't act normal. It's like you gotta know some kinda secret handshake or sumpin'."

"You come up here to get away from that man cut you," I said, only partly as a question.

"Not only that," Charlotte said. "I wanna be a cook too. Not just a cook that make stuff but a chef. I wanna own my own restaurant. You know my mama was the best cook in our whole town, and I learned from her. Back where I come from, you could only cook for a house fulla dirty kids in a backwood shack, or up in some rich white peoples' houses. I want my own place."

"You know I got to go soon, Charlotte."

"Say that again."

"You know —"

"No, not that, just my name."

"Charlotte."

She smiled and got up to kiss me.

"You was just what I needed, baby," she said.

28

WHEN I GOT TO the hospital it was almost eight. I left Charlotte with the promise to call in a few days; just that little pledge made me feel that I might be alive and free after this mess was over.

The hospital room smelled sour, like a mound of dead skin.

Fearless was sitting at Sol's bedside speaking in low tones. That made me happy because it meant that Sol was listening and talking.

"They brought me here to die," a voice to my left said.

I turned to see an ancient white man sitting up in a bed. He was so small that he seemed like an infant allowed to sleep in a grown-up bed. The odor was coming from him.

"What?"

"They brought me here to die," he said again. "The doctors and the lawyers and Marjorie."

"Are you sick?" I asked.

He raised a skeletal hand and waved me to his bedside.

I glanced at Fearless, who had stopped talking for a moment to look in the direction of the voices. He saw me and then turned back to continue his conversation with Sol.

"They're trying to kill me," the man said after I had moved to his bedside.

"Who is?"

"They all are. They bring me here and stick me with needles and make me take poisons and hope that I die. They aren't going to operate," he said indignantly. "I don't have fever. Here, feel my forehead."

He was cool as a cucumber, as my mother often said.

"See? I'm not hot or bleeding. Why would they leave me here without my things? Why would they leave me with all these sick people's germs if they're not trying to kill me?"

I had no answer. I once heard a sermon in my uncle's church where the minister claimed that there was no Earth, only Hell and Heaven. Where we were was an upper level of Hell. And when we died, we either tumbled the rest of the way down the mountainside or rose on an angel's wings. I wasn't sure about the Heaven part, but life sure was feeling like Hell to me.

"Fearless knows," the aged gray-headed man said. "Fearless knows."

I wondered if Fearless had gotten us mixed up in yet another hopeless cause, but then I remembered the troubles we were in were of my doing.

I went to Fearless ready to ask if I had to carry that old man out on my back. But the words died in my throat when I peered over his shoulder.

Sol's face was shrunken and blue. His teeth glistened between parted lips, and he wasn't breathing. He hadn't drawn a breath in some time.

But still Fearless babbled on.

"Fearless."

No reply.

"Fearless!"

"What? What you want, Paris?"

"Who are you talkin' to, man? He's dead."

"I know that. You think I don't know a dead man?"

"Then who are you talking to?"

"His soul," Fearless said. There was a hint of embarrassment in his voice.

"What?"

Fearless put up his hands to silence me. "My momma used to say, a long time ago when I was a boy, that when a man dies, his soul is lost at first 'cause he don't know he's dead. It wanders around and could be lost forever. But if he sees you and he knows who you are and he knows that you're talkin' to him, then he tries to answer back. But when you don't answer, he knows that he must be a spirit. Your voice becomes the messenger, and he realizes what has happent an' he knows to go for Heaven."

Then, instead of getting up and talking to me about our business, he turned back to Sol and started muttering again. I sat in a chair far away from the tiny man and waited until my watch said eight-thirty, then I went to Fearless again.

"How long you plan to keep this up?" I asked.

"Momma said to do it till dawn."

"Visitors' hours end at nine, Fearless. We don't want the nurse to see you hoverin' over no corpse."

246

Fearless hesitated, then he turned away from his divine mission. "I guess that's enough. I think he must'a heard me."

"Yeah," I said. "Now let's get the fuck outta here."

"WHEN DID he die?' I asked Fearless in the parking lot.

"I don't know. I mean, he was dead when I got there."

"And the nurse didn't come in to see him?"

"No. He was dead," Fearless assured me.

"But how could that be? Aren't the nurses supposed to check?"

"How should I know?" Fearless said defensively. "Maybe they looked in and saw that he looked peaceful. I don't know."

"So he didn't say nuthin'?" I asked.

"How he gonna say somethin' if he's dead, Paris?"

I had no reply, no question to follow up. I wanted Sol to be alive more than anything. He was the only one who really knew about the money everybody was after. And that was the only reason I was still looking for answers. At least with some cash, I could rent another bookstore. But now that he was dead, I knew that it was time to move on.

"You want to go down to Louisiana and visit my mother?" I asked.

"Sure," Fearless said. "Right after I find who killed Sol and Fanny."

"The trouble is too deep," I said. "It's time for us to split."

"You go on, Paris. It's my word on the line here."

"Your word what? You didn't promise to find out who killed them."

"But I promised to protect Fanny, and I didn't. I bet because she wasn't comin' here, that's why Sol died."

"Mr. Jones," I said as a plea.

"You go on, man. You didn't promise."

"I was with you, wasn't I? I got you here. Maybe I even think you're right, but I'm scared, man, scared to death with all these men fightin' and killin'." The truth came out of me without my intention.

Fearless put his steely hand on my shoulder.

"You scared, but you ain't no coward, Paris. Uh-uh. Matter'a fact, you a hero."

"What?" I never knew Fearless to try and play anybody, much less me, his best friend.

"Yeah. Hero is just bein' brave when there's trouble. An' bein' brave means to face your fears and do it anyway. Shoot. You can't call me a hero 'cause I ain't scared'a nuthin' on God's blue Earth."

He got me again. Shamed me into going in on something that I should have left alone.

"You go on home," I said. "I'm'a go over and see Gella and the fool. I'll be back later on."

29 GELLA GREETED ME at the door looking over my shoulder for Fearless. He had that kind of effect on people; that's why I never wanted him to meet my girlfriends before we were solid.

"He couldn't come," I said.

Gella smiled, realizing she had been rude. "Come in, Mr. Minton."

The tiny house was neat and sweet smelling. I imagined that gawky Gella had spent the whole day cleaning, trying to wipe away the stigma of death.

I remembered that Sol was dead and wondered if she had been notified. I decided to leave it up to the hospital. It wasn't my job to announce death, and anyway, I wouldn't want any evidence that I was the first one to know. It struck me as strange that the nursing staff was unaware of Sol's passing for so long.

Being safe was still my motto, regardless of Fearless calling me a hero.

"Please have a seat, Mr. Minton."

"Paris," I said while lowering myself onto a brown leather chair.

From the outside the Greenspans' house looked like a plaster castle painted a dull orange. But inside the layout was the same as Sol and Fanny's house. One contractor must have built tract homes for miles. Back in my little parish in Louisiana every home was different. We were poor, but at least we were different, I thought. That's how jealousy works sometimes.

I was jealous of the fine wood furnishings and the long, plush drapes that covered an entire wall. There was a grandfather clock with a brass pendulum that must have weighed half a pound and gold-brown carpeting so thick that you'd think you were standing on an ancient pine forest floor.

Her skinny neck had a gold chain on it, and the diamond of her engagement ring was no chip like the wedding stones you found around where I lived.

For a moment I felt sorry that I didn't send Fearless. Why shouldn't he be in that house and have that woman draped on him like that chain when her husband finally decided to come home? Why couldn't he take her on the couch, and on the floor, while that sap of a husband gawked and whined?

I felt the beginnings of an erection as I sat there looking at that red-eyed, sorrowful young woman, but there was no love in my heart. Maybe it was the past few days of danger and mayhem that stripped away the bonds of my rage.

"Is something wrong?" Gella asked me in that slightly nasal voice.

She saw the rage and aggression in my eyes. That recognition doused my anger — and my ardor.

"It's been a tough few days," I said.

"Yes it has."

Gella reached for a small, framed photograph that sat on the coffee table. She looked at it and then handed it over to me. It was a picture of Fanny in a fancy green dress. She was laughing very hard and leaning over to the side like she'd done with me and Fearless that first night. It was a very different picture from the ones in Fanny's bedroom.

"Uncle Sol gave it to me before they arrested him," she said. "When he gave it to me, he said, 'Isn't she beautiful?'"

"She was a wonderful woman." I handed the frame back. Then I said, "What's this about your husband?"

"It's like I said on the phone." Gella perched on the end of the matching brown sofa. "For a whole day he wouldn't eat or talk. Then, when I was washing dishes, he got in his car and drove off."

"Did he say anything before he left?"

Gella shook her head the way one does when faced with an impossible math problem. "He didn't seem to know that I was there except once."

"What happened then?"

"He sat up and looked at me."

"Is that all?"

"It was in his eyes," Gella said, her voice skating near grief. "He was begging me with his eyes. There were tears, and he tried to say something . . ."

"What did the police say?"

"What?"

"What did the police say about Fanny?"

"Oh," Gella said. Maybe she had forgotten about the death of her aunt, maybe she wanted to forget. "They wanted to know if there was any trouble in the family. They asked where Morris was when Sol was attacked."

"Where was he?" I asked.

"At work. He has a part-time night job working for a man named Minor."

"Zev," I said.

"Yes. Do you know him?"

"He came to Fanny's right after we found her, you had already left for the hospital. Said he wanted to say hi."

"That's strange."

"Why?"

"I didn't think that they knew Mr. Minor. I'm sure they didn't."

"He said he knew them back in the old country, that him and Sol lived in the same town."

"He never met Sol since Morris worked for him," Gella said. "And Morris never told me that he was a landsman."

"What does your husband do for this guy?" I asked.

"He's learning to be an insurance agent."

"What kinda insurance?"

"Art."

"Say what?"

"Mr. Minor writes policies for expensive paintings and sculptures. It's a very good business." There was pride in her voice, pride for her smart husband and his good choices. "Morris is already making more money in his night job than he does at the bank."

"You got somethin' to drink?" I asked.

The Greenspan kitchen looked even more like Fanny's, even the wallpaper was the same. The only difference was that where Fanny had mismatched dishes and cookware, Gella had copper pots and dishes all with the same deep blue floral pattern.

She poured me a shot of peach schnapps in a cute little crystal thimble. Gella didn't understand drinking the way her auntie did. I was sitting in the alcove, her standing before me. I downed the shot and put the thimble down in plain view, hoping that she'd get the hint.

"Sol is dead," she said.

"When?"

"They called just before you got here. He died in his bed. Heart attack."

I remembered what the maternity nurse, Rya McKenzie, had said about heart attacks but kept my silence on the subject.

"What did we do to deserve this?" she asked.

I got up and put my arms around her. She was a little taller than I, but still she got her head on my shoulder. I realized what Fearless meant about being there for someone who needs it. It was a small lesson on a bad day, and I wondered if I would remember it later on.

We stood there breathing, sobbing, being silent in the embrace. I was thinking about what I had to do next to keep out of trouble and to help Fearless realize that we were in over our heads. I pulled half away from the clinch, still holding on to her upper arms.

"He have any friends?" I asked.

"Sol?"

"Morris."

"Oh." That was a more difficult question. "Morris never had many friends. He was too serious for the young people who came to shul. He was always nervous and shy about how big he was. He was all the time saying how people made fun of him."

"You got somethin' to eat in the icebox?" I asked about food because I didn't want to hear any more about how her Sad Sack husband didn't have any friends and because I didn't want to run him down in front of probably the only person who ever loved him since his mother.

"Oh yes," she said brightly.

There was leftover meat loaf and stuffed cabbage that Fanny had made for them four days before. That and a Cel-Ray soda from the Jewish market was my dinner.

"She was a great cook," Gella said, trying not to cry over the food. "They were both wonderful. He saved my father and me from the Nazis. He was a great man who would die for what is right."

She switched over from meat loaf to heroism in wartime so quickly that I almost missed the meaning of her words.

"Some people said that it was because my father was rich that Sol saved us. But all our money was stolen by a man named Zimmerman. Sol knew that."

"Who's Zimmerman?"

"A Jew who worked with the SS men that sought out and deported Jews. They knew that some Jews had hidden their jewelry and valuables from German banks because they didn't want to be robbed by the Nazis. Zimmerman came to my father and offered him our freedom for Papa's art collection. But my father found out that Zimmerman lied and ran with me. After the war my father was broken. He lived with Sol and Fanny until he died."

There was nothing for me to say. Sol and Fanny were saints.

"There's a man named Jonas," Gella said after a while.

"Who's he?"

"Simon," she said. "I think that's his first name. He's one of Mo's friends. He's not Jewish and so . . ." She let her own ideas of race and separation hang in the air a moment.

"Would Morris go to see his friend if he was upset? Somebody to talk to and drink with?" I suggested, indicating my empty glass.

"I don't know," she said, shaking her head. "Maybe."

"Did you call him and ask?"

"I don't know his telephone number. Morris never writes numbers down, he has a perfect memory." She was proud of him, and scared for him, but still she wouldn't call this non-Jewish man.

"You want me to see if I can find this Simon guy and ask him somethin'?"

GELLA BROUGHT ME the phone book. Simon was the only Jonas out of over eighty thousand entries.

"Is he married?" I asked Gella.

"No."

Maybe it wasn't only his religion she didn't like, I thought. "Well then maybe I better go knock on his door."

I stood up, and so did Gella.

"What's wrong?" I asked her.

"Nothing."

"Don't you want me to go?"

"Yes, but . . ."

"Don't you want me to find Morris?"

"I'm afraid."

"You think he might be with another woman?"

"No."

"What then?"

"I want to go with."

"You mean ride with me down to Culver City in the middle'a the night?"

She nodded innocently.

"I cain't do that."

"But I must go."

"Why?"

"Hedva was killed in her own home. In her own house."

I looked around Gella's identical dwelling and knew that she was right.

"Listen," I said. "You might not know this, but cops like to get target practice on Negro men when they see 'em with white women. You get me?"

She nodded.

"So you have to lay low in the backseat if you gonna ride with me, okay?"

"Yes."

I wanted her to say something else, something to reassure me, but I didn't know what that could be.

"Okay then. Now go get that bottle'a schnapps, close it tight, and bring it along."

"You want to bring liquor to find Morris?"

"Medicine," I said. "Just in case you or me, or Morris when we find him, gets a case'a the nerves."

30

I WAS DRIVING in a white neighborhood in the middle of the night with an open bottle of peach schnapps in the glove compartment, a married white woman hiding in the backseat, and a stolen .38-caliber pistol next to the gearshift on the floor. It was a far cry from my bookstore days, selling *Popular Mechanics* and *Batman*.

"Tell me somethin'," I called to the backseat.

"Yes, Mr. Minton."

"Why you gonna trust me?"

"What do you mean?" she asked.

I didn't know if it was the question or the articulation of black English versus her own Europeanized English that she wondered about.

"I mean, why would you call me or Fearless when your husband goes missin'? Why not call somebody you know, or the cops?"

"I don't know many people," she said. "Just Hedva and Sol, and Morris. We don't have many friends. And the police didn't like Morris. That's why he was upset, because they weren't trying to find the black man who stabbed Sol."

"I'm a black man."

"But Fanny trusted you. She told me that it wasn't you who came after Sol. And I can see that you and Fearless are good men, not murderers."

I have never been as certain of anything as Gella was of me.

SIMON JONAS LIVED on the left side of a one-story two-family house on Cassidy in Culver City. The light was on, but that didn't mean that Morris Greenspan was around. Gella didn't want to go to Jonas's door, so I went alone.

"Yeah?" a very large and blond specimen of Americana said. He answered after the fourth ring. "What do you want?"

"Morris Greenspan."

"Who the fuck are you, nigger?" He enjoyed the last word. It brought a grin to his big mouth. He was wearing blue jeans and no shirt. His skin was streaked with oily grime.

"Byron Leeds," I said in an amiable enough tone. "I'm a friend of the aunt and uncle of his wife. He drove off, and his wife hasn't seen him. She said you and him were friends, and, well, I was in the neighborhood."

"His aunt got killed," Jonas said. Light began to dawn on his filthy face. "Hey. He said it was a nigger did it, stabbed his uncle too."

"When did he tell you that?"

"What you say?"

Mr. Jonas and I were at a crossroads. He was measuring my size and disposition while glancing behind me to see if I had come alone. I, on the other hand, had split into two separate personalities. The first and foremost of these was the one that felt an intense hatred for the blond mechanic who hated me and insulted me without the slightest knowledge of my personal worth.

The second character in my internal drama was experiencing pure amazement at this hatred I felt. I never knew that such an emotion was in me. My whole life I had merely been cautious of whites, like I was cautious in a thunderstorm. I didn't hate lightning but merely took cover when rumblings came in off the gulf.

"I said, tell me when Morris talked to you about his uncle."

"Or what?"

Simon Jonas reached out for me as he asked his question. I, in turn, leaned away from the clumsy lunge, stuck my hand into my pocket, and pulled out Sol Tannenbaum's .38.

"Or no more Simon," I said, pointing the muzzle at one blue eye.

The fear that came into that eye was immediate and absolute.

"Wh-wh-wh-what do you want?" His voice, his posture, even the color of his grimy face changed just that quickly.

"Morris Greenspan," I said again.

Someone might think that I would feel on top of the world at a moment like that. There I was, alone with the drop on somebody who represented the enemy of the spirit of my whole race in this inhospitable country. But all I was thinking was that with that gun in my hand, there was a good chance for it to go off.

"I don't know where Mo is," he stammered.

"Has he been here today?"

"Yeh. Yeh. We had a drink about noon."

"Where'd he go?"

"I don't know. Really."

"Guess."

"He's got a girl."

"A girlfriend?"

"Yuh. A girlfriend named Lily. He said that he was fed up. He said that he was tired of trying so hard and that he was going to leave, go away, maybe to Mexico."

"And you think he went with this Lily?"

Simon didn't answer. I don't think he even heard me. The skin about his eyes had begun to cringe, telling me in its wordless way that it was time for the gun to go off.

"Simon."

"What?"

"Where does Lily live?"

"I don't know." He was near tears. "I'm sorry."

Then came the hard part. I wanted to get out of there without getting killed. The blond bully was six two at least, and he did hard labor for a living. I was five eight, a bookseller by trade, and a bookworm by nature. I didn't think that I could swing the piece of iron in my hand hard enough to stun the mechanic. And I had to believe that he had a gun somewhere in his little apartment. If I just walked away, he'd get to that gun before I could drive off. I was pretty sure that I could nail the guy point blank, but at six paces away I might as well have been packing a cap gun.

Killing him was the best option, that was my first thought. But there was Gella sitting in the car. I couldn't expect her to be quiet about murder. So then I thought about wounding him, shooting him in the thigh, after that maybe hitting him in the head.

Then I came to my senses. I brought up my left hand to steady my aim. Tears sprouted from Simon Jonas's eyes, and the high-pitched sound of a small animal came out of his throat.

"Get down on your belly, boy," I said.

The little animal screeched from under his tongue.

"Get down."

Simon did a belly flop right there in his doorway. The moment he was down I turned tail and ran for the car. I jumped into the driver's seat, slipped the key into the ignition, and turned over the engine in record speed. I had taken four sharp turns before Gella could sit up in the backseat.

"What happened?" she asked.

"Get down!"

She obliged and asked again, "What happened?"

"He doesn't know where Morris is, but he saw him."

"When?" she sat up again.

"At lunchtime."

"Was he all right?"

"I guess not if he left you all alone. But Simon seemed to think that he was just fine."

"Where did he go?"

"Don't know."

"Did you ask?"

"Why you think I was there?"

"Why were you running?"

"Because Jonas is a big white boy not too pleased with a black man ringin' his bell in the middle'a the night."

"You're scared?" she said. "But you have the gun."

"And so you think I can just go up and down the street shooting anybody I want?"

"I just think that you don't need to be scared."

"Jonas didn't know where Morris was," I said, not wanting to discuss my lack of bravery, "but I'd like to look around the office he has with Minor. Do you have a key somewhere?"

"There's a duplicate key in the big plant outside the front door," she said. "Mo leaves it there because he forgets to bring his sometimes."

IT WAS a four-story office building made from brick; not tenement or factory brick, but solid, English-manor-house blocks. They were red, even in the night, and flawless. There was no fancy entranceway, but the door was flanked by five-foot pine trees set in gigantic terra-cotta pots. There were three windows stacked above the front door, each looking into the hallway of that floor. There was a dim light shining somewhere on three.

"What floor does Morris work on?" I asked Gella. We were parked across the street from the building, on Melrose. There was nobody out at that time of night.

"Two," she said.

"So the key is in that pot on the right?"

"Under the inside lip of the one on the right as you face the door," she said, obviously parroting something that her husband had told her many times, "toward the back."

"Okay. I'm'a go in alone."

"I'll come with," she said.

"No."

"Why not?"

I had the whole ride up from Culver City to think about that question. I didn't want Gella to find out about Lily unless she absolutely had to; not that I cared that he had a girl on the side or even how Gella would feel about that, but we were in a tight situation, people were getting killed, and I didn't need any excess passion boiling in the backseat if the cops pulled us over.

"I'm gonna leave the key in the ignition," I said, "so that if we have to leave fast again, I can just jump in and hit it. But if I leave the keys and ain't nobody in the car, then when we come out, there might not be a vehicle to get away with. That won't do."

"But there's no one to run from here," she argued.

"Maybe not for you alone, but if you're with a black man, at night, in a closed office building, going through a man's papers and such without his permission — then maybe there might be a reason to move fast." By the time I had gotten through that mouthful I had convinced myself.

"Can I turn on the radio?" she asked in defeat.

"Knock yourself out."

THE KEY WAS where it was supposed to be, which made me think that I was not where I should have been. Everything so far that had worked out right had ended up wrong. I went through the front door anyway.

The second floor was dark. The key that opened the office building was also designed to work on the Minor Insurance Company door. The office was one middle-size room with two desks, one ash and the other constructed from sheet steel that was painted light gray.

I knew from first glance that the wooden desk belonged to Morris; it was as sloppy as he was. It was covered with candy bar wrappers, *Men at War* magazines, and a thin layer of dirt comprised of eraser dust, crumbs, and good old L.A. soot. He had a few files for insurance policies in one of the lower drawers. Mostly art items were covered: paintings, rare books, and the like. The policies were all pretty thick, mainly with pages detailing the authenticity of the piece covered. Some of the histories dated back to the sixteenth century. The values attached to these works of art were staggering.

Morris was the executing agent on all of them. He was also the signatory agent of a dozen or more European and British insurance companies. I knew that Morris couldn't have been the agent of such expensive policies. Therefore he had to be a patsy; a big dodo sitting on a swan's clutch.

I went through every gritty, chocolate-stained file but came up empty. No Lily or secret apartment to be found.

I had to jimmy the file drawer on Minor's desk. At first I was surprised that the boss would have taken the uglier piece of furniture for himself, but then I realized that it was for the enhanced security. I wouldn't have bothered at all except that I had a notion.

Minor's lower drawers had more policies. These also listed Morris Greenspan as the agent. Rodin, Kandinsky, Picasso were but a few of the names that I recognized from the cheap art picture paperbacks I sold in my store. Policies ranged from tens of thousands to hundreds of thousands of dollars. The owners were people from around the world. I sifted among the files and folders until I came upon a policy for a set of jewelers' tools. I took Sol's newspaper clipping from my wallet and checked it against the last entry on the documentation section — the dates coincided with the auction that caught Sol's attention. The sale was brokered by Lawson and Widlow, the accounting firm Sol had worked for. Ten or eleven other policies had Lawson and Widlow mentioned one way or another; brokers, gallery representatives, collateral holders.

There was fraud in there somewhere, I was certain of that; not that I cared. All I wanted was the cost to set up a new bookstore. The rest they, whoever they were, could keep.

I knew that Minor had something to do with the bond; that's why he came to see Fanny. Or maybe he knew that Fanny was dead and he intended to search the house personally. There was nothing about it in his desk. The only connection I could make to Sol and Fanny were Lawson and Widlow, the article that Sol had clipped, and the fact that Morris Greenspan coincidentally worked for Minor.

The putz, as Fanny called him, wasn't there, but I didn't expect that. The way I figured it he was at Lily's house unleashing his laments upon her bosom. The only reasons I helped Gella were that I hoped she could get me closer to the bond and to keep Fearless from getting distracted. It would have been good to have found an address or number for Lily. That way I might have had some leverage over Morris; maybe I could have even turned him against Minor.

Then a thought hit me. Most of the time a married man taps on a woman he has easy access to. Wedlock keeps him from going out every night prowling the bars and nightclubs; he meets his girlfriends at work or next door. *Maybe Lily works on the third floor,* I thought. *Maybe that light up there is them.*

LIGHT FROM a single bulb spilled out from the crack into the gloomy hallway. To my disappointment the word JANITOR was stenciled on the red-brown door. There was no sound coming from anywhere.

I pulled the door open, expecting to see a deep-basined sink and a worn-out collection of mops and brooms.

I wondered how long he knew about the exposed beam that ran across the ceiling of the third-floor hopper room; the perfect timber to hold the rope firmly.

His face was darker than mine, and his inelegant hands were now stiff from the onset of rigor mortis. His skin was room temperature. The pants were unzipped and his grayish pink penis poked out. Morris looked as uncomfortable in death as he had in life. Under his feet was an overturned step ladder he had used to reach up with the rope and then kicked away to end his life. In the corner was a dwindling puddle that had the strong stench of urine. In the opposite corner was a cream-colored envelope that, I found, held the suicide note.

A few weeks later, when I was taking a forced vacation, it came to me that the piss in the corner was Morris's last act of sloppy rebellion, the comment that summed up his life and then evaporated. The suicide letter was just a footnote to that metaphor.

I squatted down outside of the janitor's door and read the five sheets of small, surprisingly neat, print. Then I read it again. The words were craftily penned, but the mind that wrote them was still a mess.

Morris was filled with fears and hallucinations, delusions of grandeur and deep self-hatred. His girlfriend, it seemed, was a prostitute, his dreams empty and pitiful.

I'm a fast reader, so I read the letter a third time and then put it in my pocket. I went all the way down to the front door and then stopped. Ever since Elana had come into my store I had been making the wrong decisions, going in the wrong direction. Therefore my next choice had to be considered. What would I say to Gella Greenspan? If I told her about her husband, she would want to call a hospital, and they would call the police. The police would want to know her movements that night, and those movements included me. Simon Jonas would be happy to press charges of assault, and if I didn't ditch the pistol, they'd also have me on theft. On the other hand, if I didn't tell her, it would be up to strangers, cold-hearted cops who'd just as likely accuse her of some crime connected to the idiot's demise.

Pat Boone was fumbling a note when I opened the door to the car. Gella was asleep in the passenger's seat. The sound startled her, but when she saw my face she smiled.

"Did you find anything?"

"No," I said. "Nothing."

31 | FEARLESS AND DORTHEA were asleep in the bedroom when I got back to our apartment at a little past five. I'd dropped Gella off at her place twenty minutes earlier. When we neared her house she worried that maybe Morris came home while she was gone and that he'd be worried about her. I kept my silence, telling myself that it would be less painful this way.

"Paris?" Fearless said from the bed.

"What time is it?" Dorthea groaned.

"Go back to sleep," Fearless told her.

He threw on his clothes and met me in the kitchen of our little unit. I breathed Morris's suicide in a whisper. It wasn't until we got in the car and were driving that I told him the rest.

"And you didn't tell her that her husband was upstairs," he said, "dead?"

"I told you, man. It was nighttime, and they had already called her about Sol. And the dude was stone-cold dead. She couldn't'a helped him. How would it have been good for her to see the husband she loved with his neck stretched out a foot long on a hemp rope, his dick stuck out, and his piss all over the floor?"

"I don't know about all that," Fearless chided, "and neither do you. All I know is that a man's wife deserves to know when he's dead."

"He left a suicide note too," I said.

"He did?"

"Yeah. I took it."

"Now why you wanna do that?"

"'Cause sometimes I must think that I'm you," I said.

"What's that s'posed to mean?"

"First off, he wrote it to a prostitute named Lily. The whole thing was written to her."

"Girlfriend?"

"By the hour," I said. "And that ain't all. Morris the one killed Fanny."

"No." Fearless turned to me in wonder.

"Morris wrote it down that he told her on the drive over to her house that the man he had been working for, Zev Minor, a man she had never met, was actually a guy named Zimmerman. He was feeling guilty over what happened to Sol and scared about what might happen still. Fanny went a little crazy when Morris told her that. She screamed at him and yelled at him and said that she was going to raise hell. He dropped her off and then got scared. He said that he went to his car and then came back to knock on the door, but she wouldn't let him in.

"And then he went around to the back to kill her?" Fearless asked.

"No. At least he said it was just to talk her out of going to the police. It seems that the policies that Minor had been writing weren't exactly legal and Morris was listed as the agent for all of them. He said that he went to the back door, but she wouldn't let him in. Then she said she was calling the police. When he saw her pick up the phone he went crazy. He broke the window in with a rock. After that he said that he didn't remember anything until he came back when we were there."

"I don't get it," Fearless said. "Why would Fanny go to the police? She said she didn't like the cops. An' even if she would go, why would she tell on her own family? I mean, I know she didn't like the boy, but damn."

"It's 'cause of Minor. Morris wrote it in the note," I said. "He said that he'd been working for the man who called himself Minor. But his name was really Zimmerman, a Jew that worked with the Nazis to fool wealthy Jews who had hidden their wealth from the Germans. He told the Jews that they could buy their freedom, but it was a lie."

I glanced over at Fearless. His jawbones were standing out because of his clenched teeth. No black man liked the notion of the concentration camps; we had lived in labor camps the first 250 years of our residence in America. And for Fearless it was even worse; he had actually seen the camps. He knew the price of this treachery firsthand.

"Why would Gella's husband work for a man like that?"

"He didn't know at first. Minor came to him after Sol was convicted and gave him a part-time job working as an art insurance agent. Then, after a few months went by, Minor told Morris that he was working secretly for the Israeli government. He said that Sol had embezzled money that was meant to go to Israel. Sol was already in prison, and Minor wanted Morris to find out from Fanny what he'd done with the money. Slowly Morris figured out that Minor was Zimmerman, but by then he got greedy. Morris tried to find out from Fanny where the money was. But Sol was too slick, he had covered up his business. Fanny didn't know anything, and there were no records left to be found."

"And where was this money that Sol could steal it?" asked Fearless.

"I don't know for sure, but as close as I can figure, Minor was selling off the art treasures through Lawson and Widlow and then giving the buyers some kinda fake history through his insurance company. Lawson and Widlow must have been holding the money, and when Sol found that out, he embezzled it and converted it into bonds. When Morris couldn't get a line on the dough, Minor came up with Plan B."

"Leon," Fearless said with conviction.

I nodded. "Reverend Grove went to Lawson and Widlow with the bond he was holdin' for Elana. They went to Minor or Zimmerman or whatever you wanna call him. He must'a told them about Leon's deal with Sol, and Minor went to work getting Leon outta prison."

"All that was in the note?" Fearless asked.

"Naw. Just about Minor, and Morris workin' for him. I been figurin' the rest out myself. Minor figured that the bond was linked somehow to the rest of the money that Sol stole."

"But that don't make no sense, Paris," Fearless said after a long ponder.

"What?"

"Minor spendin' all that time and money to get at the bond. By the time Leon got outta jail, it should'a been gone."

"No. The bank needed Sol to cash it, and even if Elana had passed it on, she might have written the numbers down or at least remembered who she gave it to."

"Oh," Fearless said. I don't think that Fearless was incapable of understanding me, he just wasn't interested in my puzzler's mind.

"Minor and Leon still lookin', but I just might know where the bond landed."

"Oh yeah?" Fearless said.

THE EXETER HOTEL ON Hooper had a red velvet phone booth with a louvered door that shut out all noise and gave the caller a good deal of privacy. I dialed the phone number that I'd put in my pocket for safekeeping four days before.

"Pine Grove Hotel," a fresh, young female voice declared.

I hung up.

"JOHN MANLY," I said to the hotel clerk.

"And to what is this pertaining?" the snooty, suited white man asked.

"He the one wanna see me, man." I was being needlessly argumentative. "Just tell him that I have something to tell him about Sol Tannenbaum."

"Maybe you'd prefer to leave a message," the coal-eyed, hollow-chested clerk suggested.

"Maybe you don't understand English," Fearless said.

The clerk dialed a few numbers. He picked at the cord nervously while shooting glances at my friend. I thought he was calling for help, but instead he said, "Mr. Manly? I have two men down here who want to talk to you about a Mr. Tannenbaum."

I smiled and nodded.

"But sir," the clerk said. "Wouldn't you prefer to come down and meet them first?"

The clerk didn't like the answer he was getting.

"Yes sir. I'll send them up directly." He put the phone down behind the counter somewhere, then took up a brass bell, which he shook, causing a shrill ring.

A Negro bellman came running from somewhere. Ignoring us he spoke to the hotel clerk. "Yes, Mr. Corman?"

"Not you, Randolph. I want Billings."

"Yes sir," Randy said, and he darted away.

While we waited, Mr. Corman became very interested in a loose thread on his jacket sleeve. He took out a pair of scissors and tried to see if he could cut the errant strand at the root. But the run was halfway between his wrist and elbow and it was impossible to hold the thread and cut it at the same time. It was a dilemma. He couldn't cut the string without taking off his jacket and couldn't take off his jacket while standing at the front desk. But he couldn't leave his desk with two Negroes standing there unattended.

"Are we waiting for something?" I asked.

Mr. Corman concentrated on his sleeve.

A new bellman, white this time, came to the desk.

"Yes, Mr. Corman?" he asked, just as fawning as Randolph had been.

"See these gentlemen up to three-twenty-two."

"Yes sir."

The walk through the lobby with its plush carpets and potted bird-of-paradise plants was even more humiliating than Corman's condescension. The women wore fine clothes and all the men had suits on. I was in the same tired slacks and loose shirt, in shoes that had done more than their share of walking. It felt like going to church in your dirty work clothes.

We didn't molest our escort. It wasn't his fault that he had to accompany us every step of the way. He knocked for us. The door was answered by a handsome and well-built white man in his late twenties. The same man I had seen bidding farewell to Sergeant Latham and Elana Love.

"Mr. Manly?" I asked affably.

"Thank you," the bellman Billings was saying to Fearless, and I realized that my friend had given our warden a tip.

"Mr. —?" Manly hesitated.

"Minton," I said. "And this is Mr. Jones. May we come in?"

"What is this about?"

"It's about a Jewish fortune stolen by Nazis and one turncoat Jew named —"

"Come in," the man who answered to the name John Manly said. He backed up, ushering us into the sitting room of a large suite. A yellow couch and four blue chairs were arranged around a table with all kinds of official-looking papers on it. The room was heavy with strange-smelling tobacco smoke. It wasn't an American blend.

From a side door two more men entered. One was short with heavily muscled arms. He wore a gray T-shirt and ocher pants with no shoes. He had a big belly and a hawkish nose. He wasn't happy to see us, but from the look of that scowl, I doubted if much made him happy. The third man, and the youngest of the three, was taller and sleeker than Fearless. His skin was pale, and he wore a small black cap on the back of his head.

"This is Ari," Manly said, pointing at the shorter man, "and Lev."

We stood there for a moment, wondering what manners to follow.

"Would you gentlemen like to sit down?" Manly asked us.

Fearless moved for a blue chair, I followed suit. Manly took a seat on the yellow couch, but Lev and Ari stayed on their feet.

A pair of glass doors led out to a vine-encircled patio. The sun shone in, slightly green from the vines.

"What do you have to tell us?" Manly inquired.

I was getting ready to launch into the business at hand, but Fearless beat me to it.

"Sol an' Fanny Tannenbaum's dead," he said, "an' I don't like it one bit. They was good people, and I promised to look after 'em. I got a pretty good idea'a who killed 'em, but I want to get the man that was the cause of their death."

Manly glanced at the stocky Ari. The latter hunched his shoulders and turned down his lips.

"That has nothing to do with us," Manly said.

"That's a bunch'a shit," Fearless said. "You want the lost money, the money that Sol took. Whoever killed him was after that. An' if it's you, I'm'a find it out."

I came for a parley and found myself on the verge of war.

"Vat do ve care about you?" Ari said in a surprisingly high voice.

Fearless stood up.

"You don't wanna know what I can do." The *motherfucker* wasn't said, but everyone in that room heard it.

Ari looked like he wanted to test Fearless's claim.

"We didn't have anything to do with the Tannenbaums' deaths." Manly was tense but still thinking.

"What do you know about a man named Zimmerman?" Fearless asked.

I didn't think that the atmosphere could stand any more tension, but the mention of that name caused tremors in all three of our hosts.

"Vat do you know about Zimmerman?" Ari demanded.

"I think it was him caused Sol and Fanny's killing," Fearless said. "You know I do, 'cause if I didn't, I'd'a come in here with my guns blazin'."

"Zimmerman," Lev uttered his first word since we entered. "Zimmerman."

"Why'ont you two guys sit down here with us?" Fearless demanded. "Either we gonna fight or we gonna talk."

Ari was still taking Fearless's measure when Lev took a seat.

"Sit down, Ari," Manly said.

"I want the finder's fee," I said.

Maybe I was a little hoarse, because Manly asked, "What did you say?"

"The finder's fee," I said, clearing my throat as I did so. "I want the finder's fee."

"Vat is it you do for this?" Ari asked.

"We know how you can get to the money," Fearless said with absolute confidence. "But we don't tell you a thing unless you tell us about Zimmerman."

"If you're talking about the bond that Hedva Tannenbaum gave the woman, it is useless," Lev said. "The policeman brought her here with it. We took the number and our people checked it.

It was a single issue. Tannenbaum had no other dealings with that bank."

"I ain't talkin' 'bout no bond," Fearless said. "I'm talkin' 'bout the money, the money you guys is lookin' for."

"Why would we believe that you can help us?" Manly asked Fearless.

"Morris Greenspan killed himself last night," Fearless said. "He left a note. He been workin' for a man called hisself Minor, and then he fount out what Sol did with the money. But then he fount out who Minor was."

There was a question in John Manly's gaze.

"Zimmerman," I replied.

Manly sat back and considered. There was an arrogant twist to his lips. He looked at each of his friends, making eye movements that I couldn't read.

"Where is this note?" Manly cocked his head to the side as if he were trying to see if the suicide note was hanging out of one of our pockets.

"Where's Zimmerman?" Fearless asked.

Manly answered, "We will pay you to tell us where the money is," not as an offer but as a foregone conclusion.

That sounded like a good first step to me. All we had to do was talk about a number; no thugs or blood or blackjacks.

Fearless stood up and said, "Come on, Paris."

Ari stood up too.

"No," Manly said. "Sit down, both of you."

There wasn't much give in either of the gladiators. So I asked a question.

"Where you guys from?"

"We are foreigners," Manly said.

"From Israel, I bet."

That somehow broke the standoff. Both Fearless and Ari took their seats.

"We are here to reclaim the wealth of our people," Lev said. His strained voice warbled with emotion that he bore like an open wound.

"Lev —" Manly began, but he was stopped by an upheld hand. I was surprised to see that the pale kid was the senior statesman among the bunch.

"This man, this Abraham Zimmerman, he helped the Nazis to steal it, and we are here to get it back."

"Steal what?" I asked. I was pretty sure of the answer, but I wanted to see what they would say.

"They took everything," Lev said. "The gold from our teeth, the hair from our heads. They took our pocket watches and our wallets. And if you were rich and you hid your jewels and paintings and furs, then Zimmerman was sent in to sell your freedom for what you had hidden away. He and his Nazi friends hid them again . . ." Lev's words trailed off, and he stared into space.

"Where is Zimmerman?" Fearless said, always wanting to cut to the chase.

"We don't know," Lev said after making the grimace of a man swallowing a bitter draft.

"What's this all about?" I asked the pale kid. Somehow I felt a connection with him.

"Zimmerman is a Jew . . . ," Lev began.

When Ari heard this, he spat on the floor.

"We already know the part about Zimmerman robbing the

rich Jews who thought they could buy their way out of the slaughterhouse," I said.

Lev caught the last word and looked into my eyes.

"Yes," he said. "Many of those wealthy men had converted their money into art treasures and gold. David Tannenbaum found out about the sale —"

"— of those jewelry-making tools that the Rothschild's jewelers had at one time," I said, finishing the sentence.

"He knew that these tools had belonged to his nephew and so contacted our government," Lev said, continuing, "but they told him that we could do nothing without proof."

"Why don't you just go over to those accountants and make 'em give it up?" Fearless suggested.

Squat, muscle-bound Ari grunted in agreement.

"The American government frowns on agents of foreign powers threatening their citizens," Lev explained. "We have no proof that this property was stolen. There were only thirty families that these Nazis and their dog, Zimmerman, took from. And they are all dead. The treasures were private property, and the papers of ownership were part of the devil's bargain. Our actions must be beyond criticism. So we ask for help from those who sympathize with our goals."

"That include hirin' a crooked cop to scare Fanny Tannenbaum and kill Conrad Till?" I asked, none too friendly.

"Do you know Israel?" Lev asked.

"What you read in the papers," I said.

"We made our own nation," the pale leader intoned. "We have taken back our lives and our history even though they have tried to destroy us all."

"If you and Sol believe in the same thing, why didn't you just ask him for the money?" I knew about Israel; I knew about Marcus Garvey too, and I didn't have the heart to hear about Garvey's dream coming true in another man's world.

"We did," Lev said. "We did, but like I told you, we are not official. We could not prove to him who we were, and no official of our government would vouch for us."

"If he didn't believe you, then why should we?" I asked.

"All you have to believe is our money," Ari said derisively.

"What about Till?" Fearless asked.

Lev brought the upturned palms of his hands up to the level of his shoulders. "We read that he died of a heart attack."

"You know better than that," I said.

"We are not murderers, Mr. Minton. We would not kill a man who has not committed a crime against us. The policeman was, how do you say, suggested to us by people we know. We did not trust him. We did not tell him to kill. We only wanted the bond that Fanny Tannenbaum gave to Leon Douglas."

"Okay," I said. "Now here you guys is livin' in the lap'a luxury, fresh off the boat from Israel, don't know a damn thing and ain't got no friends to help you, except one crooked cop; but still you go lookin' for a bond changed hands between Sol Tannenbaum and Leon Douglas's girlfriend. That don't even add up to numbers, man."

John Manly spoke up then. "Mr. Latham was not an honest man, but he was a good detective. When David Tannenbaum was still in prison, the good sergeant found out that Leon Douglas was his protector. When Leon was released, Latham became suspicious. He was already keeping an eye on Hedva and David through a friend of his who was a policeman in their neighborhood."

Ari muttered something in Fanny's tongue. I didn't understand a single word except for *svartza*.

"You ain't listenin' to me, brother," Fearless said. "We want the dude caused it all; we want him to pay for what he did. Money's nice — we could all use some, I'm sure — but this is about making the traitor Jew pay for what he did."

"But we don't know where he is," Manly insisted.

"If we did, we would have him already," Lev added.

"Are you after the thief or the money he stole?" Fearless impressed me with his question.

Lev hesitated a moment too long before replying, "Both of course."

"You tell us where to find Zimmerman, and we give you the suicide note," Fearless said.

The men were all silent. I couldn't tell the mood of the room, so I decided to concentrate on the kid. If a fight broke out, I figured I could take him — at least I could try.

"He's with his old Nazi overboss, Otto Holderlin," John Manly added. "If we knew where he was, we would demand his arrest. But I doubt that we will find him."

"Why's that?" I asked.

"From what we could find out, his accountants were moving his monies to Equador, Brazil, and Panama. Herr Zimmerman is moving south for the weather."

"How much you pay for the money if we lead you to it?" I asked.

"Thirty thousand dollars."

"But you don't get a thing," Fearless said to the Israelis, "till we see about Zimmerman."

32

"THAT SOUNDS pretty okay, huh, Paris?" Fearless said on our way down the block to our car.

"What?"

"Thirty thousand. Even split three ways you could still start a new bookstore with that kinda scratch."

"That was just talk, Fearless. We don't know where the money is. And what the fuck were you doin' in there anyways?"

"Pushin 'em a little," Fearless said almost innocently. "Pushin 'em to work with us on this thing."

"Why you after Zimmerman? You don't know him. You ain't even ever met him."

"It's Zimmerman had Sol killed."

"You don't know that."

"Yes I do, Paris. And he gonna pay."

"Pay how?"

"With blood and money, his freedom or his life," Fearless said.

"And what's all this stuff about money?"

"It ain't about money, it's about the man who destroyed Fanny and Sol."

"Morris killed Fanny."

"'Cause Zimmerman drove him crazy."

"What does that have to do with you tellin' them spies up there that we know where the money is? Now they gonna be after us."

"Not after I told 'em I lied," Fearless said.

"And what if they don't believe you?"

"You give 'em the note that Morris wrote and say you sorry."

HALF AN HOUR LATER we cruised past Gella's home. Three black-and-white police cruisers were parked out front.

"I guess they must'a found Morris," I said.

"She must be hurtin' over that," Fearless said. "That was the last family she had in life." There was an indictment in his tone.

"And how would me draggin' her upstairs to see his corpse make it hurt any less?"

"You could have comforted her, Paris."

"No, no. That's you, Mr. Jones. You the one talk to corpses and kiss married women under their husbands' noses. It's you who walks into a room full'a spies and puts *our* lives on the line. Me, I just hold tight and try not to get washed overboard."

Fearless's response to my tirade was to light up a cigarette. "Where to now?" he asked half a Camel later.

"Milo might have something, but he could wait. There's one thing in all this that don't fit," I said. "It might be a long shot, but then again, maybe not."

I drove back to south L.A., back to a nameless alley off of Slauson. It was mostly backyards and trash cans in that alley, but there was one doorway that led to a flight of rickety unpainted stairs. At the top of those stairs was a hallway of apartments. The front of the building, on Avalon, was condemned, but the landlord, a man named Mofass, let the units illegally for fifteen dollars a month.

Theodore Wally had lived in number three since his mother died six years earlier. I knew that because I had a girlfriend who used to live there until she got TB and went back to Lake Charles.

Wally took a long time to let us in. We heard him scurrying around in there. When he opened the door, he had on pants and nothing else. His yellow chest was almost concave, and the hickey on his neck was so purple that it might have bled. I imagined some fat girl pinning him down with her girth while sucking mercilessly on his neck.

"Mr. Minton," he said, near tears it seemed. "Fearless. What can I do for you?"

"Let us in, Wally," I said.

"I-I-It's n-n-not really a good t-t-time for me," he stuttered. "The house is a mess and . . . and . . . and I got a cold. I promised my uncle that I'd help him move."

"Move it, man," I said.

Theodore made room, and we came into his wreck of a home. His once-upholstered sofa showed its cotton stuffing and at least one spring. The wood floor was uncovered, unpainted, and unswept. There was a console radio against the wall and a boarded-up window that allowed a few shafts of sunlight to poke through. The room was longer than it was wide, and it wasn't that long. There were two chairs and a table with a hot plate and various dirty dishes thereupon. But there was also a tall glass vase holding three long-stemmed white roses that were as big as apples and lovelier than summer clouds. They released an odd but still sweet odor that seemed familiar but not like roses.

"What you want, Mr. Minton?"

"Call me Paris," I said.

"Okay."

"Call me Paris."

"Okay . . . Paris."

"Now talk to me about my store," I said.

"What you mean?" The clerk hunched up one shoulder and listed to that side. He smiled like a fool who couldn't possibly know anything. But that act wasn't going to work on me.

Fearless strolled over to one of the chairs and sat down. The movement seemed to alarm Wally.

"What you talkin' 'bout Mr. — I mean, Paris?"

"I mean that dude beat on me didn't burn down my store. He said he didn't, and he had no reason to lie. So somebody else must'a did it."

"I don't know who did it," Wally claimed.

"Now that's a lie."

He was trembling there in front of us, looking around as if he expected some accomplice to jump out and save his life. But no one jumped, and we were still there.

Wally belched loudly. His face contorted with nausea.

"Why you quit that market?" I asked.

Theodore tried to look me in the eye, but he couldn't. He struggled against tears and was mostly successful.

"I'm sorry," he whispered. And then, when he'd gained more of a mastery over his tears, "I'm sorry," in a surer tone.

"That's okay, man," I said. "That's okay. Just tell me what you know. 'Cause you know I plan to get my due."

Theodore Wally was as scared a man as I had ever seen. He was trembling, near tears and full of gas, but still he managed to maintain the semblance of a man standing his ground. I couldn't understand why he was so afraid.

"I'm sorry I burned down your bookstore, Paris," he said.

"What! *You?*"

"He told me to, and I did it 'cause I always did what he said. Mr. Antonio was like my father, you know. I been with him fourteen years, since I was a kid."

"*You* did it?"

"I told him about the man, the man who hit you. I told him that I saw you drive off, and then I saw that man go after you in his car with bull horns. He said to wait till late, an' if you didn't come back to burn down your store. He paid me, but I couldn't stand it, so I quit. He gave me eight hundred dollars. But you can have it, Mr. Minton." With that he fell on his knees and reached under the sofa, coming out with a manila envelope. He ripped the paper pouch open and grabbed at the tens and twenties as they fell. He went down on his knees again, gathering the money up. When he had gotten it in two fistfuls, he held them up to me and said, "Take it. Please take it and forgive me."

"Damn," Fearless said.

I knew what he was thinking, that I had gotten into more trouble in one day than he had in a lifetime. It made me mad, so mad that I slapped the clerk with the back of my hand.

It wasn't a hard slap, but it caused Theodore to bleed from the corner of his mouth.

"Take it," he said again.

"How could you do that to me, man?"

"He told me that you'd get the insurance. He said that his lease was up and that he needed to buy the lot next door or he was gonna go outta business. He said you'd get the insurance and that nobody'd get hurt if you was gone. It wasn't until after that I found out you didn't have any insurance."

"Even if I did, where was I gonna get more books? Where was I gonna have a new store if the one I had burned down?"

"He used to send my momma groceries when she was sick," Wally said. "He said it was all gonna be okay. Just take the money. Take it please."

I slapped him again.

Fearless was shaking his head.

I hit Wally with my fist, and he fell down upon his knees. The money went every which way. He crawled among the bills gathering and bleeding on them at the same time.

"Why you think I'm in all this shit? Huh? Why you think I'm out here riskin' my life? It's 'cause you burned down my store. If I'd'a come home to my place, I would'a let it drop. I would'a let Fearless outta jail and give him a place to stay till everything was okay."

Theodore wasn't listening. All he did was grab at the money, weeping blood.

There was an iron crowbar in the corner, next to the window. I picked it up.

"You the one messed up my life!" I yelled.

I didn't even feel my arm rising above my head. I had no idea I was swinging the crowbar until something stopped the sweep of my arm.

"Paris," Fearless said. His powerful grip had stayed the execution.

"What?"

"Take the money, man."

Theodore had gathered the cash again. He clutched it in both hands. I couldn't take it, so Fearless collected it for me.

While he was straightening out the bills I asked, "How much did you say it is?"

"Eight hundred dollars," Wally said, "near about."

"To burn down my life?"

"I'm sorry."

"I bet ya he paid you more than that," I said. "'Cause you had to pay somethin' for them flowers and that monkey bite."

"I got them from my girlfriend," he said, finding some backbone. "She kiss me for nuthin' and tried to make my house like a home."

By then there was the ice of murder in my veins. Not murder that I wanted to commit, but the murder I had almost done. I had almost killed Theodore, and that frightened me. I never believed it when people said that they lost control, that they blacked out like Morris said and killed without volition. Until that very moment I believed that a man made his own decisions, that the excuse of passion was just a lawyer's lie.

• • •

I WAS TOO worked up to drive, so Fearless took the wheel. He cruised down Slauson, keeping quiet while I fumed.

After a few blocks I said, "Damn. Damn."

"He couldn't help it, Paris. You know Antonio been good to him. He probably never even read a book."

"What difference does that make?"

"He didn't know what he was burnin', man."

"Let's go see Milo," I said to my friend. "Maybe he got somethin' for us."

"Whatever you say, Paris."

33

MILO WAS LEANING back in his chair with his fingers laced across his belly and a smile on his lips. He wasn't on the phone or reading. He wasn't doing a thing. I got the feeling that he was sitting there, being smug with himself, waiting for us to arrive and hear his glad song.

"Fearless. Paris. How you'all boys doin'?"

"I hope you don't choke on that canary you swallowed," I said.

"It's more like a goose, son. The goose that lays the golden egg."

"Where's Loretta?" Fearless asked.

"I thought it was best if she took a few days off," Milo said, his voice suggesting more.

"I'll bite," I said.

"I went to see Lawson and Widlow," Milo admitted. "I took a business card that said my name was Brown. I told them that I had a client named Love who had found a bearer bond worth a few thousand dollars to the owner."

I could see that Milo intended to earn his thirty-three percent.

"And what did they say?" I asked.

The bailbondsman sat forward. "At first they acted like they weren't too concerned. But when I suggested shopping the bond around, they said that that wouldn't be such a good idea. They let it drop that I could get in trouble if the wrong people found out about the bond. I said maybe I should go to the police. They offered me a finder's fee right then and there."

"How much?" Fearless asked.

"Five thousand dollars."

"What then, Milo?" I wanted to know.

"I said some names then. Leon Douglas. Fanny and Sol Tannenbaum. I said that that wasn't all, and I wanted some real money for my client or they was gonna be up to their elbows in J. Edgar."

"So where'd you leave it?"

"I got a answerin' service under the name'a Brown at a switchboard downtown. I gave Widlow the number and told him to call me inside of a day."

"Have they called yet?"

"I was waitin' for you'n Fearless to come 'fore I checked." With that he picked up the receiver and dialed. He waited no more than the span of a ring and said, "Brown, sixteen-sixty-four."

Milo looked up and started snapping his fingers at me. He made the motion of writing and pointed at Loretta's desk. I ran over, finding a yellow pencil and an unused envelope. I brought these back to Milo's desk.

"Hold on, hold on," Milo was saying into the receiver. "I got to get a pencil. All right, go on. Yeah. Three-*two*-one? Oh. Uh-huh. Is that all? Well then I thank you."

Milo frowned at the words he had written down, then he smiled and said, "They wanna meet us at their office tonight at eight-fifteen. They said that the security guard'll meet us at the side door in the alley and let us upstairs. What do you think about that?"

"We ain't got the bond," I said.

"A sheer technicality, my boy," Milo responded cheerfully. "If Lawson and Widlow are still looking, it means that your girl-friend hasn't brought it to them yet."

"The bond's worthless," I said. "Well, not worthless, but only worth the face value."

"How would you know that?"

I related the improbable tale of two American Negroes and the Israeli secret service.

Milo wasn't phased. "Well," he said. "Lawson and Widlow don't know that. We just jack up the price to ten or fifteen thousand and let them find out on their own."

"Yeah," Fearless added. "But we tell 'em that it ain't no deal unless we sit down with Zimmerman."

"Why complicate matters, Mr. Jones?" Milo asked. "Get the money and get out, that's what I say."

"Money ain't everything, Milo."

Milo tried to argue, but Fearless wouldn't budge.

MILO GAVE Fearless a small .32-caliber pistol that he had taken as a payment from a man charged with distributing counterfeit bills. It was not the kind of weapon Fearless commonly used.

"I usually like somethin' wit' more bite," he said. "But in a sitchiation like this, somethin' small is even better."

"Situation like what?" I asked. We were driving toward downtown. Fearless was testing different places to conceal his weapon. He tried his belt, the sleeve of his windbreaker, even in the elastic of his sock.

"Whenever a man tell ya he gonna meet you at the side door, you know he got somethin' t'hide," Fearless said. "An' if he's hidin' one thing, then he might be hidin' somethin' else. An' then you got to worry. Me, I don't like to worry, so I just hide somethin' myself." With that he shoved the pistol in his pocket and shrugged.

"Well, you just keep that thing in your pocket, Mr. Jones," Milo said from the backseat. "This here is just business. Plain and simple business."

"Okay," Fearless replied.

I remembered something that my uncle Lonnie used to say. *Trouble with a friend who stand by you in time' a need is that you usually got to be in trouble to enjoy his company.*

LAWSON AND WIDLOW'S OFFICE was in a six-story stone building on Wilshire. There was a big glass door and vines trained to cover the walls. The windows were large. Garish floodlights bathed the edifice so that it looked official and important on the otherwise dark street.

A big and brawny white man met us at the side door. His face was bland with smallish features. It wasn't a face that I recognized, but still I thought that I'd seen him before.

"What, three?" he asked. "There's only supposed to be one."

His accent sounded European, but I was no expert. It was familiar, though I couldn't remember where I'd heard the cadence before.

"These are my partners," Milo said in an officious tone, as though he expected the stranger to hop out of the way. He was acting like a black man who had never experienced racism, who expected his due with no arguments or questions.

The white man didn't like the idea of partners but finally decided that he couldn't make us disappear.

"Come," he said gruffly.

We followed him up three narrow and unlit flights of carpeted stairs. Everywhere was dark until we arrived on the fourth floor, where a light shone from behind a glass door at the end of the hall. Our chaperone opened the door and ushered us in with a gesture of his hand.

Fearless was the first one through the door, then Milo and me, followed by the big man. We all three had different reactions to what we found there.

Fearless swiveled his head around to get the lay of the land. Milo looked at the small suited man behind the desk and sputtered, "What's this supposed to mean?"

I was proud that I didn't let the fear I felt come out when I greeted our host.

"Hello, Mr. Minor," I said. "I wondered when you'd show up again."

The little man squinted at me. "Rome? No, Paris. You were at the Tannenbaum's house, no?"

"Yes," I said.

"Hey, brother," Fearless said.

When I looked to my right to see who it was that Fearless was greeting, I felt a clenching spasm down in my bowels. Leon

Douglas, his eye still puffy and his jaw swollen, stood next to another evil-looking black man. The stranger was taller by an inch and twenty pounds lighter than Leon. He wore a cowboy hat.

Both men glared at us.

"What is the meaning of this?" Milo said again. "Where's Mr. Widlow?"

"Mr. Widlow suggested to me that the principals should work out the specifics of this transaction," the little man said. "Sit down, gentlemen."

Fearless grabbed the chair closest to Leon and his friend, who stood against the wall on our right. The big white man who let us in leaned against the door behind us.

Minor was seated at a vast maple desk that was empty of papers or books or anything else to distract the eye. All he had was a lamp with an opaque green glass shade. Mr. Minor/Zimmerman smiled and nodded.

"How is Sol?" he asked.

"Dead," Fearless said.

"We have business, yes?" our host asked. Sol's death was not even worth his notice.

"Who are you?" Milo asked.

"I am Zev Minor." I would have never known it was a lie from his delivery. He was just a feeble uncle too old and weary to waste time trying to fool you. "And this is Mr. Christopher," he said, gesturing to the man behind us.

Fearless had his head turned away from Minor. He was pretending to read the titles on a shelf of books. That way our back was covered.

"I think you already know Mr. Douglas. His friend's name is Mr. Tricks."

"Just Tricks," the cowboy said.

"We represent Lawson and Widlow in this business about the bond." The last three words betrayed the gravity of his interest.

It was then that I remembered where I had seen Mr. Christopher. He was the big man leaving the Messenger of the Divine storefront on the night I was so cold and sleepy.

"This is totally unacceptable," Milo said, sputtering as he spoke. "I was to meet Mr. Widlow, and I expect to meet with him . . ."

Milo kept talking because he sensed danger. Words were Milo's weapons, so he pulled them out. I wasn't concerned about the bailbondsman or his fears, but when I looked over at Fearless, I saw that his hand had edged nearer to his gun pocket. Fearless was preparing to fight for his life. I could see that in his posture and the almost imperceptible furrow at the center of his brow. I wasn't worried about Fearless though — if anybody could survive that kind of battle, he could, but the odds for me and Milo weren't so good.

Under the fear of impending death and with the recognition of Christopher, who I would have bet was the Nazi Holderlin, everything else fell into place in my mind. I wondered if the nearness of death caused some chemical reaction in the brain that increased intelligence, as some scientists say that adrenaline increases physical strength in times of great stress.

I sat forward and said, "We know where Elana Love is at, and she has the bond."

"Where?" Leon asked from the sidelines.

"My colleague has a good question, Mr. Minton," Minor said.

"What's it worth?" I asked.

The little man pressed out his lips and shrugged. "My patience is wearing thin, my friend. Sol Tannenbaum stole my money.

It took me many years to get to this moment. Don't press your luck."

"You mean the art treasures you stole from the poor people that Mr. Christopher sent to the gas chamber?"

Mr. Christopher said something in German.

"What'd he say?" Leon demanded. "I told you muthahfuck-ahs I don't want you talkin' that shit around me."

Fearless's hand was at the opening of his pocket.

I felt my own pistol pressing into my stomach at the belt line.

I wanted to get us up on our feet and going through the door. That was a natural advantage that I was sure Fearless could capitalize on.

"We could take you to her," I suggested to Minor, "but we'd have to get something for that."

"Why bother, Paris?" Fearless said. "Go on, tell him."

I turned to Fearless, speechless.

Fearless smiled.

"Tell him what the Israeli guys said." Fearless leaned forward across the desk, reaching into his pocket as he did so. "Elana took the bond to these Israeli guys been lookin' for you. She showed 'em the bond, and they found out that it wasn't part'a the big money you lost." Fearless nodded toward Leon and Tricks. "That means he don't need you no more, Leon. If there ain't no treasure, then there ain't no cut. He'll probably tell that fancy lawyer you got to cut you loose."

"What's he sayin', Minor?" Leon said.

"It's nothing. It's a trick."

"That cop, that Latham, he was workin' for the Israelis," Fearless went on. "He took Elana there before Grove called you. You know I ain't lyin'."

Minor's eyes showed uncertainty. I remember thinking that Fearless had probably succeeded in getting us killed.

Mr. Christopher chose that unfortunate moment to practice his German.

"I told you to talk English," Leon shouted. He pulled a pistol from under his shirt.

"Get down!" Fearless screamed.

He grabbed my chair, upturning it into Milo. We both tumbled over, shouting. Mr. Christopher shouted something else in German. One shot was fired. I was turned on my back, facing Minor, who stood erect like a soldier holding a pistol at arm's length. He fired and I turned, expecting to see Fearless die.

He was already firing when the bullet entered his forehead. Then the tall and slender black man named Tricks fell straight down in a heap.

Fearless, was on my lips when I realized that it was the cowboy who'd gotten shot. Leon had pressed Mr. Christopher against the far wall and was just firing the bullet into that man's temple. With terrible quickness he fired randomly in my direction. I didn't know if he'd hit me or not, but Milo screamed out loud. Two more shots fired. I grabbed for my pistol, but I pulled it out with such force that it went flying out of my grasp into a far corner. Fearless was bleeding, but the baby gun was in his hand rapping out reports. Leon lowered his gun and got a strange look on his face. When he remembered that he was supposed to be shooting, the gun was already too heavy. He slumped down and expired, beaten for the second time in a row.

Suddenly I remembered Minor.

"Fearless! Watch out!" I yelled.

I stumbled up on top of the desk and then fell right on the corpse of the traitor. The shot from Tricks's gun had found the mark.

"Shit!" Fearless shouted.

"I'm dyin'," Milo moaned.

Both men were bleeding — Fearless from his left hand and Milo from his upper arm. I went to Milo and pulled off his jacket, then I ripped the shirt off his back. I wadded the shirt up and pressed it against the wound.

"Hold it tight," I told him.

"I can't," he cried.

"You don't and you'll keep on bleedin'," I said. "An' you know there's only so much you got to give."

Milo grabbed the bandage, and I went to Fearless. He was holding a handkerchief on the wound of his left hand and searching the floor with his eyes.

"Damn!" Fearless cursed. "Damn!"

"What, man? What!" I cried.

"My goddamned baby finger," Fearless said. "Muthahfuckah shot it off!"

"We got to go, man!"

"Not without my finger."

"What?"

Fearless grabbed my shirt with his good hand and pulled me up close. "Wake up, Paris. That finger got my fingerprint on it."

I took a deep breath, and in that forced semblance of calm I said, "You get Milo to the bottom of the stairs. I'll find the finger and be down in a minute."

Milo yelled in pain when Fearless helped him to his feet. They struggled over the four dead men, climbed through the door, and went shuffling and groaning down the hall.

I turned on the overhead light and searched the bloody scene. I looked all over the floor, under the desk, and even under the four corpses. I was in a kind of shock, sifting around. I got lost there among the dead. At one point I sat down on the floor next to Tricks. He had collapsed into a seated position, looking like a puppet waiting for someone to pull his string. I looked at him, wondering who he was and what had brought him to this final moment. Then I thought that if I was lucky, I'd read about it in tomorrow's evening edition; if not, I'd find out at my trial.

Down on the floor, next to the man's knee, was a finger, a curved little digit with a wad of bulging red flesh pressing out where the knuckle should have been. I picked it up and put it in my pocket. Then I got to my feet. I retrieved my discarded pistol and headed for the stairs.

As I walked from the room, Tricks fell over on his side.

34

I JOINED Fearless and Milo, who were hunkered down by the side door. Being the only man not wounded, I was elected to get the car. I drove up to the sidewalk, and Fearless hustled Milo out and into the backseat. They both laid low back there while I drove down the fairly empty streets.

We weren't out of the woods yet. There I was, a black man driving down the streets of white Los Angeles with no reason that a cop could imagine — except mischief. And what could I say if he pulled us over and found two wounded men in the backseat?

"Fearless."

"Yeah, Paris?"

"You still got that gun?"

"Naw, man. I wiped it off and dropped it next to the big white dude while you was workin' on Milo's arm."

That was one thing at least. My pistol hadn't even been fired.

Maybe, if we got away, the cops wouldn't suspect that there had been others in the room.

"Take Hauser down to Olympic and hang a right," Milo said. "Take it to Sierra Bonita and go all the way south down to three blocks past Venice. It's the only two-story house on the block."

I KNOCKED ON the front door. After a few seconds Loretta Kuroko said, "Who is it?"

"It's Paris, Lo. Me and Milo and Fearless."

The door opened. Loretta was wearing a blue terrycloth bathrobe. Beyond her were two small Japanese, a man and a woman, huddled together.

"What happened?"

I told her about the wounds but not how they were inflicted. She had me drive through the driveway and into the backyard. From there we went through the back door and into the kitchen. Loretta's parents didn't speak any English, but they showed surprisingly little fear of blood and gunshot wounds or desperate men in the middle of the night. Both Fearless and Milo were washed up and bandaged within a quarter of an hour. Milo, who knew enough Japanese to say *may I* and *thank you,* made his bed on Loretta's couch.

Fearless and I said our thank-you's and left. I dropped Fearless off at Dorthea's and then drove over to our apartment at Fontanelle's court, where I slept fitfully until late the next morning.

When I got up, I knew what I had to do.

So, dressed in the same funky clothes, I drove over to an alley off Slauson and climbed the back stairs to the third floor.

Theodore Wally's door was unlocked, but that didn't matter much because you can't steal from a dead man.

The bullet wound had been fatal but not immediately so. He had been cleaned off and bandaged and put into the ratty sofa's foldout bed. The covers were pulled up to his chin. His skin was still warm.

There was a bloodstain in the middle of the floor. That's where they shot him and left him to die. I sat on the side of the bed and lowered my face into my hands. I don't know how long I sat like that.

When I felt a gentle breeze on my skin I looked up, and Love was standing there. She wore a yellow dress with low-heeled orange shoes. Her pocketbook was black though. The fact that she hadn't color-coordinated her bag was the only clue that she was pressured or rushed.

"I'm surprised you came back," I said.

"I'm surprised you did too." She closed the door, and when she turned back, there was a small pistol in her hand.

"Wally tell you that we were here 'fore you killed him?"

"I was hiding behind the sofa," she said. "When you almost beat him to death."

"I smelled your perfume," I said. "But I mistook it for roses at first. And I had the club in my hand, but I didn't kill him."

"Neither did I."

"Then who?"

"Leon," she said with distaste. "Leon or his friend Tricks. I don't know which one because they were both here together."

"So why are you still breathing?"

"I wasn't here. I came in after they had shot him." Her sorrow seemed sincere. "He went to meet them, to make a deal about the bond. I guess they followed him after they met, and they left him for dead."

"How'd you hook up wit' Wally?" I asked.

"I was looking for you like I said before, and I remembered him from the day he helped you. I saw his profile, and you told me that he worked at the store. He was all sad. I talked to him a little bit, he was nice. Then, when I went out to look for you, Leon grabbed me."

"Then you were with me and Fearless and then with Latham," I said. "So how'd Wally fit in all that?"

"I wanted to find you again," she said. "I thought Theodore could help me, but he was so upset when I went to the store that I offered to take him out for a coffee. He decided right then to quit his job. He wrote a note, and we went off together. He was very sad about what he did to you. I gave him a shoulder to cry on and offered to help him."

"Some help," I said.

"I tried to save him."

"A doctor would have been better."

"He didn't want a doctor," she said. "He wanted the money from the bond and the police would have messed all that up."

I grunted, and Elana looked away. She wanted the money so bad that she had a dead man begging for it.

"You gonna shoot me?" I asked.

"Only if you want me to," she said.

"No thanks."

"Why don't you join me, Paris? We could make this money together. We could split it," she smiled, "or share."

"I don't know if I like the odds."

"What odds?"

"I was sitting outside of the motel when Latham and Brother Grove got laid low. I saw you driving in the opposite direction."

"When Bernard fell asleep I called Father Vincent. He said he'd call Grove," she explained, "but he brought that big white German dude. They were gonna rob us, but somebody called Latham and warned him. The pig, he ran out with my bag 'cause he thought the bond was in there."

"But I bet you took it out while he was sleeping off that thing you do with your tongue."

I regretted what I said immediately because it made her angry. And it doesn't pay to make a woman angry when she has a gun pointed at your head.

"No thank you, Elana," I said. "I don't think I could survive a partnership with you. But you could tell me something."

"What?"

"Why you messin' around with Leon when you already been to see the Israeli guys?"

My knowledge of her actions disconcerted Elana a little. But she was a smart enough cookie to keep cool even in surprise.

"They say they payin' like two percent for a finder's fee. But Leon's connection was talkin' about a share." She hesitated a minute and then continued, "You could get your friend, Paris, we could go to Leon and get him to tell who the connection is. You might as well, 'cause you know Leon'll try an' kill the both of you after you shamed him like you did."

"Lawson and Widlow," I said.

"Say what?"

"Lawson and Widlow. Accounting. Somewhere in Beverly Hills. That's Leon's connection. It's on me."

Elana got that tight look around her eyes. Every time I'd seen it before, she was soon to figure out my angle or meaning. But not that time.

"You wanna come with me?" she asked.

"Not for a hundred thousand dollars," I said.

She almost said something. But words failed.

"Where's your friend?" she asked, moving away from the door cautiously.

"Fearless is in his girlfriend's arms. I wish I was too."

"Why you tellin' me about Leon's connection?" she demanded.

I gestured at the cooling corpse. "I done had enough shit."

For the next few seconds my life was in the balance. Killing me might have been a good idea. But I had played my best card. I didn't want any more to do with Elana Love. Sitting there next to Theodore was the safest thing I could do. The money, even if we could have found it, stolen from doomed men, was itself a kind of doom. Maybe Elana Love could ride that kind of storm. I sure couldn't.

"You're a fool, Paris." Elana Love was neither the first nor the last woman to think so or say it.

I nodded.

She backed toward the door and let herself out.

I DON'T KNOW what happened for a while after that. I suppose that Elana went to the accountants' offices and saw the aftermath of the carnage we had witnessed. Maybe, after a day or so, she was able to speak to the principals. I doubt if that meeting did much for her wealth.

But that's all supposition, because on the drive back to

Fontanelle's court I was stopped by the police. The uniforms detained me until two plainclothes cops arrived.

There was a portly man in a green suit with a snaky little partner who wore a houndstooth jacket and coal-gray pants.

"Paris Minton?" the snaky cop asked.

I held out my wrists and they obliged without even a kick or slap to show who was in charge.

I expected the charges to be conspiracy, theft, maybe breaking and entering, and certainly murder. And so I was surprised down at the precinct at Seventy-seventh Street to hear, "You are being held because we suspect you for the arson of your landlord's property."

I used my one phone call to ring Charlotte.

"They got me in the can, baby," I told her. "But the charges are wrong, and I can prove it, I think." I asked her to call Milo and tell him. I knew that he'd tell Fearless. That was everyone who mattered.

The county jail was full, so they transferred me to a facility down around Redondo Beach. I had a cell that looked over the ocean and chess partners that could beat me now and then.

There was even a small library. It was like visiting a spa after what I had been through.

They brought me before a public defender who told me that the owner of the store I rented caused such a stink that they were leaning on me.

"They want you on an insurance angle," the milky-faced kid told me.

"But I didn't have insurance," I said.

"They think somebody hired you to set the fire," he said.

"But how could that be?"

"It happens all the time," he assured me.

"But, Mr. Defender. You sayin' that the owner is puttin' on the pressure, and so they brace me 'cause they think somebody paid me to set the fire for the insurance."

"I don't get your meaning," the kid said.

I knew I was in trouble then.

He didn't stay long. He resented having to come down to Redondo. The cops didn't like the drive either. So between the lag in visits and the lack of interest in their own case, I spent six weeks in the can. There was some mixup in the transfer records, so even Milo couldn't find me.

Finally I was brought back to Los Angeles for a meeting with the prosecutor. It seems that my lawyer, whose name I don't think I ever knew, had decided I was guilty and that, because my record was clean, I could probably get some kind of reduced sentence.

The prosecutor was young too but she had a little more on the ball.

"But he doesn't have insurance," the chubby prosecutor said, trying to understand what she was reading while my lawyer talked deal. I remember that she wore a navy jacket and skirt with a brilliant white blouse and string tie like the cowboys wear.

"It's the owner," my lawyer offered as if their roles were reversed.

"But," the prosecutor said, now talking to herself, "then why aren't we trying him?"

My lawyer wasn't smart enough to supply an answer.

They drove me back out to Redondo, where I sat in a cell with a man dying from TB. That was another three weeks. Then they let me go on the streets of Redondo.

"Can I have bus fare?" I asked the guard who was giving me my clothes back.

He handed me a dime.

"I have to call L.A.," I said, thinking he'd take pity and give me enough for the station-to-station call.

He was not so inclined.

WHEN MILO ANSWERED the phone my heart sank.

"Collect call to anyone from Paris Minton," the operator said sternly. I was hoping for Loretta to answer. She, I knew, would at least accept the call.

"Of course," Milo said jovially.

"Do you accept the charges, sir?" the woman asked.

"Yes I do." And then, "Paris, where are you?"

35

MILO CALLED FEARLESS and told him where I was. Fearless picked me up, in a brand-new Ford Crown Victoria, at the city library three hours after I called.

We had already said our hellos, and I explained the dumb charges that held me in jail.

"Why Milo take my call?" I asked Fearless. "I mean he never takes a collect call unless it's from one'a them bounty hunters."

"Open the glove compartment," was Fearless's reply.

There was a fat envelope there with my name on it. I was loathe to touch it.

"Go on," Fearless encouraged me.

It held a thick wad of cash.

"Thirteen thousand," Fearless said. "Plus the eight hundred from poor Wally and the five hundred I owed you for my fine."

"What is it?"

"It's a present from Gella Greenspan."

"What?"

"After I got to Dorthea's I called Gella to see how she was and to tell her somethin'," Fearless said. "But she was arrested just like you. They wanted to charge her with the murder of her husband or her auntie or both, but they couldn't figure out how to make the charge stick and they had to let her go."

"Oh."

"Yeah," Fearless said, grinning. He was never much on sarcasm. "And then I told her what Sol said."

"When did Sol say somethin'?"

"Oh yeah. Sol wasn't dead when I got to the hospital. He told me about the money he stoled before he passed."

"He told you?"

"You see, he put the money in a bank in Montreal — that's in Canada — under Gella's name, but he didn't tell nobody. The account number and everything was in a picture he framed and gave her. It was a picture of Fanny laughing and wearing a green dress."

"But, but what about the bond that Elana Love had?" I asked. "What did that have to do with it?"

"Oh yeah," Fearless said. "Sol said that that bond was just practice."

"Practice?"

"Yeah. He wanted to see how to convert dollars to another country's money. That was all it had to do with the millions."

"I don't get this, man. Why he wanna tell you?"

"He liked me 'cause I came with Fanny. And he wanted to make sure that Gella got the finder's fee. So I went to her and she wanted to give the money to Israel like Sol wanted, so we went to Manly. Only they had already kicked him and his boys outta the country."

"Say what?"

"They were over here pretendin' to be architects or sumpin'. A rich Jewish guy friendly with the Jewish government signed their papers. He the one own that hotel they was in. Anyway the cops looked into Latham's death and came up with Manly and his boys. But then Gella decided to go over there on her own."

"She left the country?"

"But she give us one-half of one percent. Forty thousand dollars."

Fearless drove along, chatting happily. He had bought his mother and sister houses, and he owned the Ford he was driving. I did the math on one-half of one percent. The solution made me sweat.

THAT WAS some months ago. The police drop by my new bookstore on Florence now and then and ask me about the old landlord and that fire. Antonio took a ninety-nine-year lease on the lot and put up a new Superette. That burned down too, under suspicious circumstances. All the suspicion was cast on me, but no one could prove it.

I still see Charlotte, and sometimes Fearless and I get together for drinks. He's broke and needs a loan now and then, but I don't mind.

He hasn't gotten in any trouble, and I'm hoping that he doesn't. But I know that if he does, I'll have to help him, because Fearless is my friend.